Sage Advice

Senior Year at Cromer High
BOOK ONE

CORI COOPER

This one's for you, Kristi,
because of years of encouragement,
and the very bestest advice!

The Cromer Chronicles

ADVICE COLUMN
Sage Advice

Dear Sage,

I am not confrontational. Whenever things get tense, my tongue swells up, and I can't say a single word. How can I be braver?
Signed, Not Braveheart

Dear Braveheart,

The words, "I'm not confrontational," are just words. They aren't facts. It's not like you can look up the word "brave" in the dictionary and the definition says, "Not you."
Omar Bradley said, "Bravery is the capacity to perform properly even when scared half to death."
You can be brave and run away. You can also be brave and face something hard. What if you are brave already? Think about it. It's pretty dang brave to ask advice from someone you don't even know. What if I'm right about that?
Love, Sage

Chapter 1

I walked into the student council room forty-five minutes before the meeting was scheduled to begin. In my arms, I carried two boxes from Jenson's Café filled with fried and glazed goodness. Nobody could resist a pastry from Jenson's.

But it wasn't bribery.

Okay, it was kind of bribery.

I set the boxes on the table next to the podium so I could survey the room with my most critical eye. It was in serious need of some Feng Shui. Chairs, lights, smells... I wrinkled my nose. As much as I loved the scent of stale coffee and ancient printer fumes, this was totally not going to work.

I pulled a new bottle of body spray out of my bag. There was a good chance I'd use the whole thing making this room tolerable, but no worries. I had two more at home. I sprayed directly on the seat of each nasty plastic chair, as well as up the back. Then I spun around the room with my finger pumping the nozzle.

I wished we had pink poufs or at least velvety cushions for the student council to sit on. It was a well-known fact that people made better decisions when they were full of sugar and sitting on comfortable chairs. The most I could do was push all the desks to the corner and arrange the chairs in a semi-circle that faced the front of the room.

That was much better.

Cozier.

It just needed a little something-something more.

I dug through my purse for the glittery pink tablecloth that I'm convinced makes the world a better place. I draped it over my shoulder while I moved the bakery boxes to a chair. I swung the tablecloth into the air and watched in awed satisfaction as it transformed the nasty fake-wood table into a thing of joy and beauty forever.

I smoothed the top of the tablecloth and checked the length all around to make sure the sides were even. Then I replaced the bakery boxes and stacked matching napkins nearby. I hefted an insulated drink dispenser of hot cocoa and carefully placed it on the table across from my mom's cutest porcelain teacups, which I moved into the shape of a smiley face.

A vase of artificial zinnias was just the thing to brighten the podium. I turned off the horrible fluorescent lights that gave the entire room a lime green tint and put my hands on my hips to scan my work. There wasn't a thing more I could do to prepare.

It was ready.

Better than ready. It was perfect.

Now I just needed to make sure I was perfect. Vince Lomabardi said, "If we chase perfection, we can attain excellence." I was holding onto that because I needed excellence today.

Excellence and success.

I retrieved my bag and headed to the nearest bathroom. It was still too early for students to be in the school, but I passed a few teachers who smiled and wished me a good morning.

I sincerely hoped it would be.

In the bathroom, I fluffed my hair and secured it with a round of hairspray, then pulled out my makeup compact. There wasn't really a need to touch up mascara or lip gloss, but I did both anyway. Just for fun. It made me feel better, like I had truly done all I could.

I twirled on the toes of my heeled booties to make sure everything was tucked, wrinkle-free, and fabulous. With my fuchsia skinny jeans and embroidered peasant top that cinched at the waist, I was ready to conquer the world. I blew myself a kiss and pulled my purse over my shoulder.

On my way back to the student council room, I almost bumped into Mrs. Larsen as she came out of the teacher's lounge.

"Pyper. Hello, dear."

"Good morning, Mrs. Larsen!" I fell into step beside her, shortening my strides to keep her pace as we headed back to the classroom. "Thank you for letting me call this extra meeting."

"Of course." She smiled, but her forehead creased. "Though, I admit, I'm curious. Will you tell me what this is all about now?"

I shook my head, my hair brushing across my lower back. "It's super important to me that it doesn't leak out ahead of time."

"I see." Mrs. Larsen nodded. "Well then, I will be content with being surprised."

I thanked her and stood back so that she could enter the student council room ahead of me. She stepped through the doorway, then stopped so suddenly I bumped into her back and had to grab the sides of the door to keep from falling on my rear.

I peeked over Mrs. Larsen's shoulder so I could see what made her block traffic. If one of those stinking boys miraculously got here early and wrecked my hard work, they were seriously going to wish they'd slept in.

Oh, good. It was all the way I left it. Except that Leah, student council president extraordinaire, was now standing next to the door, in the process of flipping the lights back on. It happened too fast to stop her. Under the fluorescents, my hard work looked droopy and sad.

"What is all this?" Mrs. Larsen lifted a hand to her cheek.

Leah placed her fists on her hips in a signature power pose. "I have no idea. I just got here."

I hurried to the horrible light switch and pulled it back down, making the room look amazing once again. "I came early to set up. I wanted this meeting to be different."

"Different how?" Leah pursed her lips. "It looks like you're recruiting for beauty college."

"Do people recruit for beauty colleges?" Mrs. Larsen raised her eyebrow.

Leah waved one hand. "You know what I mean. What is that smell?"

"Honeysuckle Wildflower. It's dreamy." I moved to the front of the room and perched on the edge of one of the chairs behind the podium so that I would be in place when the rest of the group arrived.

"Okay, it does smell good," Lean admitted. "Why did you go to so much trouble? It's just a bunch of guys; they won't notice anything. Except the food. Food was a good idea."

"Thank you," I said without answering any of her other questions. We talked about this just a few days ago. She knew why I went to so much trouble; she just had too many things in her brain to remember. As soon as the meeting started, it would come back.

Speaking of...

I pulled my notes from my purse and began reviewing them. It was just something to do to keep the nerves down while I waited. I knew exactly what I was going to say. Brooklynn and I spent three hours last night arguing the issue from all sides. I was beyond prepared.

"Stop, you neanderthals! Wait for the meeting to start!" Leah screeched as she held off three lowerclassmen officers trying to get to the refreshment table. At the moment, her physics book was working to keep them back, it probably weighed more than a freshman, but she was definitely in need of some backup.

"Hey, guys?" I stood to get their attention. All three of them stopped flailing their arms toward the food and looked at me. "I left a poster in my car; would you mind getting it for me?" I lifted my car keys to eye level. Each of their heads swung from side to side with the movement of the keys. "It's super important. It's in the backseat."

The sophomore class secretary snatched the keys out of my hand. "Which car is yours?"

"Idiot," said the freshman vice president as he punched the sophomore's arm. "It's the bright pink one. Everyone knows that."

"Beauty," I nodded. "Be nice to her, and hurry. We're going to start soon."

They dashed out of the room without a backward glance.

Leah crossed her arms. "Ten to one they go for a joy ride, and you never see your car again."

"Ten to one none of them have their permits yet because all they want to do is play video games."

"Salty!" Leah raised her hand for a high five.

I gave her palm a satisfying smack.

Within the five or so minutes it took for the guys to return with my keys and the poster, the room had pretty much filled.

"Thanks," I said as I stashed my keys back in my purse and pulled out some putty to hang my poster behind the podium.

"Ugh." The senior class secretary shielded his eyes when I turned around. "So much pink."

"Whatever," I said, rolling my eyes at him. "It's perfect."

"Why did you hang up a blank posterboard?" He gestured to the poster. "I don't get it."

No surprise there. I ignored him, took a seat, and waited for Leah to call everyone to order.

She stood at the podium but leaned way over to talk to Mrs. Larsen. As soon as I settled into my chair, she straightened and banged her fist like a gavel. Everyone snapped to attention.

"I think we're all here, so let's get started."

"Yeah, why are we here?" The bleary-eyed sophomore class president took a swig of something from a water bottle and wiped his arm across his mouth.

Gross.

While Leah explained the purpose of our meeting for those fellas who didn't listen or read their emails—a.k.a all of them-- I stared at the lowerclassmen. Actually, *they* didn't have to be here. This only concerned the juniors and seniors. We didn't need the entire council.

Although, I suppose the sooner I got people to change their thinking, the better.

A second later, Leah turned the time over to me. I stepped up to the podium and laid my palms flat on top so I wouldn't be tempted to drum my fingers. It was a nervous habit. Not that I was nervous; it was just that habits have a way of showing up when it was least convenient.

"Thank you, Leah." I flashed a brilliant smile that hovered over my fellow student council members. "I know it's early. Thank you, guys, for coming. I asked Leah to set up this extra meeting to discuss an idea. I put together a proposal—"

"I have a proposal for you, Pyper!" the junior class vice president called out.

I tried to keep my smile loose and flowy, even though I could feel the corners of my mouth tightening. "I'm sure it's super serious and not at all immature, Jack. How about you email it to Leah, and we can talk about it at the next meeting? For now..." I stepped up to my poster and tugged so that the blank board fell away, revealing my glitter glue masterpiece underneath. "I'd like to propose that we cancel prom this year."

There, I said it.

I raised one arm to draw their eyes to the shimmering letters that spelled out "prom," then I took a thick sharpie from the podium and drew a black X over the word to emphasize my point. I surveyed the effect with satisfaction before I turned to look at the student council again.

It was difficult to tell if they were with me or not. Half the group looked confused, a fourth was half asleep, and the rest were scrolling on their cell phones.

Super helpful.

"Let me tell you why." I glanced over my notes. "Number one: prom is a huge drain on the school budget. If we eliminate prom, we could do so many other things."

I paused to let their minds run wild with the possibilities. What could we do with that money? Get drinking fountains that actually worked? Revamp the cafeteria options? Get new sports uniforms and a mascot costume that didn't smell like fancy French cheese?

A few heads nodded, giving me a boost of confidence.

"Number two: the highest amount of underage drinking, arrests, and vandalism happen over prom weekend. I researched the town statistics from the last ten years."

The junior class secretary raised his hand. "I have a question for Pyper."

"Proceed," Leah said, waving her arm majestically.

"Yes?" My pinkie finger started drumming before I knew what was happening. I straightened it out and pressed it into the podium.

"Do you really think people would stop doing those things if there wasn't a prom?"

Because he asked in a curious voice and not a skeptical one, I decided to answer with equal politeness.

"That's a really good question. No, I don't think canceling prom will stop all the bad things in the world, but I do think it will make a difference. Anyway, it would be interesting to find out, wouldn't it?"

I directed this question to Sam, the freshman class president. He was a next-level genius taking senior advanced chemistry and he was also my lab partner. I knew how much he loved the scientific method. He had notebooks covered with elemental symbols that resembled hearts.

He looked away when I caught his eye.

In fact, no one was giving me any attention. Their heads were bowed, examining their Nikes, Vans, and Docs.

This was my fault. I should have known better than to overestimate their capacity. I needed to appeal to them at their level.

I moved my notes to the side. "Think of it this way: if we cancel prom, it will save you so much money. Carson?"

He jumped like someone pinched his bottom. "Yeah?"

"You went to prom last year, right? How much did it cost you?"

His eyes whirled while he did some mental math. "Uh, like, six hundred dollars. But we did the limo thing, so, there's that."

"And where do you work?"

Carson ducked his head. "Taco Bell."

"Part-time?"

"No, uh, like, ten hours a week."

I took a second to do my own mental math. "Think about this, guys. Carson spent the same amount on prom as he makes working almost an entire month at Taco Bell."

I let that sink in.

Then bit back a smile as the murmuring began.

Leah stood up to bang on the podium some more. "Guys, stick with us."

When the room quieted enough for my voice to carry, I appealed to them with my most earnest tone. "Is it worth it? Is prom worth the time, the expense, the headache, the mess?"

I gazed around the room, listening to their whispers as I let them process my proposal.

"She is so hot."

"Do you think she'd go out with me?"

"She has a boyfriend, idiot. He's in *college*."

Okay, those were not the kind of whispers I was hoping for.

I placed one hand over my heart. "I truly believe that our school, our student body, and yes, our town as a whole, would be better off if we totally quit prom, not just this year, but permanently." I nodded at Leah, who scrambled to her feet and stood beside me.

Using her presidential voice, she said, "I'd like to call for a vote of no more prom at Cromer High School."

I waited a second to see if any of the guys would second it. When they didn't, my heart sank.

"I second it," I said, giving them all my most disappointed face.

"All in favor?" Leah raised her hand to remind them what to do, then lowered it to the podium. I stared at the freckles sprinkled from her wrist to her elbow.

Why was her hand lying there like a slug?

Why wasn't it raised in the air?

I raised mine as high as I could and stared at her pointedly. Leah did not look at me.

And neither did anyone else in the student council. I thought horrible things about each of them in the seconds that followed.

"All opposed?"

I didn't bother checking who raised their hand. There were too many to count, and Leah's vote was the only one that mattered to me.

I leaned sideways to hiss. "Why are you raising your hand, traitor? I thought we were in this together. What happened to female power against the male-dominated student council?"

"I know, I know. But, it's prom..." She shrugged. "And Will texted me this morning—"

"Will Davis?" I interrupted.

"Yes! I have the perfect dress, and it's our senior year, and..." Her voice trailed off when it became obvious that I wasn't listening.

I was going to destroy Will.

For multiple reasons.

Who asks someone to prom over text?

Leah tallied the votes, even though I was ridiculously outnumbered, and read off the stats. It was beyond dismal. The disappointment enveloped me like stinky perfume. I couldn't blame Leah, not really. Of course, a girl would jump at the chance to dress up like a Disney princess and have someone buy her dinner. That made total sense. It was the rest of the room that I took issue with. What guy wants to go to prom, really?

I fell into my seat behind the podium as Mrs. Larsen replaced Leah at the front of the room.

"Thank you, girls. It warms my heart to see the judicial process in motion."

I snorted.

"So," Mrs. Larsen went on, "it's interesting that prom is the topic of our meeting this morning because I have some news about the prom committee."

I perked up. Her voice didn't sound like it was good news. Maybe this was my salvation. Prom was only a week away. If something happened to the committee, it was way too late to get a new one.

No prom committee, no prom.

"Kathy just texted that she has mono—"

"Crap!" Max, the senior vice president and Kathy's boyfriend, pulled out his phone. "Are you serious? I have a game this weekend. Crap."

The other guys ribbed him for way longer than was necessary before Mrs. Larsen called them back to order.

"Without Kathy, we have a huge hole in the prom committee." Mrs. Larsen said. "The good news is Leah's committee took the biggest job, so we don't have to worry about scrambling to decorate. So, moving forward, I'd like to propose that we appoint Pyper to fill Kathy's place as head of the prom committee."

Wait, what?

I stared at Mrs. Larsen. There was no way I heard what I just heard.

"I second it." Carson waved his hand with an evil grin. I knew he was a jerk; it was his genetic lot in life. But this was next-level jerkiness.

"All in favor?"

The room disappeared into a mass of raised arms.

Were they kidding me?

I was suddenly on my feet without making the decision to get there. "Can I refuse?"

"You've been elected." Mrs. Larsen waved her hand to indicate the judicial process in process.

I scowled.

She placed a hand on my shoulder. "I know how you feel about prom, Pyper, but you're the only person in this room I can trust to pull this dance together. You're creative, and you know how to get things done. Prom is important to the students in this school. I know you'll put your personal feelings aside to make this happen; I have full confidence in you."

Oh, fabulous. How was I supposed to say no to that? "Fine, I'll do it."

She patted my slumpy shoulder a few times. "Attagirl. You know what they say: if you can't beat them, join them. You might have fun."

Yeah.

I sincerely doubted it.

ADVICE COLUMN
Sage Advice

Dear Sage Advice,
One of my friends ditches school all the time, and she comes back with all these awesome stories of all the fun things she does. I want to ditch, too, but I don't want to break the rules. Is ditching school wrong?
Sincerely, FOMO

Dear FOMO,
I'd love to give you permission to ditch school. Really, I just want you to be happy. But I can't do that.
Do you really want to ditch? Or do you just want to have those fun experiences your friend is having when she ditches? Because you can always do fun things after school hours, not to mention weekends and holidays. You know?
Love, Sage

Chapter 2

I meandered through the hall, making my way to the parking lot while I wondered who came up with that stupid quote about making lemonade when life gives you lemons. What was I supposed to make when life gave me a room full of cavemen, a traitor of a student council president, and a teacher who must hate me deep down inside?

A mess. That was all.

One big, hot mess.

I replayed the entire meeting in my head, trying to figure out what went wrong. Brooklynn and I spent hours on those notes, we even got her five brothers to help us. I thought it was fool proof. It should have been. I don't get what happened in there.

This was a terrible way to start the day.

"Hey, Pyper!"

"How's it going, Pyper?"

"Pyper, hi!"

I smiled and waved at my fellow students like everything was peachy when in reality, I wanted to throw each and every one of them in the garbage can, even the people who were totally innocent and didn't just vote against me. They were all prom-loving sheep. I bet they never once considered how stupid prom is.

All those flowers that had to die for boutonnieres and wrist corsages that sagged by the end of the night. All the money wasted on tux rentals that ended up with punch stains, and dresses that were only worn once. All the time spent trying to transform the gym from sweaty sock central into a dreamland. And all the drama of who asked who and who didn't.

It was so stupid. Every part of it was so stupid.

I unlocked my car and shoved my poster into the back seat. That, an empty thermos, dirty teacups, and a half-empty bottle of body spray were all I had to show for my hard work.

With a sigh, I reached for my economics textbook and tucked it into my bag. Then I sighed and tilted my face towards the sunshine.

It succeeded in melting a part of my disappointment enough that I almost smiled. Except just as my lips began to tilt upwards, something caught my eye.

Wait a second.

Was that Moe, Brooklynn's truck?

I shielded my eyes and peered forward.

It totally was. And, more than that, there was someone sitting in the driver's seat.

My heart began thumping to the ear-splitting bass of the lifted truck that pulled into the spot beside me. I ignored the group of guys inside, especially when they started whistling and calling to me.

I had more important things to pay attention to at the moment.

All week, Brooklynn was stressing over the huge math test she has third period. Yesterday during lunch, my tacos got cold while I drilled her on the multiplication table. No matter how many times I tried to tell her that the table had not been on any of our tests since, like, the third grade, she insisted that she wanted to be prepared if it happened to pop-up.

Brooklynn always spent the morning before a test in the library. What was she doing in her truck?

I flung my purse over my shoulder and hurried across the parking lot to the passenger side of Brooklynn's truck. I yanked the door open and was halfway in the seat before I realized there was already someone sitting there.

"Carly!" I cried. Surprise made me stumble and almost fall onto the asphalt. I steadied myself on the door handle just in time. "What's going on? What are you guys doing?" I glanced at Brooklynn, who shrugged.

Carly slid across the bench seat so I could squish into the truck. I shut the door behind me and then gave them both my full attention. Carly sniffed twice, her body rounding over her knees. The look on her face smooshed my heart out like Play-Doh. Something was seriously wrong here.

"Never mind. Don't answer any of that." I wrapped my arms around Carly, pressing her face into my shoulder. She shuddered, and muffled sobs quivered down her back like waves.

I mouthed a barrage of silent questions at Brooklynn. "What happened? What's wrong with her? What's going on?"

Brooklynn just shook her head.

Apparently, my questions would have to wait.

I smoothed Carly's thick, auburn curls away from her forehead. The need to fix things swelled up inside of me, and it took every effort to swallow the urge to demand explanations and produce a massive list of solutions. Instead, I racked my brain for reasons why Carly might be crying like her heart was destroyed.

She was fine at school the day before. More than fine, actually; she'd been bouncing off the walls with excitement. She had a date with Simon that afternoon.

Oh.

Simon.

I can't believe I didn't figure that out sooner. This was about a guy. Of course it was about a guy.

It was *always* about a guy.

The first bell rang and echoed from the high school building to the parking lot like a pinball arcade game. By the time the sound reached us, it was faint enough to ignore.

And that is exactly what I did.

Who could think about tardiness and pink slips when one of their best friends had navy blue mascara dripping down both sides of her face?

"I'm so sorry," Carly said as she lifted her head with a sniff. "I'm making us late for school." She rummaged through her purse for a tissue but couldn't find one, so she rubbed the sleeve of her sweater across her face. The gesture made her look more like a toddler than a high school senior.

I pulled a travel pack of tissues out of the side pocket of my purse and placed them on Carly's lap. "Here, use these. Mascara is crazy hard to get out of clothes."

"Really? How do you know?" Carly pulled a wad of tissues out of the package and blew her nose.

I was so not answering that.

I took another tissue and used it to dab around Carly's eyes. "Do you have eyeliner with you? If I just touch this up, you'll look perfect." I'd learned a couple of eyeliner tricks that made puffy eyes look normal.

Carly rummaged until she found her periwinkle-colored makeup kit and handed it to me. I used a clip to keep her hair away from her face, then proceeded to fix her eyeliner. Since I had all the tools, I went ahead and redid the rest of her face, too. When that was done, I flipped the visor mirror down so Carly could see.

"All better." I tucked her hair behind her ear. She looked perfect, better than new. But I knew this was a temporary solution. If she started crying again, she'd go right back to being a mess.

I had to do something.

"Would you look at this weather?" I leaned forward and pretended to scrutinize the sky through the windshield. "It's just the worst. I totally think it's going to snow."

Brooklynn's forehead wrinkled. "Pyper, the sun is shining."

"Snow day!" I buckled Carly into the middle seat and then pulled the passenger seat belt over my lap until it clicked.

"What?" Carly blinked.

"To the mall!" I cried, raising my purse into the air.

"Seriously?" Brooklynn pressed her lips together. "What about school?"

"Don't worry. We can be back for your test. There's plenty of time."

Carly looked from Brooklynn to me, her head moving side to side like she was trying to work a kink out of her neck. I stretched my smile bigger and raised both eyebrows.

Brooklynn sighed and put her key in the ignition.

"Yay!" I squealed as Moe rumbled to life. Although he was slow and slightly arthritic, he was a reliable little truck. I loved him almost as much as I loved my Beauty—especially now that he was the vehicle taking us to a better place.

Everything looks brighter at the mall.

It took only five minutes for Brooklynn to drive us there, and I filled every second with nonsensical chatter. I didn't want Brooklynn to have a chance to decide that this was a terrible idea. We were going to have so much fun that all of us would have to forget our troubles.

By the time Brooklynn parked us outside the main entrance, Carly perked up enough to put on some bright red lipstick. I decided to take fifty-two percent of the credit for her rapid improvement. Thirty-five percent belonged to the mall itself, and the last thirteen percent to the coconut-scented hand cream I insisted Carly try as we drove.

I tumbled out of the truck while Carly tried to tame her fantastic curls. I barely had my feet under me when Brooklynn jerked my arm.

"Wha-?"

She held a finger to her lips and pulled me around to the back of the truck.

"What's up?" I whispered.

"I need you to promise me something." Brooklynn leaned so far forward that she destroyed my personal space bubble.

I totally didn't know she had that many freckles on her nose.

"I'm serious, Pyper. You have to promise."

"Okay, sure. What is it?"

"Promise me that no matter what happens—" Brooklynn paused. It felt like I was streaming a mystery movie and the Internet crashed right at the climatic reveal. My left wrist twitched against my leg.

"—we will get back to school in time for my math test."

It took way longer than it should have for Brooklynn's words to make sense inside my brain. When it finally all came together, I swatted her arm.

"Brooklynn! Seriously? You're still thinking about your math test?"

She crossed her arms against her chest and looked away. "My grades are seriously important to me, Pyper. You know that."

I did know that.

Regret flicked across my face like a stray hair, making me want to sneeze. I placed a hand on Brooklynn's shoulder until she would look at me again.

"I'm sorry, Brookie. I get it. And I promise we will get back to school with plenty of time for you to take your test."

Brooklynn's shoulders dropped three inches. "Thank you."

I darted my eyes over the truck bed where I could see Carly through the window, trying to pull a hair band around the ginormous messy bun she made. "Did she tell you what happened?"

Brooklynn shook her head. "There wasn't really time. She was waiting when I pulled up. Probably for you, but since you weren't around—"

"Yeah, I was in that student council meeting."

"That's right," she said, snapping her fingers. "How did it go?"

"We'll talk later. This is about Carly. What happened when you pulled up?"

Brooklynn eyed me for a moment longer, then gave in. "She jumped in Moe as soon as I stopped and just exploded into tears. I couldn't understand a single thing she said until you got there."

Poor Brooklynn. She lived with her dad and five brothers. She must have felt like she was on an alien planet with Carly sobbing all over her truck.

Carly chose that moment to join us. "Ready?" A smile squished her eyes until they almost disappeared.

I couldn't help but smile back. "You know it. Let's do this!"

As we walked across the parking lot, I leaned down to Brooklynn—I was probably a full foot taller than her with my wedges on—and whispered, "But seriously. Look how happy Carly is now. Best idea ever?"

"Okay, yes. You win. Best idea ever."

"Yay!" I nudged her with my elbow. "You should say that again. And maybe a little louder. I love those words so much!"

Brooklynn took a few long steps to get away from me, glancing over her shoulder with a sassy grin. I let her go even though I really would have loved to hear those words again. Carly held the mall doors open, waiting for us to enter.

"It smells fruity," Brooklynn said, wrinkling her nose as she looked around at the gleaming storefronts. The mall was understandably overwhelming for a girl who bought most of her clothes from her dad's sporting goods store. For me, it was like my birthday and Christmas at the same time. I couldn't stop a grin from spreading across my face.

Carly turned to me. "Where should we start, Pyper?"

I pursed my lips to give the impression of deep contemplation, but there was never a doubt in my mind where to begin. My feet started walking in the direction of my sole. I mean soul.

"Pyper?" Brooklynn asked, jogging to catch up to my long-legged stride. She gave me her best grimace, but I ignored it. Everything, even suspense, deserves a chance to grow and flourish in this world. It's good for us to have to wait for things.

For this reason, and because I was really enjoying the drama, I didn't reveal our destination until we stood directly in front of the window display of Glorious. Then I stopped walking and waved my arms around to the funky beat that only I could hear.

"Shoes, of course!"

The
Cromer Chronicles

ADVICE COLUMN
Sage Advice

Dear Sage,
I think I'm invisible. Seriously. No one ever notices me. People talk over me all the time, they forget my name, and once, someone sat on me at a football game. I don't need a ton of attention; I'd just like to feel like I matter.
Sincerely, Invisible

Dear Invisible,
Right off the top of my head, I can advise you to wear brighter clothes and stand up super straight, but I know that's not the real problem. I think what you're saying is you feel like no one sees you. You disappear into the background sometimes. This is a super relatable problem. A lot of people feel this way. So, my suggestion to you is to put aside your own feelings and look for others who seem lost and lonely. Notice them and reach out. I guarantee that when you think about others, they will start to think about you.
Love, Sage

Chapter 3

Time went by way too fast as we visited all my favorite stores and shopped our feelings away.

Well, I did, anyway.

The mall worked its magic on me thoroughly. By the time we got to the food court for some much-needed refreshment, I was so hyped up that I almost forgot we came to the mall for a reason other than the coral tulle skirt and matching wedges I had in my shopping bags.

Brooklynn snagged us a table while Carly and I went to Greedy Cow for ice cream.

"Have you been here before?" I asked Carly. She stared at the menu with her eyes popping out of her head.

"No. Wow, there are so many choices. How do you know which one to get?"

I pulled out my phone to scan the QR code on the counter. When the images loaded, I enlarged the pictures and showed Carly. It was easier to choose when you could see what everything looked like.

Greedy Cow didn't mess around. You either got plain soft serve or one of their milkshake creations with cookies, candies, and sprinkles all arranged to defy gravity over your cup.

"Wow!" Carly's eyes got even bigger.

"The Chocolate Coma is divine," I said, pointing. "Oh, this one is new."

"Hullabaloo Belly Buster? What's in that?"

"There's no description. Maybe cause it's new? I don't know. Let's ask."

Carly followed me to the counter, where a guy about our age fiddled with the soft serve machine. He looked kind of familiar, but there was no way I knew him. If he went to our school, he should be there right now.

"Excuse me?" I said. "Can you tell us what's in the Hullabaloo Belly Buster?"

Carly giggled as I flubbed over the tongue-twisting consonants.

The guy looked at me, then his eyes flicked to a point above my head. "Uh, yeah. Sorry about the name; my sister did that. It's vanilla ice cream with chocolate chips, a peanut butter swirl, caramel sauce, and chocolate-covered marshmallows."

"Wow," I said, letting out a breath. "Belly buster indeed."

"Yeah, it's disgusting."

"Your sister named it?" Carly looked up from the polish she was picking off her nails. "Do you own this place?"

He pointed to the sign above the soft serve machine. "Family owned and operated since nineteen ninety-five. What can I get for you?"

Carly squirmed and turned to me. "I don't know."

"I'm getting Strawberry Shortcake," I told her with an encouraging smile. It was the same thing I always got because it was so yummy. If she couldn't make up her mind, Strawberry Shortcake was the way to go.

Carly scrolled through the ice cream images on my phone. "Oh, I don't know. There are so many choices. What does Brooklynn want?"

"The peanut butter one." I pointed it out to Carly, then turned to the guy behind the counter. "So, we'll order the Strawberry Shortcake and Peanut Butter Thunder from Down Under. Can you get those started while my friend decides?"

"No problem."

He went to work and Carly stared at the menu. After a few minutes of listening to the blender whirl, I noticed that Carly wasn't looking at the phone anymore.

"Did you decide?"

"What?" She blinked, slowly focusing on my face.

I repeated my question.

"Oh, I got distracted." She leaned closer and whispered. "That guy is so cute. At least, I think he's cute. Do you think he's cute?"

I glanced at the back of his head. "Great hairline. His hair will probably turn white before he goes bald."

Carly giggled, covering her mouth to keep from catching his attention. "I get it. No one can compare to your perfect boyfriend, huh? When do I get to meet this dreamsicle?"

If I had my way, never.

"I love that pink cardigan you just bought," I said, smoothly steering the subject in a different direction. "I think it's so tragic that most redheads won't wear pink."

Carly nodded absently while she chewed the side of her lip. "Can I ask you a question?"

Unless it has to do with my supposed boyfriend or the cute ice cream guy, sure.

I pressed my lips into a tight smile and answered, "Of course."

"Jason is real, isn't he?"

It seemed that subject change didn't work as smoothly as I thought. I opened my mouth to try again, but Carly kept talking over me. "I mean, it's not that I think he's made up. Everyone at school talks about your hot college boyfriend, but I've never met him. He never visits. You don't have any pictures of him. You never talk about him. You're so gorgeous; I bet you could have any guy at school. I just hate to think you're wasting yourself in a relationship that isn't making you happy."

Oh, wow.

It was like a *Teen Queen* magazine advice column regurgitated out of Carly's mouth.

I took a deep breath to get rid of the buzzing sound that started in my left ear. "Stop, Carly, I'm blushing! You're gorgeous, too, you know? I'd give my wedges for your hair."

Carly ducked her head and smoothed a few stray hairs into her messy bun. She let the silence reign for so long that I thought for sure she'd forgotten all about her question. Then she said, "Jason does make you happy, doesn't he?"

I sighed.

"I don't need a guy to make me happy, Car. I'm not even sure that's possible." It was suddenly exhausting to filter my thoughts. I opened my mouth so they could stop pounding inside my head. "And even if there was no Jason, I wouldn't date any of the guys at our school. Dating in high school is such a waste. Guy's brains don't connect until they're twenty-five, did you know? Nobody's got time to wait for that."

Carly's eyes widened.

I smiled sweetly. "Dating is what people do before they get married. I just think it makes more sense to wait to start all that when you're ready to get married. Like at thirty-five."

"You don't think people should date until they're thirty-five?" Carly sucked in a sharp breath.

I shrugged one shoulder. "Maybe forty."

Carly clamped her mouth closed as the guy behind the counter turned around. He set the peanut butter shake in front of us and finished it off with a swirl of whipped cream, a couple of Nutter Butters, and a cookie straw.

"That is so beautiful!" Carly licked her lips. "I think I want that one, too."

"Car?" I touched her shoulder. "You are kinda allergic to peanuts."

"Right." She tipped her head to the side. "Can you make this one without peanuts?"

The guy thought for a minute. "If you get the Chocolate Coma, it's similar but without the peanut butter."

"Does it still have cookies?"

He nodded. "Oreos."

"Perfect. I'll have that one. Thanks."

I glanced at Brooklynn to see how she was holding up. She'd pulled her math book out of her hobo bag and was hunched over it like a gargoyle.

"I'm going to take this to Brooklynn before it starts to melt." I reached for the milkshake, but Carly beat me to it.

"I'll take it."

Which left me alone with my thoughts. My least favorite place to be. Without Carly or shopping to distract me, my thoughts were as obnoxious as ever.

Why didn't the student council agree with me? It was probably stupid, but I thought that a room full of guys would be on my side. They don't care about prom. My dad once told me that he put his tux on in his car ten minutes before he picked up his date because he spent the day river rafting.

All five of Brooklynn's older brothers ranted for an hour about how expensive prom was. That wouldn't mean a whole lot because her brothers have a flair for exaggeration, but Tyler was only a year older than us, so the memory was still fresh for him.

Maybe the stupidness of prom was one of those things that guys didn't figure out until they were done with high school. Like how to use a belt or the intricacies of personal hygiene.

This just proved what I knew all along: you could not count on high school guys.

"Here you go." The Greedy Cow guy brought my shake and Carly's to the counter, then swirled whipped cream on top of both and sprinkled some nuts on mine only. To finish them off, he jabbed in some cookies and the straws. It was mesmerizing to watch him work, and the perfect thing to pull me away from my thoughts.

When he finished, he went to the register and pushed a bunch of buttons while I dug my credit card out of my wallet.

"Okay, Pyper. That will be twenty-six dollars and thirty-two cents."

My hand faltered. "Do we know each other?"

I hadn't given him my credit card yet, and I don't think Carly said my name.

I searched his face for something familiar, but nothing about him stood out. His hair was somewhere between brown and blond, and his eyes were muddy brown. He was neither tan nor pale, not fat or skinny. He wore faded jeans and a brown t-shirt with the Greedy Cow logo. He would have been the most frustrating character to look for in a search-and-find picture. He could blend in anywhere.

A light flush crept up his neck and stopped just below his jawline. He pushed his hair off his totally normally proportioned forehead. "Yeah, sort of. I mean, we had Speech and Debate together last semester."

I nodded, trying to place him.

"And also, English 9, 10 and 11."

Wait, what?

"Oh, and we have econ together. But that's it," he finished with a shrug.

"Wait, we have econ together this semester? Like, at Cromer?"

He nodded.

I pursed my lips. "Why aren't you at school right now?"

He leaned forward, his eyes crinkling at the corners. "Why aren't you?"

I tapped my credit card on the counter. "Because I'm ditching first and second period today. And you?"

His grin widened. "I have on-the-job second period. I go to econ, work here through lunch, and then go back to school for third and fourth."

Okay, that sounded legit.

I rearranged my face into a Miss America smile. "Right, of course. Remind me what your name is? Senior moment." It wasn't my best joke attempt, but I thought I made it work.

"Landen."

I tapped my fist against my leg. I sort of thought his name would ring a bell. I could say, '*Oh yeah! Landen Jingleheimer Schmidt. How silly of me. Remember that time we did that one thing? So fun.*'

But I had nothing.

He gave a short laugh. "I guess I'm not all that memorable."

"You make a really great milkshake, though." I held one out like a toast to emphasize my point.

"That's something," he muttered as he took my credit card and swiped it on the machine. A moment later, he slid the card, receipts, and a pen across the counter.

I signed quickly, handing him the merchant copy. "Thanks for the ice cream, Landen." I emphasized his name.

"Yep. See ya, Pyper."

I grabbed the two milkshakes, then got out of there as fast as I could. I sipped my milkshake to distract myself and made a face. It tasted like strawberries and shame.

Okay, get a grip, Pyper.

It made sense that I didn't know who he was. I didn't pay attention to any of the guys at my school. They weren't worth it.

Even though I believed this with all my heart, my stomach continued to clench in an uncomfortable way.

What advice would I give someone else in this situation?

I squinted and walked slower to give myself time to think. I would tell them not to worry about it. People forget things all the time. If I felt like I needed to do something, I could apologize as soon as I saw Landen in class again. Then, it was up to him if he wanted to be offended forever or forgive my brain slip.

No big deal.

I straightened my shoulders and tossed my head. Really, I couldn't care less if he hated me forever. He was just some random high school guy.

ADVICE COLUMN
Sage Advice

Dear Sage Advice,

I hate it when guys treat me like an object. You know what I mean? I was at the movies with my sister, and this guy in the snack line totally flirted with me the whole entire time we waited. Then, he went into the theatre and sat next to a girl, put his arm around her, and smiled at me. What's that about?

It's so faux that guys think they can flirt with one girl and mack on another. I wanted to punch him in the face. Why do guys do stuff like that?

Signed,

More Than a Flirt Fling

Dear More Than a Flirt Thing,

If I could answer that question, I think I would solve one of the great mysteries of the universe. I don't know why guys do stuff like that, and even if I did, it wouldn't help. We can't control what other people do; we can only check ourselves. So, my advice to you is to be very, very careful who you flirt with. I'd even suggest waiting until after high school to flirt and date. By then, guys will theoretically have matured, and your chances of being treated the way you deserve will increase.

It might be worth a try.

Love, Sage

Chapter 4

"All right, Car. Time to talk." I pushed my empty milkshake cup to the side and fixed Carly with my best spill-your-guts stare. I'd given her space for as long as it took us to eat ice cream and discuss the movie posters on the wall of the food court.

Brooklynn's leg jiggled against the table. She'd finished her peanut butter shake ages ago. Living with all guys meant that she learned to eat fast or not at all.

Carly twirled her spoon through the remains of chocolate ice cream without looking up.

"Come on, Carly. You know you always feel better when you talk things out," I encouraged.

She shifted in her chair. "I had a date with Simon last night."

Brooklynn and I nodded. We already knew that. Simon called her at lunch yesterday to ask her out. Carly was so excited when she hung up that she couldn't finish her lunch. All she talked about the rest of the day was how hot it was when Simon did things spontaneously. She was a little out of control, honestly. Talking about Simon's impromptu date plans totally eclipsed our day.

Carly stopped playing with her spoon and rested her chin on her arms. "He was so bossy about getting together. He didn't give me time to say yes or no. I mean, not that I would have said no, but..."

Yeah, I remembered that bossy thing, too. Even yesterday I thought it sounded suspicious. Thursday is not typically a rocking date night.

"I put my Algebra homework on hold to go out with him. My mom and dad were both working at the café, so they didn't check in with me. I never did finish it. I'm probably going to fail math."

"Don't worry about that," Brooklynn said.

I nodded. "Brook can totally help you."

"Thanks, girls." Carly closed her eyes for a moment. When she opened them back up, tears glistened in the corners. "Simon picked me up at six for dinner. He was super distracted the whole time we drove. He would start to ask me a question but not finish it, and when I asked him one, I had to repeat it three times."

I tried not to interrupt. I had to literally bite the inside of my cheeks. Before Carly started dating Simon about a month ago, she asked my opinion about him. I told her that he seemed to go on a lot of dates.

Well, that's what I meant to say, anyway. What came out was something like, "The dude is a player, sister. Run for the hills." Carly laughed at first, then got offended when I tried to bring up evidence, so I dropped it. I wanted to remind her of that conversation now. Not to prove I was right; I already knew that I was. I just wanted her to understand for the future that if she'd taken me more seriously then, she would have been spared this heartache now.

"Do you remember the date Simon and I had right before this one? I told you about it, right? Where he kissed me for the first time?"

Brooklynn nodded. I grimaced.

"It was so amazing." Carly stared at the ceiling. "I thought maybe he was, like, remembering that and was overcome with emotion, so he couldn't concentrate. I thought he was about to tell me he loved me, or that he wanted to take me to prom, finally, or something else life-changing. I couldn't wait to hear what he was going to say."

Carly blew her nose. "So, we finally pulled into the parking lot of that burger place on Seventh. What's it called?"

Brooklynn and I looked at each other.

"The fast food place?" I wrinkled my nose.

Brooklynn added, "Big Bubba Burgers?"

"That's the one." Sadness wrapped around each word as it left Carly's mouth.

"That's where he took you on your big, spontaneous date?" My words came out harsh and jagged.

Carly didn't seem to notice. "I thought maybe it was a joke. When I asked him what we were doing there, he snapped, 'Eating dinner' like I was a big, fat dummy. Then he pulled into one of the parking stalls and stopped the car. I started to unbuckle, and he snapped at me again."

"Why?" Brooklynn asked. Her face was scrunched, trying to figure this all out.

"Because we weren't going in. He only stopped so we could decide what to order because he thinks it's super annoying when people take forever at the drive-thru window."

"That is just wrong," Brooklynn said as she stretched back in her chair.

"Yeah, it was a mess. I honestly don't even remember what I told him to order for me. I was kind of in a daze. He didn't order anything for himself. He just tossed the food at me and then started driving again." Carly rubbed her eyes. "Back to my house."

"Wait." Brooklynn slapped her palms on the table. "That was it?"

"I was still trying to choke the food down when he pulled into my driveway. He stared at me the whole time I chewed, and when I swallowed the last bite, he said, 'Thanks for the date. Have a good night.'"

"What?" I sputtered.

"What happened next?" Brooklynn curled her hands into fists and then tucked them into her armpits like she was trying to remove the temptation to punch someone.

"I thanked him for dinner and went inside."

"Carly!" Brooklynn exclaimed. "You can't let him walk all over you like that! You have to stand up for yourself. He was a major jerk, and you let him get away with it!"

I didn't say anything. I just watched Carly's face.

"I know, okay! I was so confused and hurt and... I didn't know what to do, and he was looking at me so impatiently that I was kind of scared to say anything. It was like he was a total stranger. I thought we were getting serious. I thought he really liked me. I mean, he kissed me. That means something, right? I thought we would be together forever."

I bit back all the words I wanted to say. There were so many pushing against the back of my teeth. Big, tough words that would totally put Simon in his place. But I knew none of them would help Carly right now.

Brooklynn pursed her lips. "So, is that it? You let him drive off?"

Carly shook her head. "Once I got inside, I started thinking that maybe it wasn't about me. Maybe he had a really horrible day. I mean, I am his girlfriend, you know? Maybe I could help. I started feeling sorry for him."

"Oh, Carly." I shook my head.

"I called him, but he didn't answer. I read my *Teen Queen* magazine to see if anyone else had been through something similar, and someone had! Advice Annie said it's always best to talk to the boyfriend when there are issues."

"You could have called me," I reminded her.

"Pyper," she said, patting my hand, "you are great for choosing outfits and picking out shoes, but you know nothing about guys. You've dated the same one forever."

I pressed my lips together, avoiding Brooklynn's eyes. It wasn't Carly's fault she thought that. Her family moved here at the beginning of the year. There's no way she could have known what I was like before now.

And I sure as suede was not going to talk about it.

"It was only seven," Carly went on, "so I decided to walk to Simon's house and talk to him. I wanted to find out what was going on. Simon's little brother answered the door. He told me Simon was gone. Then he said Simon was sick. Then he said something about Peru. Obviously, Simon didn't want to talk to me. I didn't push it, but I was feeling pretty awful when I walked away. About halfway down the driveway, his sister, Maggie, whispered at me from behind the hedges. She's a freshman. Do you know her?"

I shook my head, but Brooklynn nodded. "I tutored her in science last semester," Brooklynn said. "She's really nice."

"She is!" Carly brightened. "We totally clicked the first time I met her, but Simon always told her to bug off when I was over there. Anyway, Maggie stopped me and explained what was going on."

A heavy silence hung over our table. Carly fiddled with her spoon again. A tingle started in my toes and continued moving up my body until I couldn't hold it in another second.

"Carly! There are so many red flags here. Can't you see that? Why do guys like Simon think they can treat girls this way? Take my advice: dump him, and good riddance. It is time to move on." I paused for breath.

Carly shook her head. "I don't really have a choice. Not after what Maggie told me."

"What did Maggie say, exactly?" Brooklynn asked. "I mean, is there more? That date was bad enough."

Carly leaned forward to rest her chin on her hands. "Maggie told me Simon has a girlfriend. They're super serious. She goes to one of the other high schools. They've been dating for over a year."

"He has a girlfriend?" I set my hands in my lap where I could twist my rings around my fingers without Brooklynn or Carly seeing how agitated I was. "But, he goes out with girls at school all the time."

"Maggie said their parents made a rule about one-on-one dating. Like, none of them are supposed to do it at all until they graduate from high school."

Now that was what I was talking about! Why didn't all the parents have a rule like that? No exclusive dating in high school was the best idea ever. It was just unfortunate that the only people who saw things my way were Slimy Simon's parents.

"They had a family meeting a few months ago when they found out about Simon's girlfriend. They said he can keep seeing her, but he has to date other girls in between."

"What does that mean, exactly?" Brooklynn asked.

"When he goes out with his girlfriend, he has to go on a date with someone else before he can go on a date with her again."

I didn't say it out loud, but I actually thought that was a really good idea. I mean, it would have been a good idea if Simon hadn't taken it, twisted it, and turned it to the dark side.

"Maggie said Simon was super mad about it. Their parents said he could choose. He could stop seeing his girlfriend completely, or he could start dating other girls in between. He agreed to date other people, but Maggie said she had never seen him so angry. Pretty soon after that was when he asked me out for the first time."

"You have got to be kidding me," Brooklynn groaned.

Yeah, agreed.

"I wish I was." Carly twirled a strand of hair that escaped from her messy bun. "I guess Simon and his parents had another huge fight yesterday morning because Harlee's prom is tonight."

"Harlee?"

"Who's Harlee?" Brooklynn asked.

"His girlfriend," Carly said miserably.

Brooklynn barked out a laugh. "How in the world did he keep that straight?"

"He didn't," Carly said. "He called me Harlee all the time, but I thought it was, like, a cute lisp or something. I think that's why he kept dating me in between dates with her, because if he slipped and said his girlfriend's name it wouldn't be as noticeable as it would be if my name was Georgianna or something. So..." she waved her finger in the air, "yay for Carly."

"Wait," Brooklyn held up one hand. "I totally don't get this. Why did he kiss you if he's so crazy butt in love with Harlee?"

Carly's eyes welled with tears again. "I don't know. I wish I could ask Advice Annie or Suggestion Sally. They would be able to explain it to me."

I let out a huff of breath but kept my opinions to myself. Carly was in enough pain right now without me adding to it.

"Jerk," Brooklynn said as she shredded her napkin. "Jerk, jerk, jerk. Jerky McJerkerson."

Tears slid down to Carly's chin, then dripped onto her lap. "I really wanted to go to prom. I've already picked out the perfect dress."

"Well," Brooklynn dragged the word out until the syllables tripled. She widened her eyes at me and gestured to Carly with her head. Obviously, she wanted me to say something comforting, but the truth was, I thought it was a great idea for Carly to miss prom.

"Why don't we have a girl's night?" I suggested, pepping my voice to sound contagiously enthusiastic. "We could watch Matthew Mc-Conau-hottie movies and give each other mani-pedis."

"What-what?" Brooklynn looked alarmed.

I waved a hand at her. "I'll explain later."

"Oh, goody." Brooklynn rolled her eyes. "Carly, I still don't get something. Why did Simon bother taking you out on such a lame last-minute date? What was the point of that?"

Carly shrugged. "Simon gave Harlee a ride home from school on Tuesday, and his parents counted that as a date, so he wouldn't be able to take her to prom tonight if he didn't go on a date with someone else first."

"Unbelievable," I said as I sat back, shaking my head. "Someone needs to tell Harlee what Simon is doing. This is so wrong."

"She knows," Carly said.

I looked at her. "She what?"

"She knows. She doesn't care. It solves their problem."

Of all the things Carly had told us so far, this one hit me the hardest. How could a girl knowingly do that to another girl? High school and dating were hard enough without us turning on each other.

Maybe I would feel different if Simon and Harlee had told the other girl, in this case Carly, what the situation was, that she was just a filler date. Leading her on the way they did was so messed up on so many levels.

Too mean.

Too cruel.

For just a second, I wondered what Harlee would think about that magical kiss the other night between Simon and Carly? I was willing to bet she wasn't on board for that.

"This completely stinks." Brooklynn dug through my purse and pushed another packet of tissues toward Carly. All our napkins and tissues now formed a pile of navy-blue mascara-streaked sogginess next to Carly's cup.

I was totally going to have to redo her face again before we went back to school.

"Thanks." Carly's voice disappeared into the sound of her blowing her nose.

"You know what?" I said after she was done.

"What?"

"It's a good thing this happened."

"Huh?" She stopped wiping her eyes to stare at me.

"Simon is a horrible person. It's better you found that out after dating him for a couple weeks, instead of a couple years."

"I guess." Carly looked at the crumpled tissue in her hand. "I really loved him, Pyper. I don't ever want to see another guy again. I wish they would all disappear."

I knew exactly how she felt. I leaned forward with all the earnestness I could gather. "Carly, let me give you some advice. Take a break from dating for a while. Before Simon, you were dating Josh, and before him was Tristan, and then Farley, and that guy with the Vespa..."

"Devon," Brooklynn said.

"Dylan." Carly's eyes clouded over. "He had great hair."

"And before that was John. Actually, have you ever not had a boyfriend?"

Carly gave a watery smile. "I like boys."

"Yeah," Brooklynn said, poking Carly arm, "so do I, but I'm not constantly dating one."

"Why not?" Carly blinked. "It's super fun."

"Obviously." Brooklynn looked pointedly at the pile of tissues. "I'm seriously missing out."

"Well, this part isn't great." Carly added the tissue from her fist to the pile. "But falling in love is so fun."

I didn't like the look in her eyes. "You don't need a guy to have fun."

"Hey," Brooklyn said, "if you don't think you can give guys up all the way, maybe you can have a celebrity crush. Chris Pine is totally hot!"

"He's as old as my dad," Carly said, wrinkling her nose.

"Someone else, then. What about that guy who plays Aladdin?"

"Maybe."

I really needed Carly to hear me. "Put dating on hold, Car. We graduate in, like, six weeks. You could take a break for that long. It's worth it. Guys our age are heartless and selfish. They only—"

I didn't get to finish.

At that moment, a man appeared at my side, holding a tray of chicken nuggets and waffle fries in the air near his ear, like we were in a fancy restaurant. He was older, in his forties maybe, with thinning hair, a stud in one ear, and bulging arm muscles.

"Excuse me, miss."

He set the food down in front of me. My face must have shown all the confusion I felt because he smiled and went on.

"I work at Chick Fil-A." He gestured over his shoulder. "My employee over there wanted you to have this on the house. He thought you looked sad." His deep brown eyes disappeared into the folds of his smile.

"Oh my gosh! That is *so* adorable!" Carly gushed.

I glanced at the chicken, and then at the man. What was he talking about? I didn't look sad. I was fine. Perfect, even.

The man winked, then walked away, whistling.

Brooklynn nudged my arm.

"Um, thank you," I called.

He waved one hand in the air without turning around. When he reached the restaurant's counter, another guy popped up from behind the counter. They started whispering, shooting glances our way.

"Pyper!" Carly leaned across the table. "I could die. This is *so* sweet."

"No," I blinked. "No, it's not. It's weird. And it's probably for you anyway. You were the one crying. He got confused."

Brooklyn swiped a fry and stuck it in her mouth. "I think the chicken guy is in loooooooove with you."

"Wow. Okay, no." I pushed the food toward her and pulled out my phone to check the time. Brooklynn dug right in while Carly dropped her chin to her hand again, this time with a dreamy sigh, and gazed into the distance.

"As soon as Brooklynn finishes eating, let's get back to school," I said, tucking my phone away. We still had plenty of time, but I was suddenly done with the mall for today.

Instead of answering, Carly stood up and scooped the tissues up into her hands. She threw them away and brushed her hands on her skirt.

"You know what?" she said, her eyes roaming the tables and chairs of the food court. I couldn't tell what she was looking for, and honestly, I wasn't sure I wanted to know. She reached for her new cardigan and yanked it over her sweater. "Simon is a jerk! What he did was messed up. I am totally better off without him."

Brooklynn stopped with a fry halfway to her mouth. Ketchup dripped steadily onto the table.

"I deserve better," Carly said as she buttoned the last button of her cardigan and rested her palms on the table.

"Yes," I said cautiously. There was something not quite right about the glint in Carly's eyes. "You do."

"So, I'm going to go find him."

"Who?" Brooklynn choked.

Brooklynn and I looked at each other.

"The guy that's going to treat me better than Simon. The guy I deserve." Carly looked down at us. "I realized something when that man brought you that free food, Pyper. There are nice guys out there. I just need to find one of them. So, who can I date instead of Simon?"

"Who can you date instead?" I stared at her. "Are you serious?"

"I want to go to my senior prom." Carly craned her neck to look at each person who walked by our table. "I've been dreaming about it since I was twelve. I need a date."

Brooklynn shoved the empty chicken nugget wrapper away and raised her hands in the air. "I'm done. I feel sick."

So did I.

"Carly," I said, "are you sure a new boyfriend is the best idea? You are kind of on the rebound. People don't usually make great decisions when they are on the rebound, you know?"

"This isn't like that."

I stood up so Carly would stop looking down at me. "You can't just choose a guy like you would a shirt out of your closet and expect him to fit. Prom is next week; you need way more time to get to know someone before you start dating them."

I finally caught Carly's attention; her head tipped to the side. "I thought dating *was* a way to get to know people."

I shook my head. "If you're out on a date with someone, you're already semi-committed. What if the guy is a creeper? What if he only eats Sour Patch Kids and never brushes his teeth?"

"I love Sour Patch Kids," Brooklynn said.

I shot her a not-helping look. This was serious. I had to get through to Carly. Why did she think that because I don't date high school guys, I don't know anything? The opposite is true: because I'm not blinded by dating, I can see things more clearly than other girls.

"Carly." I gave her my best, shiniest smile. "It's not like your only options are to go to prom or sit at home by yourself until you're eighty. You want to go to prom?" I swallowed the bile that rose in my throat. "Great! Let's go to prom together. You, me, and Brooklynn."

"You don't go to prom with friends!" Carly sputtered. "That's, like, against the law. Prom is supposed to be romantic."

Brooklynn raised an eyebrow. "Prom is in eight days, Carly. Do you really think that's enough time to meet *and* fall in love with another guy?"

"Anything is possible if you believe."

Brooklynn lifted her hands in the air. "I give. There is no reasoning with this girl."

Carly headed towards the exit doors. "Let's get back to school so I can find myself a date."

Her tinkling laugh felt like a slap in the face.

ADVICE COLUMN
Sage Advice

Dear Sage,
Is it weird that my mom is my best friend? Some of my friends at school think it's weird that I tell my mom everything. Am I the only teenager in the world that likes her mom?
Sincerely, Momma's Girl

Dear Momma's Girl,
From one momma's girl to another, yay for you! Don't let the haters get you down. I think you will always be glad you are close to your mom.
Love, Sage

Chapter 5

"I'm home!" I called as I walked through the front door. Out of habit, I slipped off my shoes and put them and my purse into the metal basket my mom had mounted on the entryway wall. There was one for me and one for each of my three siblings, all appropriately labeled with our names from oldest to youngest.

Pyper, Roxie, Kai, Gavin.

I hung my purse and shopping bag on the hook under my name, then slipped off my shoes.

"Pyyyyyyyyyyyyyyyyyyyyyyyyyyyyypa!"

Gavin careened down the hall, slipping and sliding in his socks, with his superhero cape flying behind him. I caught him in my arms right before he hit the wall. Gavin to the rescue, indeed!

"You home, you home, you home!" he yelled.

"Hey, Trouble!" I lifted Gavin up, cradled him in my arms and bounced him up and down. "Where's Mom?"

"Kitchen." He wiggled and giggled until I set him on his feet. I held on long enough to plant a big, noisy smooch on the top of his head. Only when he ran away did I notice he was completely covered in powdered sugar.

And now, so was I.

"Comeoncomeoncomeon," he called, waving his arms at me as he skidded across the tile. Puffs of powdered sugar drifted from him like pixie dust.

"Pyper?" My mom stepped into the hall, wiping her hands on a dish towel. "Gavin said it was you, but I thought he was joking."

Gavin was going through this phase where he thought it was hilarious to trick people. Just the day before, he had spent, like, five minutes trying to convince me that a bright blue hippo was sleeping in my bed.

It wasn't.

I checked.

I reached out and tickled Gavin as he ran circles around Mom and me. "He seems to be feeling better."

"He is, thank goodness." My mom's smile illuminated all the freckles that were scattered across her nose. "His fever broke around nine, and we both took a three-hour nap. Life. Is. Good."

"Speaking of good, what are you making? It smells super yummy."

My mom flushed. "Come see!"

I followed her into the kitchen.

It was a disaster.

Mom moved around the kitchen island. "I was watching *The Great British Baking Show* last night while I laid on the couch with Gavin. They made these layered sponge cakes with custard in the middle. It just looked so good. There was leftover custard from the eclairs yesterday, so that's what we're doing. Just waiting for the sponge cake to cool." She opened the fridge and poked at the cakes inside with her finger.

The clock chimed obnoxiously loud while I eased onto one of the barstools. I had to test it before I put my full weight on it. Gavin liked to use the stool as a merry-go-round for his stuffed animals, so that meant sitting on a bar stool in my house was one of those at-your-own-risk things.

"Wait a sec." My mom turned around and looked at me. "Did that clock just chime one o'clock?"

"Confession." I moved the plastic wrap and swiped some custard from the bowl before my mom could stop me. I sucked it off my finger with my eyes closed, completely losing my train of thought. It was that good, like putting a cloud of happiness in my mouth. I reached for more, but this time my mom was too fast for me.

"Confession?" My mom tightened the plastic wrap and moved the bowl away from me. She leaned forward, elbows on the counter, and her piercing mom eyes searching the inner crevices of my soul.

"I sort of skipped school today."

"Okay." Mom stepped around the counter and sat on one of the chairs by the kitchen table. Gavin climbed into her lap, sucking his first two fingers. "Tell me a story."

So, I told her everything that had happened that morning, everything from my bitter failure and humiliating new assignment on the prom committee, to Carly's tragedy.

"Let me make sure I understand." Mom's eyes narrowed in concentration. "Carly decided to flirt with a random guy to try to get a prom date?"

"Yep."

My mom shook her head but didn't say anything. It wasn't necessary. I knew what she was thinking because it was the same thing that Brooklynn and I had been thinking. I could see it in her eyes.

"But the thing is, Mom, it worked. She texted me like five seconds after we got back to school and said that she did it."

"Someone asked her to prom that quickly?" My mom's eyebrows scrunched into the wrinkles on her forehead. Worry wrinkles. She claims she started to get those when I turned thirteen.

"Well, no. Not yet. But she got Travis' phone number and if she has his number that fast, then it's only a matter of time." I pulled a loose string that was hanging off my shirt; the snap was strangely satisfying.

"Do you know this Travis? Is he a nice boy?"

I hesitated. "He plays football."

"Okay," my mom said as she tipped her head to the side. "That didn't exactly answer my question."

"He has very white teeth. His face is totally symmetrical."

"Pyper!" my mom laughed.

I sighed. "He's friends with Jason."

"Oh." My mom's face drooped. "Jason."

"Yeah."

"Honey?" Mom twisted her wedding ring around her finger three times. "Since the subject came up, we should probably talk about Memorial Day."

It was suddenly hard to swallow.

Mom pressed her lips together. "Dad and I have been trying to figure out what to do. The Mylers are our friends. It doesn't seem right to stay home this year without a good reason."

"We could just re-enact Pukeageddon."

"Stop." Mom made a face. "Don't even tempt the fates. Last year was the worst Memorial Day weekend we have ever experienced. I do not want to go through that again." She shuddered. "Anyway, your dad and I feel like we need to go."

That sounded way worse than puking all weekend. "Do *I* have to go?" I ran my nail over a drip of frosting that had congealed to the countertop, chipping it away until not a speck remained.

Mom took a deep breath. "Dad and I decided to leave that up to you. Obviously, we want you to be with the family. It's been almost a year; do you think you could-"

"No." I gritted my teeth and felt the muscle in my cheek twitch.

A long silence followed, then Mom cleared her throat. "So, tell me some more about this student council meeting. Why do you think they voted you down?"

Because they are idiots.

I took a deep breath and let it out with the words. "I don't know."

"You're disappointed," Mom said, tipping her head to the side, "but you don't seem surprised."

"No," I said, shaking my head. "I think deep down I knew no one was going to go for it. But I had to try." I let out a long breath and looked at my mom. "Why don't people listen to me? I told Carly when she started dating Simon that he was a jerk, and it turns out he was even worse than I thought. Of course, I didn't know specifically that he was double-dip dating, but I knew enough about him to know he was going to break her heart. I'm trying so hard to save people from themselves. It's just frustrating, you know? And Travis? He is not anywhere near my list of top ten most trustable guys."

"Oh, Pyper. Is anyone on that list?"

"No." I shook my head. "No one is. Not even close. But if I could find enough trustworthy guys to make a list, Travis would definitely not be on it. Why won't people listen to me, Mom?"

My mom chewed her lower lip.

"Just say it."

"Do you feel that Travis isn't a good person just because he's Jason's friend?"

That was the easiest question of all time. Of course I did. Two guys couldn't spend that much time together and not be similar in all the wrong ways. But I couldn't say that to my mom. She would psychoanalyze my reasons.

It came down to this: I would rather err on the side of thinking all guys were jerks and be wrong, than trust one and get hurt.

I smiled, straightening my shoulders. "You know, Mom, Shakespeare said, 'Trust a few.'"

Of course, that wasn't his whole quote, just the part that served my purpose.

"That's true." My mom was chewing her lip again. "But M.K. Soni said, 'Life without trust is life in turmoil.'"

My smile dropped.

"Pyper, you have a heart of gold. You are such a good friend. You're always looking for ways to help others, and you give fantastic advice. However, I wonder if you are projecting your experience with Jason on this situation with your friends. You seem to assume that everyone is going to have the same experience you did. They might not, you see? Just because Jason—"

I stood up and went to the sink for a sponge to start cleaning the kitchen. It was a filthy mess. There was a pile of powdered sugar next to the toaster that I decided to tackle first, but it refused to wipe up. It either left a streak of white goo, or the sugar dissolved, making the counter look clean and feel sticky.

"Pyper? I know you hate talking about this," my mom said softly.

"It's fine." I rinsed off the sponge, then went back to the counter to have another go at the mess.

"Is it?" Mom tipped her head to the side. "I've noticed that you get twitchy whenever someone mentions Jason."

"I'm not twitchy. I'm helping. You're welcome."

Mom tugged my wrist. "Honey, I think you still have some big feelings."

Feelings. I hated those things. Right now it felt like two hands were squeezing my belly. "I've got this. I'm fine."

She nodded but didn't let go. "When I have big feelings that are all jumbled or scary, I mentally picture myself catching them in a glass jar like Kai used to do with caterpillars."

I walked back to the sink and turned on the water to rinse the sponge again. The cold water ran over my palms, cooling me down. I glanced at my mom and noticed that Gavin's eyelashes fluttered, and his fingers were drooping out of his open mouth, along with a thin string of drool. He snorted in his sleep and shifted slightly.

Which was just the cutest thing ever.

I smiled.

My mom continued, encouraged by my smile. "I mentally stick the jar on a windowsill so I can clearly see what is happening inside. It's so much easier to identify what I'm feeling when I separate from it and look at it objectively. I make better decisions when I act based on what is really happening and not on muddled feelings. You see?"

My mom stood up, holding Gavin in her arms, and left to put him in bed. I knew she was also giving me space to process because that is how my mom rolls.

I guess it couldn't hurt to take her advice.

I mentally built a butterfly net out of glitter strands and a sparkly, pink handle. I thought that might be the most effective tool for this exercise. I then swooped it through my mind, gathering all the thoughts that were fluttering around in there, and I deposited them into a large, glass jar.

Then I got stuck.

Jason's face swirled around the jar like an angry hornet, stirring up a black dust that coated all my other thoughts.

"Hey." My mom came up behind me and put her arm across my shoulders. "You okay?"

It took me a minute to answer. I was still trying to swat that circling hornet in my mind.

"I'm fine," I said. "Perfect. Do you want some help finishing up dessert?"

"Hmmm." My mom squinted in a way that made me think she wasn't going to let me get out of this that easily. Then, she surprised me by changing the subject.

Again.

"Let's talk about you skipping school today. How are your grades?"

"A's."

"Did you miss anything important, like tests or study guides or presentations?"

"I don't think so."

My mom raised an eyebrow.

"In economics, we were finishing up a unit before we start group projects. We haven't picked the groups yet. I have a free period next, then lunch. Third period is English, and we are just watching the movie *Romeo and Juliet*."

"Which one?" Mom's voice rose in alarm.

"The newer one. Then I have chemistry, which I'm pretty sure was a lecture today. I'll ask my lab partner for his notes so I can catch up."

Mom studied me for a moment longer, then reached for a serving tray. "In the future, will you text or call me *before* you decide to skip school, so we can talk about it?"

"Yes, I will. Sorry."

My mom grabbed a dish towel from the counter and flicked me with it. "Now go get that cake out of the fridge and help me finish it."

While we worked, my mom explained that she baked the cake in a cookie sheet so that it would be thin and easy to layer. I couldn't see the vision yet, but I was happy to set the cake on the counter and cut circles out of it with a cookie cutter. I slowly placed the circles on the counter next to my mom. She spread raspberry jam on one side, then handed it back to me. I topped it with that fantastic custard, then put it on the serving tray. We continued this way until there were six mini cakes, stacked three high each. Then, we piped fluffy clouds of whipped cream on the top and artistically arranged raspberries. When we were done, my mom stood back to eye the finished product.

It was breathtaking.

"I wish we had mint leaves," my mom said, looking out the kitchen window to the dormant herb garden. Her mint wouldn't grow back all the way until June or July.

"I'll go get some," I said, already turning towards the entryway.

"Oh, no. That's silly to go all the way to the grocery store for mint leaves." Mom squinted at the cakes again.

"Yeah, I'm going."

"Really?" My mom looked at me with a half-smile.

I nodded.

"Thank you. I know it's silly—"

"Mom!" I struck a pose. "There is nothing silly about wanting something to look beautiful. I need to get more cereal anyway. Kai ate all my Lucky Charms. I'll be back in a blink."

"You're the best Pyper in the world!" My mom called as I walked out of the kitchen.

I kissed my hand and waved it over my shoulder.

The
Cromer Chronicles

ADVICE COLUMN
Sage Advice

Dear Sage,

My stupid ex-boyfriend won't take the hint that we're over. He is totally following me. I keep seeing him all over town, and every time I see him, he's with a different girl. All blondes, like me. It's so obvious he can't let me go and it's ridiculous.

I don't want to see him anymore! That's why I broke up with him! How can I get him to stop?

Sincerely, Sick of Ex-Sightings

Dear Sick of Ex,

A simple solution is to change your routine and see if he keeps showing up at the same places you go.

If he doesn't, then the problem is solved!

Otherwise, it sounds like you need to take up a hobby. If you are involved with something new and super fun, you won't care what your ex is doing and who he's with.

Food for thought.

Love, Sage

Chapter 6

On my way to the grocery store, I realized that if I took my time shopping, then I could stop by the middle school and pick up Roxie on the way home. She loved it when I did that. Well, what she really loved was not riding the bus, but I was totally going to pretend it was me that made the experience super fun.

I parked Beauty farther away from the store than I normally would. Since I had extra time, I decided it would be good to get some more steps in. It was satisfying to see five digits on my fitness watch at the end of the day.

A cool breeze swept my hair off my shoulders and twisted it around my head. I smoothed it back into a bun and secured it with a pen from my purse.

I took a cart that someone had left in the middle of an empty parking space and pushed it toward the grocery store. On my way through the doors, I paused to smile at a little girl who was gripping the handle of a miniature cart alongside her mother. It was adorable.

Until she stuck her tongue out at me.

I grinned as I passed by, wishing her mother the best of luck with that.

I pushed my cart towards the produce aisle. It took me a few minutes to find the mint. The leaves were in small, plastic packages, smushed between the lettuce and green onions. The mint in front looked grim, so I picked them up to get them out of the way and shifted through what was left with my other hand until I finally found a carton all the way in the back that looked more green than brown.

"Excuse me, miss? I think you dropped this."

I was so focused on my task that I startled. Mint packages slid toward the floor, but I caught them just in time. I turned around slowly to give my heart a chance to slow down and my brain a chance to take in the blond guy in front of me, who was wearing an employee polo.

I shifted my gaze when he moved his hand, jangling a super cute bracelet.

"No, that isn't mine," I said.

"No?" His fingers curled around the charms, clinking them together like fairy bells.

"No." I went back to the mint, trying to decide what to do. I guess Mom and I could pick the green leaves out and throw away the brown. It just seemed like a waste. There weren't very many that looked pretty.

"That's weird," he shifted from one leg to the other. "Anyway, do you need help with anything?"

I started to say no again but reconsidered the sad mint in my hand. "Do you have any mint that isn't brown? Maybe in the back?"

He took the package from me. His fingers were cold where they brushed my palm. "I'll check. Don't go anywhere."

While I waited, I browsed the fruit displays. In the time it took me to decide that strawberries were a must and that I was desperately craving bananas, the boy returned, waving a new package in the air. "You're in luck!"

I took it from him and inspected the leaves. They were crisp and the right shade of emerald green. "Perfect." I set the mint next to the bananas and looked around to see if there was anything else I needed before I moved on.

That's when I realized that the grocery guy was still standing there.

"Hey," he said, rubbing the back of his neck with one hand. "Do you need help with anything else?"

"No, thank you." This section was getting a little too crowded. I aimed my cart toward the meat counter.

"Wait. Uh, my name is Kurt, by the way. Do you think you'd want to..." His voice trailed off when I arched an eyebrow.

Seriously? He had to know how ridiculous it was to ask me out here, right now. He didn't even know my name.

I pressed my lips together, trying to look sympathetic instead of annoyed. "Kurt, you saved the day with the mint, and I appreciate it, but no, thank you. I wouldn't want to go to dinner or a movie or ice skating or..."

He coughed, his neck blotching red. "Hold on. What if I was about to ask you if you would want to save fifty percent by signing up for the membership card?"

"Is that what you were going to ask me?" I leaned my elbows on the cart handle.

"No." He rubbed his blotchy neck. "I was going to ask if you wanted to see the new Marvel movie tonight. But now I'm thinking I really should have started with the rewards thing." His face almost matched the shade of the eggplant on the shelves behind him.

I felt a tiny glimmer of sympathy. The guy was obviously embarrassed. And I had to admit—grudgingly-that it took guts to ask out a complete stranger. "Can I give you some advice?"

He blew a gust of air and nodded.

"When you want to ask a girl to do something with you, get her name first. Don't open with gimmicky things like supposedly missing bracelets. Just be natural and normal and honest. Okay?"

His eyes widened like I'd hit him on the back of the head with a mammoth zucchini.

I pulled my purse up on my shoulder and leaned forward to push my cart away.

"Wait!" Kurt reached out his hand and rested it on the side of the basket. "I'd like to start over."

I didn't really have time for this. I gave him a tight smile and tried not to look at my watch.

"Hi. My name is Kurt." He held out his hand and, after a few seconds, I shook it with the tips of my fingers. "What's your name?"

I held back a sigh. "Pyper."

"Pyper." He looked at the ceiling. "I think you're gorgeous. I noticed you the second you walked by the apples. I know this is weird because we just met, but I was hoping you'd go to the movies with me tonight." He met my eyes and smiled, the left side of his face morphing with a deep dimple. "It could be fun."

For the first time in just under a year, I felt a loosening in my belly. The way Kurt looked at me, with so much hope and expectation, put a tiny crack in the gigantic titanium boulder around my heart.

Plus, I don't know a single girl who isn't a sucker for a compliment like that.

But there was no way I could go out with him. No way. I was done with that garbage. And if, for some reason, I changed my mind about the whole dating thing, I would never go out with someone I just met. He could be a creeper, or a forty-year-old man that carried his age well, or, like, a fruitarian.

I backed away. "I'm sorry, Kurt. You seem like a nice guy, but I can't. Thanks for your help with the mint."

"Wait, still no?" His face morphed into understanding. "You have a boyfriend already, don't you?"

I turned around without answering that question. He could think whatever he wanted to think. Just like everyone else did. "I have to go; I have to pick up my sister." Then I quickly pushed my cart around the corner. I didn't stop until I passed the meat counter and found a bread display in the bakery that was big enough to hide behind. I leaned forward, letting my head drop and my eyes close.

I took a couple of deep breaths to gather myself, then straightened and shook out my shoulders. I did the right thing back there. It was fine.

And now I really needed some ice cream.

I took a detour to the cereal aisle on my way to the freezer section, where I picked up two family-sized boxes of Lucky Charms. That should hold me over for a couple weeks unless Kai raided my stash again.

Then I made my way to the frozen aisle and went straight to the tiny cartons of ice cream that came with a spoon tucked inside the lid. I chose Salted Caramel for Roxie and Strawberry Cheesecake for myself. I was contemplating some frozen fruit bars when I heard my name in an all too familiar voice.

I turned slowly, grateful that I recognized the voice and had a few extra seconds to arrange my face into a carefree and friendly smile.

"Mrs. Myler! How are you?" I leaned in close for an airy one-armed hug.

"Oh, wonderful!" She sounded so relieved that it made me wonder how she had expected me to respond. "It is so good to see you, Pyper. I've really missed having you around since Jason went to college."

Even though I stood in front of a huge freezer unit, I could feel heat begin to build at the base of my spine. I tried to think of something else to bring it to a halt before it reached my face. There would be no hiding an embarrassed flush, and tomato red was so not my color.

I cleared my throat loudly.

Too loudly.

"Well, you know. Time marches on," I shrugged. I didn't even know what I was saying. Then, I happened to look down and noticed streaks of powdered sugar all over my clothes. It was like I'd wrapped my adorable skinny jeans in strips of paper mâché.

Just fabulous.

Mrs. Myler kindly averted her eyes. "Too quickly for my taste. Have you heard from Jason lately? He made the lacrosse team. He is thriving at college. You know him; he's right at the center of everything. Such a social butterfly."

"Hm." I nodded, my eyes straying to the fruit bars. Curse them for grabbing my attention. If they hadn't, I would've been well on my way to the checkout when Mrs. Myler stepped down this aisle.

Mrs. Myler watched me with expectant eyes, but I couldn't remember what she'd just said. Had she asked me a question?

"I'm...sorry?"

"Oh," she said with a tinkling laugh. "I wondered if you hear from Jason often?"

I swallowed, trying to keep my voice light. "He's a big-time college guy now. Busy, like you said."

"Oh." Mrs. Myler shook her head, her long, leather earrings swinging near her chin. "Except, you're special. Jason would never be too busy for you!" She patted my arm, like that was supposed to be reassuring. "He should keep in touch better. I'll talk to him."

I indulged myself for a minute, picturing Jason's mom scolding him for neglecting to stay in touch with me. She'd be wagging her finger in his face, talking a mile a minute. And he? I almost laughed out loud. What would he do? Feel regret? Sorry? Ashamed?

I sincerely hoped it was all three, and more.

"No, no. It's okay. I'm terrible at keeping up on email and stuff anyway. I'll just see him on holidays or whatever."

"Yes! Memorial weekend! We are so looking forward to it."

I swallowed a wad of irritation. Why did our families have to be friends? Why did they start that dumb lake tradition? Spending Memorial Day trapped on a boat with Jason when I was trying so hard to forget that he existed was torturous just to think about. I couldn't even imagine actually doing it.

"Hm." I attempted a smile. "Well, I better run. Ice cream is melting." I gestured to my cart.

"It was lovely to run into you, dear. I really miss you."

I nodded and turned away, my smile dropping as soon as my back was to her. I knew my goodbye was abrupt, probably even borderline rude, considering our history. I mean, I'd known Mrs. Myler my whole life. I used to call her Aunt Carrie. But it was horrible to stand there, listening to her talk about our families like nothing had changed, like we could still be the best of friends.

On the other hand, maybe things hadn't changed for her. I didn't know what Jason told his mom. This could be really confusing for her. One minute, Jason and I were leaving for prom, all glowy and floaty, and the next...well, Jason should talk to his mother.

That was not my problem.

As soon as I was far enough away from Mrs. Myler, I stopped walking and breathed out a sigh of relief that was so loud that an older man at the end of the next aisle dropped a can of soup.

"You all right, girly?"

"Oh sure. Sorry." I bent to pick up the can for him before I continued to checkout.

I should have grabbed more ice cream.

The line moved quickly, which was a very good thing. My introduction to Kurt and that unexpected reunion with Mrs. Myler took more time than they should have. I hurried to Beauty and dropped the grocery bags in the back seat, then zoomed towards the middle school.

I pulled into the parking lot with seconds to spare. The front doors spewed students by the droves. I had to dodge middle schoolers my whole way to Roxie's locker. It worked out splendidly in the end; she was still switching out books when I jogged up.

"Hey, sissy poo!" I threw my arms around her from behind.

"I thought that was you," she laughed. "I could smell your coconut lotion about thirty seconds before I could see you. Are you taking me home? Please say you are. Brody just told me he found an egg salad sandwich in his locker from, like, two months ago. He's been saving it so he can play keep-away on the bus. You literally saved my life." She paused to breathe. "So, what's going on? Why are you here?"

"Do I need a reason?" I linked her arm as we turned toward the exit. "I'm just picking up my most favoritest sister in the whole wide world because I love her so very much. Oh, and I also have a surprise."

"Yay!" Roxie grinned, looking so much like me it was freaky. "I hope it's ice cream."

I stopped walking. "Seriously?"

"Does that mean you have ice cream?"

"How do you always do that? You're like a mind reader."

Roxie pulled my arm to get me moving again. "You're the mind reader. You're the one who always knows when I need ice cream."

I tugged her fish braid. "Good point. I'm pretty much the best."

"You know it!" She swatted my hand away. "Last one to the car has to sing Gavin to sleep tonight!" She let go of me and was gone so quickly that I knew I would never catch her.

When I got to Beauty, Roxie was leaning against the passenger side door, obviously gloating. "I won! You sing!"

"I demand a rematch." I unlocked the car and rifled through grocery bags to find the ice cream cartons.

Roxie shook her head. "No way."

"The competition was obviously rigged." I tossed her the Salted Caramel.

"Oh, bless you, sister!" She opened it and took an enormous bite. "Of course it was rigged. I totally cheated. It's my night, and I don't wanna sing that dumb song ever again."

I slid into the driver's seat and opened my own carton of ice cream. The scent of creamy strawberries wafted up my nose. I scooped a spoonful and held it on my tongue to savor it. Strawberry Cheesecake was an excellent choice.

Roxie kept talking. "I think Mom and Dad made this dumb rule because *they* are sick of singing to Gavin every night and don't want to admit it. Their plan failed, though. Because we all have to take turns, everyone in the whole family is going to hate 'Somewhere over the Rainbow' before Gavin grows out of it. I can't even listen to Iz sing anymore, and he's amazing." She took a bite but kept talking around it. "Did you know Kai doesn't sing? He just says the words in a really bad Scottish accent. I don't know how he thinks that counts. No one in the *Wizard of Oz* is Scottish. Munchkins aren't Scottish, witches aren't Scottish. The Tinman? So not Scottish. Our brother is weird."

I hummed the first few bars of 'Somewhere Over the Rainbow' loudly. Roxie smacked me with her notebook.

"I don't know how you can even joke. Seriously, it's the worst!"

I totally agreed. If I never heard that song again, I would be so very happy.

I balanced the ice cream carton on my knee as I started Beauty up and slowly pulled out of the middle school parking lot. With all the traffic moving at snail speeds, it was easy to finish my ice cream before it melted.

"Are you?" Roxie looked at me.

"Sorry, what?"

Roxie's sigh was more akin to a hurricane. "Would you listen? I was saying that you seem kinda off."

I'm sure her voice contained a lot more concern the first time she said it; this time it was more like she was asking me why I used her sewing scissors to cut out nail stickers.

"Pyper Sage Lewis!"

Okay, yeah. So, I was a little off.

"Sorry, Rox. I'm fine. I just-" I paused. I just what? Skipped school so one of my best friends could decide to start schmoozing more guys? Went to the store for Mom and ran into the woman I thought would one day be my mother-in-law?

Not that I would *ever* in a billion years admit that to anyone. I already destroyed all the notebooks that said Mrs. Pyper Myler. So, no evidence.

"Yes?" Roxie rapidly blinked at me. "You're just what?"

I pulled into the driveway and parked. With a sigh, I put my keys in my lap and leaned against the headrest. "It's Friday."

"Uh-huh." She nodded, sucking on the ice cream spoon even though she'd finished a long time ago.

"Friday hates me."

"It's a day, Pyper. It can't hate you."

"And yet, here we are."

Roxie's face softened. "Okay, spill it. What happened?"

I flipped the keys through my fingers. "Oh, nothing. I just ran into Mrs. Myler at the store before I picked you up." I stared straight ahead, not wanting to see the look on Roxie's face. I could feel her agitation building. It would have been no surprise to see actual steam billowing out of her ears and her nostrils flaring.

"What did you do?"

"Obviously, I talked to her."

Roxie huffed and she puffed, and she blew out another explosive breath. "About what?"

I opened my mouth to respond but didn't get a chance.

"About how her son is the biggest jerk-o of all time? Or maybe about how he's a player and a creeper, and if life were fair, he would have zits as big as his ego?"

"That's a mood," I grinned.

"Did you talk to her about the empty space where his heart should be? I don't know how they didn't notice that sooner with all this technology and stuff. Baby heart beats come up on those machines before they're born. I totally remember going with Mom when she was pregnant with Gavin. Someone should have taken care of Jason's empty heart space sooner; then none of this would have happened." She stopped talking with her hands and dropped both into her lap.

I should have bought Roxie a bigger ice cream carton.

She opened her door. "He's dead to me. I don't want to talk about it anymore. Can I go to the mall with you tomorrow? Didn't you say you were going to pick up job applications?"

My brain transitioned way faster than I expected, like it was just waiting for an excuse to stop thinking about Jason.

"Totally. That would be fabulous!"

I was going to ask Brooklynn to go with me, even though she worked at her dad's sporting goods store and didn't really need a job. This was a much better solution. It would take a lot of pretty words to get Brooklynn to go to the mall two days in a row.

"Yay!" Roxie reached for one of the grocery bags. "I really want to look at earrings. My friend has some shaped like pineapples. I love pineapples!" She hurried to the front door and opened it so she could bellow, "I'm hooooooome!"

"Hey there!" Mom was sitting on the couch flipping through a magazine. "Aw, Pyper, thanks for getting Roxie. That was thoughtful."

I tossed her the package of pristine mint leaves.

She caught it with one hand. "Have I ever told you how much I love you?"

"Every day," I called as I headed up the stairs to my room with the boxes of Lucky Charms. I'd hide them later. All of a sudden, I felt exhausted.

I flung myself on my bed and kicked off my cute booties. With a pillow bunched under my chin, I laid on my stomach with my phone out in front of me.

How was the test?

I sent the text to Brooklynn, and then scrolled through my messages while I waited to hear back from her.

Carly had sent a picture of herself in front of her closet, holding up a prom dress with her fingers crossed.

I responded with a thumbs up even though I wanted to send a half dozen caution signs and some fiery explosions.

There was also a text from Leah asking if I could get the rest of the prom committee to meet during their free periods to help with decorations.

Ugh. I'd sort of forgotten I was in charge of that now. Maybe if I ignored it, the whole thing would go away.

My phone chimed with another text from Leah when she included me in the chat thread with the rest of the prom committee.

So much for it going away.

I opened the chat and typed a short message about decorations and then, as an afterthought, asked when they could meet to finish up the rest of this prom junk.

Okay, I didn't say 'junk'.

I also didn't say any of the other descriptive four-letter words rolling through my mind. So, that's a win.

There was a text from my mom asking if I could also pick up some milk.

Oops.

Then Brooklynn made my phone chime.

Great! Aced it!

I responded with a clapping emoji, then added,

What are you doing this weekend?

Work and football game. You?

Mall with Roxie.

Mall? Again?

Mall! Always!

Gross.

A bunch of responses from members of the prom committee interrupted my conversation with Brooklynn. I scrolled through them super quick to make sure it was all good, then I let Leah know.

"Dad's home! Time for dinner," Mom called up the stairs.

Gotta go, Brookie!

See ya when I see ya!

The
Cromer Chronicles

ADVICE COLUMN
Sage Advice

Dear Sage Advice,
I've liked the same girl since the seventh grade, but she doesn't know. I can't seem to get her attention, even when I get the guts to talk to her. My timing reeks or something. I keep wondering if I should just give it up as hopeless, but I can't let her go.
Will you help me?
Sincerely, Bad Timing

Dear Bad Timing,
My advice is to drop the part where you try so hard to get her attention and just focus on being her friend. Get to know her, ask her a lot of questions, invite her to do things, show interest in her without any ulterior motives. Just start with being friends and let it grow from there if it's going to.
By the way, this works for you, too. As you get to know her better, you can find out if she really is who you think and decide if you want to be more than just friends.
There is nothing worse than giving your heart to someone who doesn't deserve it.
Love, Sage

Chapter 7

That night I dreamed my mom and I were making a cake in the shape of Jason's head. She really wanted me to use the mint leaves for his eyes, but I kept arguing that it wouldn't work because his eyes were blue. Carly waltzed through the kitchen wearing my pink wedges, dancing with a boy who changed into someone new every time they turned around. Gavin and Brooklynn followed them, throwing handfuls of powdered sugar into the air.

When I finally pulled myself out of the dream, I stared at the ceiling for a long time as I tried to figure out what it all meant. My mom believes that dreams are powerful, that they are our subconscious trying to tell us something important. With that in mind, I came to the only possible conclusion: my subconscious needed a vacation.

I reached for my phone to check the time and noticed a text from Roxie.

ARE YOU UP YET? LET'S GO, LET'S GO!!

All caps and two exclamation marks. The girl was an animal. I rubbed my bleary eyes and looked at the clock. The mall wasn't even open yet. I blinked and looked again. Just kidding. That was a nine, not a six.

Did you really just text me when we are in the same house? I'm telling Mom.

> That's going to be hard to explain since you just texted me back!

> Hm, good point. I guess we'll both be scrubbing toilets with our toothbrushes.

> I'll just use Kai's again.

> #willshereally?

> Ok, goofus. I'm coming.

> Give me a sec.

I had just put my phone on my nightstand when there was a horrific *bang* and my bedroom door slammed into the wall. That was totally going to leave a mark.

"Gavin! You stink brain! I told you to leave Pyper alone!" Roxie burst into my room right on Gavin's heels, who kept slipping through her fingers like a wet grape. They jumped onto my bed and started a wrestling match that thoroughly tangled and twisted my chenille blanket. When I tried to move out of the way, it only got worse. My legs were pinned, like a fluffy mermaid.

Roxie tried to grab Gavin again, but he executed an impressive front tuck roll in the space between the wall and my hips, landing behind my back where he huddled like a bunny. I scooted to the side to avoid Roxie's flailing arms. Gavin anticipated my move and curled into an uncomfortable lump against my back. Some flails of appendages later, I found myself squished under Roxie, who was sitting on my ear grasping for Gavin under my bent knees. When I finally freed my face enough to take a breath, I saw Kai filming the whole thing on Mom's phone as he stood in the doorway.

I yanked my arm out of its blanket prison and lobbed a sequined pillow at Kai's head. Unfortunately, he easily dodged out of the way. He had a lot of practice. We frequently threw things at his head.

Believe me, it was always deserved.

Roxie watched the graceful arc of my pillow as it soared through the air. When her eyes landed on Kai, she shrieked—probably permanently damaging our eardrums—and dove under my blankets to escape the camera. That plan would have worked a lot better if the blankets weren't twisted around my legs.

"Kai! Get out of here with that thing. If you don't, I'm going to-" Her voice was shrill, even when muffled.

"What?" Kai was laughing so hard he could hardly talk. "What are you going to do?"

If the video survived the wrath of Roxie, the people watching were going to get serious motion sickness from his shaking arms.

Roxie threw the blankets back. My legs moved with the momentum, propelling me off the bed and onto the floor, where I laid as helpless as a beached fish. Roxie stood on the edge of my bed like a super-hero, with hands on her hips and her head thrown back. I imagined a glittery cape waving behind her in the breeze of justice. With a few quick bounces-my poor mattress-she leaped into the air with her arms outstretched in front of her.

Silence filled the room. Gavin emerged from his cocoon of sheets with wide eyes. The sight before us was so weird, it was almost beauti-ful. I couldn't have looked away if I tried. Like a ring fighter jumping from the ropes to piledrive their opponent, Roxie soared through the air. I think she stayed afloat out of pure spite.

The world came back into focus with a loud *whoosh* as Roxie collided with Kai and the two of them crashed to the floor.

"What in the world?" Mom stared at the chaos in my room with an unreadable expression. "What is going on here?"

What had taken her so long? We were in desperate need of adult supervision. I tried again to kick my legs free, but it was useless. We might have to call the fire department to extract me from my buttery soft blankets.

"Well?" My mom's hands had found their way to her hips, and her left eyebrow was almost invisible it had climbed so high into her hairline. Even though I had done nothing wrong, I had a sudden urge to point my blaming finger at Kai.

Again, it was deserved.

Roxie hopped to her feet and smoothed down her striped top. "I was trying to keep Gavin from bothering Pyper. She's still waking up, and you know she takes three times as long when we rush her, so I had to chase Gavin down, but he's too fast."

"Like a ninja!" Gavin squeaked from under my sheets.

"Hey!" I protested, sitting up. My hair flew up in all directions thanks to static electricity. It looked amazing, I'm sure.

Roxie shrugged. "It's true."

I slumped against the wall, my pride partially wounded.

Mom stepped over Kai to sit on the edge of my bed. She gently pulled Gavin out and perched him on her lap. "Why were you trying to see Pyper, buddy?"

He burrowed his face into Mom's shoulder, peeking out just long enough to stick his little pink tongue in Roxie's direction. She huffed and folded her arms.

"I need Pypa."

I noticed the end of the blanket sticking out, which made it possible for me to start unraveling my chenille cage. Everyone watched, but no one moved.

"Thanks for the help, guys," I breathed as I pulled myself on the bed next to Mom and Gavin.

"It was like watching a baby bird break out of its shell," Roxie said in awe.

I tossed a pillow at her face, smacking her squarely. She was not as skilled at dodging as Kai.

"Why do you need me?" I tickled Gavin's back. He squirmed in Mom's arms until he could see me. He blinked his long eyelashes slowly.

"I need your cereal."

Roxie groaned, her face dropping into her hands. "Really, Gavin?"

"Seriously, dude. That was dumb." Kai pulled himself to his feet and kicked my pillow. "I already ate it."

"What?" I looked up. "I bought two huge boxes."

Kai leaned into the door jamb with a shrug.

Roxie pushed her leg out until it connected to the side of Kai's knee, knocking him back to the floor. He didn't even try to get up this time.

"Kai!" Mom shook her head at him. "I'm sorry, Pyper, really. But since you're up, Roxie is ready to go to the mall, and I have some errands I need you to run."

"Yay," I groaned as I pulled my blanket up over my head.

Because of Roxie's completely untrue observations about my morning routine, I got ready for the day speedy fast. Well, as soon as everyone moved their tushes out of my bedroom.

Since I would be collecting job applications, I made sure my outfit was professional while still reflecting who I am. That's very important when getting dressed because, despite what people say about not judging a book by its cover, most people totally do.

Judge a person by the way they look, I mean.

I chose a flowy skirt that hit just below my knees. Ivory-colored chiffon with pastel flowers. It was one of my very favorites, which I think makes it good luck. I paired it with an ivory tee that just barely peaked out under a coral pink cardigan, which, after some debate, I buttoned to my collarbone and wrapped with a thin, tan belt around my middle. Then I put on the coral wedges that I bought yesterday and looked in the mirror.

Perfect.

My confidence boosted a notch when I walked downstairs and Roxie gave me the thumbs-up sign. Even though she was four years younger than me, she was a rocking awesome fashionista. She made the skirt I was wearing with her own two hands after I picked out the fabric.

"What are you going to do with your hair?" Roxie asked, pursing her lips.

"Down?" I asked.

She shook her head. "Come here."

I sat down on a stool, and Roxie swept my hair to the side, then braided it loosely. She ran to get some bobby pins, which she strategically jabbed along my scalp to create a windswept look that was, frankly, brilliant.

"Pyper," Mom walked into the kitchen with Gavin on her hip. "You look beautiful! I would hire you in an instant."

"For what job?" I teased because she's my mom and has to say things like that.

"Any job! You'll do great. Have a good time, and good luck!" She followed Roxie and me to the front door and waved from the porch until Beauty carried us out of sight.

The butterflies didn't truly swarm around my belly until we walked through the front entrance of the mall. Although I had worked all summer for the last five summers, I never had to actually apply for a job before. Jason's parents owned the climbing wall in town. Because we were family friends, I didn't have to go through the interview process. I didn't even have to fill out an application. That was convenient at the time, but now it made me feel like I was a super noob at this job thing.

It would have been easier, but there was no way on this wide, green planet that I was going to ask the Mylers for a job this year. I'd rather wear taffeta and puffy sleeves every day for the rest of my life.

"Okay." I took a deep breath. "I'm going to start with the boutiques, then work my way to department stores. Last resort is the food court. Where will you be?"

Roxie's eyes darted all over, trying to take in every colorful detail that surrounded her. I could totally relate to that feeling.

"I'll stick with you for a bit," she said, and off we went.

The first boutique we came to was an accessory store. It wasn't my first choice for a job. The cashier handed me an application but added that she didn't think they were hiring. I thanked her anyway and left, feeling much better overall. The first time doing anything new is the hardest, and that wasn't bad. Totally do-able.

"I'm going to stay here." Roxie stopped at the entrance of the boutique, eyeballing a display of feather earrings.

"That didn't take long, ditcher," I smiled.

She answered by wrinkling her nose, then promptly ignored me as she searched through the earrings.

The next two boutiques were also not hiring, which was a little discouraging. I began to wonder if I should have waited until closer to summer. There were still five weeks left of school. Maybe stores didn't start evaluating their need for summer help this early.

I collected three more applications before coming to the place I really wanted to work more than any other store anywhere.

Juneberry.

I purposely put off this moment, hoping I'd be my best, most confident self by the time I got here. The guy at the counter was beautiful, just like all the Juneberry employees, but I was there for the discount and nothing more.

I smiled charmingly. "Hi!"

"Hi," he said. "Can I help you?"

"Yes, thanks. I'm here for an application. Do you know if you're hiring?" I steadied my hands by clasping them behind my back.

"You want to work here?" He raised his eyebrows.

I couldn't tell what he meant by that. Like, was Juneberry a bad place to work? Or maybe I didn't look like I would fit in? That was ridiculous. When I gave myself a makeover last year, I purposely patterned my look after the girls I'd seen working at Juneberry.

I choked on my, "Yes!" I wasn't cool enough to leave off the exclamation mark.

"Hm," he sniffed, then rifled through a stack of papers. What he handed me was more like the SATs than a job application. "We don't have very many applications here. Most people fill them out online."

I knew that. I thought it would set me apart to put in the effort to come in person. Not that I was going to explain that to him. I pulled my shoulders back and looked him in the eye when I took the papers from his hand. "Thank you."

He dismissed me without another look. "Clear the counter for paying customers."

My jaw hung loose, but I snapped it tight and pulled my braid over my shoulder. As I walked away, cradling the application to my chest, I had to wonder if all the work I did to create a perfect shell around myself was a complete waste of time. With one solid brush-off, that stupid guy made me feel just as small and pointless as Jason had.

ADVICE COLUMN
Sage Advice

Dear Sage Advice,
I don't get girls. My best friend is a girl. Usually we get along great, but now she's not talking to me. When I say not talking to me, I mean she is literally not saying a word to me at all. I don't have a clue what happened. We were eating lunch together last Tuesday and everything was fine. But then the next day, bam. I ask her a question, and nothing. Girls are the worst. No offense if you are one, but it's true.
Signed, He-man Woman Hater

Dear He-man,
Deep down you have to know why she's not talking to you. Girls don't do things like that for no reason. Consider your actions over the last few weeks and try to pinpoint where you went wrong. Then do everything you can to make it up to her.
You better be extra sweet to her until you figure it out.
Love, Sage

Chapter 8

I pulled out my phone and sent a text to Roxie.

Where are you?

She answered immediately, which was kind of amazing. She wasn't the best at remembering to turn her ringer on in the morning, and I wasn't the best at remembering to remind her.

Same store.

Still?

Don't judge.

I'm done. Going to the food court.

Meet me there?

Yep.

I put my phone away and turned the corner towards the food court. I must have been hungry because everything I saw looked amazing. Pretzels,

Chinese food, caramel apples, ice cream. Never mind that I just had breakfast less than an hour ago. I totally wanted something to eat.

When I reached the food court, Roxie was already sitting at a table. She stood and waved when she saw me.

"How did you get here so fast?"

"Magic." She wiggled her fingers in the air.

I grinned and sat down. My collection of applications fluttered like a pompom in my hand.

"Actually, I was just walking out of the store when you texted, and then I ran so I could beat you."

"Seriously?"

"You're impressed. Don't pretend like you aren't." She pointed to my hand. "That's a lot of papers."

I nodded. "Most of it is Juneberry."

"Yikes."

I set the papers on the table with a sigh. "Do you ever think you want something and then when you can almost have it, you second guess it?"

Roxie tipped her head to the side. "Vague much?"

"Right?" I sighed. "I don't think I want to work at Juneberry anymore."

"What? You love Juneberry! You've been talking about it for a month. Seriously, it was super annoying."

"Cute." I gave her a stink eye. "I did want to work there, but it feels all wrong. And now, I don't know what to do instead." I waved my hand over the applications on the table. "All the rest of these were practice. My plan was Juneberry."

"Sounds like you need some ice cream."

I laughed. "I absolutely need some ice cream."

"Yay!" Roxie stood up and clapped. "I'm going to get the one with the marshmallows roasted on a pretzel stick and graham cracker crumbs along the edge." She sighed dreamily as we walked across the food court to Greedy Cow. "Don't worry about the job thing, Pyper. You're going to figure it out and find the best job ever! Also, I like shopping with you so much better than Mom. You don't make me spend two hours in the bra section, and we get ice cream before lunch. This is my favorite day of all the days!"

I threw my arm across her shoulder and squeezed. "I love you so much."

"Duh," she grinned.

There was a bit of a line at Greedy Cow, so Roxie and I entertained ourselves by giving people makeovers.

Quietly.

"That guy." Roxie whispered. "Shave the beard; remove the viper tat trying to eat his ear; and put him in a tight, white shirt and Wranglers. Total hottie."

I snorted and covered my mouth. "Please do something about the mullet."

"Mullets are in, Pyp. Where have you been?"

I shook my head. "No way, it's never going to look good."

We moved up to the counter. "Oh, hey, Landen!" I said as loudly and obnoxiously as I could.

Roxie was wearing off on me.

"Hello, again." His smile was pretty much the twin sister of a grimace. "What can I get for you?"

My own smile wavered into a thin line. To cover my embarrassment, I gestured for Roxie to go first. "Rox?"

"Rocks?" Landen's forehead wrinkled.

I shook my head. "No, sorry. Roxie is my sister. I call her Rox. I was telling her to go first."

Landen looked at Roxie, who placed her order while bouncing on the balls of her feet. When Landen turned back at me, I was ready.

"I'll take the Hullabaloo Belly Buster."

He paused, his eyes narrowing.

"Really," I insisted. "That's what I want."

"You do not!" He started laughing. It was a deep, manly sound that filled the small shop. "You are messing with me. No one wants to eat that."

"I do too." I bit my lip to keep from smiling. "Don't question me. Don't you know the customer is always right?"

Landen set his hands on the counter. "Tell you what. I'm going to start making the Some More S'mores for your sister while you work out whatever's wrong with you, and then you can tell me what you really want."

"I already told you what I really want."

Landen shook his head and went to work. While he scooped ice cream into the blender, he kept looking over his shoulder to see if I'd come to my senses yet.

I hadn't.

Roxie pulled on my shoulder so I had to lean closer to her mouth. "You two have a thing. What's going on?"

"We do not have a thing."

She raised her eyebrows.

"It's not like that. I was here yesterday with my girls. We got shakes, and we were joking—. It's a long, stupid story. I was just trying to lighten things up because I forgot his name and it was awkward, and I think he's still mad about it. Anyway, it's nothing."

Roxie opened her mouth to answer but was interrupted by a swirl of color and the scent of apple body cream.

"Pyper! Oh my gosh! I'm glad I saw you here. So glad!"

"Dawn! Hi! What's going on?"

"I've been literally staring at these jeans for an hour trying to pick one. I need your advice. Which would you get?" As she talked, Dawn pulled three pairs of skinny jeans out of her shopping bag. Two actually; the third pair was jeggings.

I took each in turn and scrutinized while Roxie shifted from foot to foot. The first pair was a thin, stretchy material and a bright aqua color. It was kind of awesome, but maybe not so durable. The second pair was thicker and not as stretchy, which made me concerned it wouldn't be as comfortable. The jeggings looked like classic faded jeans, but they didn't have back pockets, and that, for me, was a deal breaker.

As I handed each one back to Dawn, I told her my thoughts.

She looked at the pants and sighed. "What would you do, Pyper?"

"I'd keep the aqua and return the other two," I said instantly. I'd been waiting for her to ask.

"Even though it's thinner?"

I nodded. "Maybe it won't last as long, but it will feel so good while it does. That material is like butter."

Dawn scrunched her eyebrows, then grinned. "You're so right. I love it. I'm going to do it! Thanks, Pyper! You are the best! Oh, hey, did you see Kami and Mark?"

"No. Are they here?"

"They're around the mall somewhere." She lowered her voice. "Did you know Kami hasn't spoken to Mark for over a week?"

I nodded.

"Weird, right? Now, get this. When I saw them, Kami was talking nonstop, and Mark looked like he was in mortal pain. So funny! I bet he wishes she wasn't talking to him still! Did you ever hear why Kami stopped talking to him in the first place? What was that about?"

I twitched my shoulders, so it sort of looked like I shrugged.

"Well, anyway, thanks again, Pyper. You're the best!" She gave me a one-armed squeeze, and then she was gone.

I turned back to Roxie.

"Oh, Pyper!" She clasped her hands together and fluttered her eyelashes. "I don't know if I got the right shake. I'm just not sure anymore. Help me decide!"

"Oh my gosh, Rox. When did you become such a booger?"

"Who was that girl?"

"I forgot to introduce you, sorry. I was too caught up in the dilemma."

Roxie's dimple flickered in and out of her cheek.

"Her name is Dawn," I explained. "She's a senior, too. We have a couple of classes together."

"So, you aren't, like, super good friends, and she still searched the whole mall for you?"

"I guess."

Roxie bobbed on her toes. "You don't think that's weird?"

"I give great advice."

"Pyper, with great power comes great responsibility."

"Thank you, Spider-Man."

Roxie swatted my arm. "I'm just saying. It's really cool that people care so much about what you think. Amazingly cool."

"But?"

"I just was thinking, if it were me being you, I'd be worried about giving the wrong advice. Like, what if she buys those pants and has nothing to wear them with? It's a lot of pressure to tell people what to do."

"I didn't *tell* her what to do, Rox, I gave her my opinion. It's not like she *has* to do what I say."

Roxie raised her eyebrows.

"She doesn't."

"Uh-huh. So, you don't think it's a big deal then?"

I shook my head.

"S'mores Shake." Landen flung graham crackers over the top like a wizard with pixie dust and slid the cup toward Roxie. She took it, her eyes huge.

"This is way bigger than I thought. Also, are you hiring?"

"Roxie!"

Landen ignored my screech and leaned forward. "You looking for a job?"

Roxie pulled the stick of marshmallows out of her shake and licked it. "My sister is. I think she needs to work here so I can get the employee discount and eat all the shakes she messes up."

"Nice, Roxie," I groaned. "Great recommendation."

"Just sayin'."

Landen reached under the counter and pulled out a job application, which he set in front of me. "As a matter of fact, we can always use some extra help."

I looked down at the piece of paper with the Greedy Cow logo in brown and cream. The food court was my last resort, but a job was a job.

Right?

Worst case scenario: I fill out the application, they say no, and I beg Brooklynn's dad to hire me even though I don't know the difference between a soccer ball and a volleyball.

I nodded. "Great! Can I borrow a pen?"

Landen pulled one out of the cup next to the register. Before he gave it to me, he locked me in his gaze like a tractor beam. "Before you get started on that, I am going to get out the peanut butter and caramel to start the Hullabaloo shake."

"Sounds great." I swiped for the pen, but Landen held it out of reach. "Does it?"

"Yep." I narrowed my eyes, determined to stare him down. I would have done it if Roxie hadn't stomped on my foot.

"Just tell him you want something normal already so we can go sit down," she said. "This thing weighs a ton."

While I glared at my sister, Landen tapped the pen on the counter. "So, I should start a Strawberry Shortcake shake, right?"

"Maybe I don't want Strawberry Shortcake." I snatched the pen from his grasp.

Landen backed away from the counter. "You want Strawberry Shortcake."

I started filling out the application to keep from looking at him or Roxie. "How can you be so sure?"

"Because," he said as he opened a mini fridge for a bottle of strawberry milk, "it's what you always get."

The
Cromer Chronicles

ADVICE COLUMN
Sage Advice

Dear Sage,

I love your advice column so much! Every time I read it, I feel inspired. I am really hoping you can help me. I think my boyfriend is cheating on me. I have lots of reasons why I think this, but the biggest one is he won't hang my picture up in his locker.

Please help me, Sage!

Signed, Possibly in Love With a Cheater Pants.

Dear Cheater Pants Love,

Your boyfriend might be cheating on you. That's always a possibility. But, I can tell you that if he pays attention to you, listens to you, and remembers things that are important to you, he probably isn't cheating on you. Talk to him about the locker picture. Guys aren't super perceptive; he may not realize that's important to you unless you tell him very clearly.

Use small words.

Love, Sage

Chapter 9

Monday morning, I woke up with a groan.

I was sort of hoping the weekend would last forever. After Roxie and I stuffed ourselves silly with ice cream, I gave Landen my application, came home, and proceeded to ignore my phone for the rest of the weekend.

As soon as I opened my eyes Monday morning, my phone sat on the nightstand like a mouth-breathing Hun, reminding me that it was waiting. There was nowhere to run and nowhere to hide.

I reached for it and punched in the password. My breath caught as the welcome screen revealed thirty-seven texts.

Gross.

The majority of them came from the prom group chat, which was unfortunate because that was the main thing I wanted to ignore. I opened the chat with a groan of self-pity. I knew Leah was going to ask me for a status update as soon as I saw her at school, and it would be humiliating to admit I hadn't done anything.

I scanned the responses to discover that everyone could, in fact, meet after school today. John, Nova, Brant, Will, Abby, Juan, and Tyson.

So, the prom committee was mostly guys.

Of course it was.

I sent a text confirming they should all be in the auditorium at three fifteen, then I closed my eyes.

I'd give anything to go back to sleep and pull a Rip Van Winkle until prom and graduation were over. No more prom, ever. That would be perfect. Who wants to be awake in a world where the girl who hates prom more than anything is put in charge of it?

I shoved my phone under my pillow and got out of bed so I wouldn't have to check any more messages. While I picked out my clothes and showered, I also threw myself a pity party. It was a fabulous affair with streamers of 'why me' and confetti made from frowny face emojis. It only lasted until I wiped the steam off the mirror and could see my reflection looking back at me.

"Okay, Pyper. You had your fun wallowing. Now, it's time to suck it up and get to work. You don't have to like prom to plan it. You don't have to like guys to boss them around. You can make this work."

My lips set in a determined line as I nodded.

"All right. Let's do this."

I got dressed in a pencil skirt, the t-shirt my mom bought me a few years ago when we went to see *Wicked* on Broadway, and a lime green cardigan.

I swept my hair into a high ponytail, securing the back with invisible bobby pins so I wouldn't get that weird hair lump. Then I put on some mascara and lip gloss. I rotated in front of the mirror to make sure everything looked perfect before heading downstairs with my mind full of positive self-talk. Each step towards the kitchen sounded a lot like the chanting cheerleaders at football games when we played the rival high school.

Give me a P!

Give me a Y!

Give me a-

I should have watched where I was stepping. It was silly of me, really. I'd lived in this family for seventeen years, and I knew better. There was always something underfoot.

Always.

"Eek!" I flailed my arms in airplane circles as I slid on some unknown substance across the kitchen floor. I tried to regain my balance by grabbing the refrigerator door handle, but instead of helping a girl out, the door clicked open, and a carton of orange juice fell to the ground, not splashing, thankfully, but glugging out onto the tile.

I'm sure if I watched a replay of that moment, I would have been impressed with the perfect oval shape my mouth made as I screamed, "No!" I also would have admired the graceful way I slid out of the range of the orange juice and landed modestly on my back halfway into the dining room.

Kai applauded. "Ten out of ten points, Pyper! I'll give you twenty if you can do that again. Thirty if I can film it!"

Gavin laughed so hard he choked, and my dad, without even looking up from his newspaper, whacked Gavin on the back twice. Chewed cereal sprayed all over the kitchen table.

My mom, who was loading the dishwasher, took the towel that was draped over her shoulder and tossed it to me without saying anything.

I caught it and spread it over my face to hide my shame.

Kai hummed a tune from one of his video games, the song that plays when the avatar kicks the bucket.

"That towel-over-the-face thing is not a good look for you. Totally hides your sassy blond highlights." Roxie tapped the bottom of my bootie lightly as she walked by. I could hear her rinse her dish and put it in the dishwasher. I think they probably heard it in China. There was no one in the world who made as much noise as Roxie did in the kitchen.

Except for maybe my mom.

"Come on." She tugged on my hand. "The good news is your clothes are still clean, and the day can only get better from here!"

She mimicked Mom's voice so perfectly I had to laugh as I let her help me to my feet. The towel fell from my face to the floor, so I used my foot to mop up all the orange juice I'd spilled. All I wanted was a big bowl of Lucky Charms goodness, but Kai had wrecked my dreams. I picked up the empty juice container and pointed it at his head.

"Hey, stink bug. You owe me two boxes of cereal."

Kai smiled and opened his mouth wider while he chewed, so I had the best possible view of the cereal mash he had been working on.

"Two boxes!" Gavin repeated as he flung his spoon into the air, splashing Dad and Kai with milk and bits of cereal. Dad folded his paper and set it on the table.

"Time for me to go," he said with a wink. He tossed Gavin a bunch of napkins and pulled Mom close for a kiss.

"I'm eating here!" Kai leaned over and pretended to barf under the table.

Gavin clapped, knocking over his *entire* cereal bowl this time. I had a moment of supreme satisfaction as I watched the milk roll across the table and flood onto the back of Kai's neck. He shrieked and whacked his head trying to get out of the way. He scooted his chair out from under him, so he ended up on his back, staring at my face.

"Karma," I said, dropping napkins on his face. Kai moved the napkins just enough to stick his tongue out. This alone would have been a justifiable cause to leave him there to rot in technicolored milk, but being a mature and forgiving older sister, I reached my hand out to pull him up.

"Thanks," he grumbled.

I gave him a toothy smile and a bunch more napkins, then grabbed a package of roasted almonds from the pantry.

"See ya later, gators." I kissed the top of Gavin's head and waved to Kai. I hugged my mom, promised to make good choices, and hurried out of the kitchen. Roxie joined me in the hall, where we gathered our bags and things.

"Question," Roxie said.

"Yeah?"

"Do you think our family is weird?"

I looked toward the kitchen, where sounds of Gavin shrieking with laughter and Kai making machine gun sound effects were still very audible.

"Super weird."

Roxie grinned. "Oh, good! That's what I thought, too."

We walked down the driveway to Beauty, then parted. I waited for Roxie to get to the end of the driveway and disappear behind the neighbor's hedge before I started the ignition. The middle school was in the opposite direction of my high school; otherwise, I would have driven her every morning.

When I pulled into the parking lot at school, I parked next to Brooklynn's truck and saw her sitting in the driver's seat.

Holy déjà vu, Batman.

I slowly put Beauty in park, trying to see if Carly was in the passenger side. There was no way Travis broke her heart already, right? She'd texted me about a billion photos of him playing basketball at the park with a bunch of other guys that had nothing better to do with their lives.

I got out of the car with my purse, math book, and notebook, then walked quickly to Brooklynn's window. She looked up with a smile.

Oh, good.

Smiles are good.

"Hey!" Brooklynn opened her door and stepped out. "I was just going over my history notes while I waited for you."

I laughed. "Oh my goodness, Brooklynn! History is *so* five hundred years ago."

"I kind of wish it would stay there. But, also, I've been mulling over that prom meeting. I can't figure out where we went wrong. I really thought we had it in the bag."

"Whatever," I shrugged. "I decided to make the best of it, so let's pretend like I love prom and can't wait to work with the guy-majority committee to make it the best prom ever. Yay."

Brooklyn pursed her lips. "Totally convincing."

"Thank you." I linked her arm as we started up the ramp towards the front doors. "Where's Carly?"

"Don't know. She doesn't usually text me."

I peered at Brooklynn. "She doesn't?"

"Nah. I'm sure you've noticed we don't have a ton in common."

That was a true statement. But, then, Brooklyn and I didn't have much in common, and that didn't stop us.

Brooklyn opened the school's front doors. "Why do you ask?"

"Hm?" I blinked. "Oh, I was just wondering. I haven't heard from her since Saturday…"

My brain stalled as I noticed a girl and a guy standing next to lockers in serious conversation. I paused to watch. She tensed up as he opened a locker door. When he swung the door back so she could see inside, it was lined with pictures of her. The girl squealed and threw her arms around him.

Brooklynn wiggled a finger in her ear. "Okay, now I'm deaf. Are you coming? What are you looking at?"

"Oh, nothing." I squeezed through a bunch of football players and unzipped my bag so I would be ready to exchange books as soon as I got my locker open.

"Watch it!" Brooklynn yelled.

Her locker door slammed shut the instant she opened it. The herd of footballers were boxing us in.

"Hey, guys?" I cupped my hands over my mouth and tried again. "Guys!"

Carson and Wes were the closest to me and the first to respond.

"Hey, Pyper!" Wes scooped me up in a hug that left my feet dangling, even though I am five-nine. I went limp and waited patiently for him to set me down.

There was no reasoning with Wes. I'd told him five thousand times that I wasn't a hugger, and yet, he kept on doing the hugs. Worse, I couldn't even be mad at him. He was too big and too jolly with a ridiculous number of dimples. Kind of like a young Samoan Santa Clause.

"I love you, girl," he said, dropping me to my feet. "I would marry you if you weren't so hung up on your college boy. How is the dawg?"

"Fantastic." I smoothed my skirt. "Fabulous. Couldn't be better. Hey, can you guys scoot over? We need to use our lockers here."

Carson leaned on my locker with his elbow. "I'll move if you dump Jason and go to prom with me."

I glared at him. "How about you move, or I'll assign you to the prom clean-up committee?"

Carson backed away with a smirk. "Hey, no need to get nasty."

I rolled my eyes and went to work on my lock. I ignored the guys so thoroughly that they had no choice but to gravitate farther down the hall until they found someone else to bother.

I tugged my locker open, found what I needed in my flawlessly organized locker system, and waited patiently while Brooklynn shuffled through piles of papers and empty chip bags for her notebooks.

"We're starting the group projects today; do you think we need our econ books?" Brooklyn flicked an apple seed off the cover and held it up.

I wrinkled my nose. It smelled like rotten bananas. "I have mine just in case."

Brooklynn added her book to the pile in her arms and slammed her locker door shut. "How do you know all those guys' names?"

"What guys?" I stopped to let a gaggle of girls move by.

Brooklynn waved an arm. "All those football players, you know everyone."

That wasn't exactly true. My flub with Landen the other day was proof, but I didn't need that kind of negativity on a Monday morning, so I pushed that memory far away. "'Keep your friends close and your enemies closer'. I can't remember who said that one."

"Sun Tzu." Brooklynn said as she rummaged through her bag. "He also said, 'Know thy self, know thy enemy.'"

I chewed on that thought until we got to econ, then I pushed it away, too. There were bigger things to think about right now. I paused in the doorway to survey the room. Oh fabulous, Landen sat in the seat right behind me. How had I never noticed that?

With a shake of my head, I let the shame roll down my back and cruised across the room to my assigned desk. After I arranged my book and pencils into formation, I turned and looked Landen right in the eyes, a huge smile in place.

"Hi, *Landen!*"

"Hi, *Pyper.*" His eyes laughed at me. "How are you?

I flipped my ponytail over my shoulder. "Fantastic, thanks. Are you so excited to be in econ today?"

"Are you?" His eyebrows raised.

I smacked his desk with a loud thump. "You can't answer a question with a question."

"Why not?"

"You did it again. You have to answer my question before you can ask one. It's the rules. Everyone knows this."

Landen pressed his lips together. "Are there any other rules I should know before I say anything else?"

"Landen," I said, tilting my chin down. "That was another question."

He held his hands out. "Okay, okay. I'm sorry. What was your first question?"

I gave an exaggerated sigh.

"She asked you if you're excited to be in econ today." Brooklynn stacked her book and notebooks in the middle of her desk and rested her chin on top.

"Right," Landen nodded. "The correct answer is, yes."

"You like econ?" I raised my eyebrows.

"Don't you?"

"That was a question!" I cried. "You really stink at this."

"Sorry, sorry," he laughed, raising his hands again. "I meant to say, yes. I do like econ. How about you?"

Now he was getting it.

"It's not my favorite, but we are learning to live with each other."

"Very diplomatic," Landen said. "And, by the way, asking questions is not cheating. It's called getting to know someone better."

I wrinkled my nose at him. "Unless you don't answer the question you were asked, then it's called ignoring. Getting to know someone has to go both ways or it doesn't work."

"That sounds like one of Mr. Rypkema's quotes."

"Nope, that one was all me."

Landen tapped his pencil eraser on the desk a few times. "I have a feeling you have an answer to everything."

"I do," I agreed. "But, in this case, it's common sense. You have to follow the rules, or there's no conversation. It's just monologuing. I'll show you how it's supposed to go. How was work Saturday? Now, you answer."

Landen scuffed his chair as he scooted closer to his desk. "How do you think work was on Saturday?"

I pointed my pen at him, almost jabbing it into his nose. "Now you're just being difficult. I have no idea how work was; that's why I asked."

"You could just guess." Landen leaned away from my pen.

"No, I can't, that would be assuming, and 'assumptions are the termites of relationships.'"

"Henry Winkler." Landen said, triumphantly. It was totally uncalled for. I wasn't trying to stump him; I was trying to make a point.

"Let's try this again," I said as I narrowed my eyes to look extra stern. "How was work on Saturday?"

Landen grinned. "Tell me, Pyper, what is your favorite class?"

I smacked his shoulder, causing him to reel back to get away. When he did, his elbows lifted from where they had been resting on top of his desk.

"Woa," I completely forgot what we were saying. "Why is your elbow red?" I reached forward to grab his arm and lifted it so I could look closer.

"Wait, what are you-?"

"Your elbow is ridiculously red. Why?"

Landen tried to pull away. "You are totally giving my arm a concussion."

"That's not even possible," I said. "Answer the question."

"Which one?" Landen yanked his arm out of my hands and almost fell backward. There were a few tense moments where the back legs of his chair wobbled before the front ones slammed back into the carpet.

Brooklyn applauded.

Landen tossed his hair off his forehead. "You asked me, like, three questions in a row without waiting for me to answer. Plus, you interrupted. If you interrupt, you don't hear the explanation, and then you ask a question that might have been answered if you hadn't interrupted. That's got to be against your rules."

"Oh my gosh," Brooklynn rubbed her forehead. "Your conversation is hurting my brain."

"Food dye from work," Landen said.

Will scooted into his seat behind Brooklynn just as the bell rang. "What's going on, guys?"

Brooklynn twisted around. "They are talking about the proper way to talk to each other."

"What?" Will squinted.

Brooklynn jabbed her finger in the air. "Exactly."

"Landen doesn't know how to answer a question without asking a question," I explained.

"So?" Will shrugged.

Landen leaned back in his chair, threading his fingers together behind his head. "I answered your question. You never answered mine."

"Free period." I shot him a snarky grin.

He quirked an eyebrow. "That's my sister's favorite class, too. Why do you people choose a free period over an actual class? What do you do with that time? Don't you get bored?"

I stared at him.

"What?"

"Okay." I shook my head. "I can't even talk to you anymore. You threw, like, a billion questions at me all at once."

"Three, not a billion. And you did that first. I thought that meant it was allowed."

I turned to face the front of the classroom, pretending that whatever Mr. Rypkema was writing on the board was super fascinating and deserved my whole attention. Landen tugged my ponytail.

"Cool."

"What?" I swung around.

"Work was cool." He raised an eyebrow. "Right?"

I looked at him for a second and then smirked as his words sank in. "Ice cream is cool. So punny."

Brooklynn rolled her eyes and leaned over her desk to copy the quote from the board. Mr. Rypkema started every class period with a series of quotes. We were supposed to choose one that spoke to us and write it down to think about throughout the day. I stared at the board but didn't register any words.

Landen poked my back with a pen. "You never answered my question. What do you do during your free period?"

"Oh, it changes every day," I finally said, being as vague as vague could be. Mr. Rypkema was nearing the end of the white board, which meant class was about to start. Landen opened his mouth just as Mr. Rypkema faced the class.

Whew.

While Mr. Rypkema welcomed us to another exciting day in economics, my mind wandered to my conversation with Landen. It was totally ridiculous and convoluted, but kind of fun, too. I tried to think of why it felt different. There were words and voices and funky school smells, but I didn't get that tight feeling like someone was wrapping their iron fist around my heart the way I did when I talked to other guys or when I thought about Jason.

It was interesting and strange.

After a few minutes, I noticed how very, very quiet the classroom was. I blinked as I looked around. Every eye was on me instead of on the teacher.

I sat up straighter and smiled like I knew what was going on.

"Announcements?" Mr. Rypkema prompted. "From student council?"

"Oh!" I jumped out of my chair and stood, smoothing out the front of my skirt. "Yes! As you all know, prom is this Friday. If you don't already have a date, it is way too late now, so you might as well help the prom committee this week. If you have a free period, we're working on decorations every day. If you have time after school, there is a committee meeting in the auditorium. Thanks." I saluted and sat down.

Mr. Rypkema nodded. "Thank you, Pyper."

I started scribbling quotes in my notebook and was almost done when my phone vibrated. I could feel it squirming in my bag next to my leg.

We're not technically supposed to use our phones during class, so I ignored it at first. That got harder when it went off two more times. I eased it out and hid it under my desk to check my messages. They were all from Brooklynn. I peeked over at her and saw her staring at Mr. Rypkema like she was paying attention, but her phone rested in her lap under her desk.

Pyper!

Why did you say that?

I wish you hadn't said that.

What?

I typed without looking down.

I could sense movement from the corner of my eye. My phone wiggled in my hands.

About prom.

Why did you say it's too late?

I started to reply when Mr. Rypkema turned around again. I dropped my phone into my purse. Brooklynn and I would just have to finish this conversation later. The last thing I needed now was my phone confiscated for the rest of the day.

I tried to focus on what Mr. Rypkema was saying about our group projects. Something-something, thirty percent of our grade. We were supposed to pick an occupation and make a realistic cost-of-living budget based on the average income of that occupation.

That didn't sound so bad. In fact, it sounded kind of fun.

Also, I think I said that last part out loud.

Mr. Rypkema waited for the chittering to die down before he spoke. "I'm glad you think so, Pyper, but, 'I don't need your approval, darling. That's for insecure people.'"

"What?" I blinked.

"Look it up," Mr. Rypkema said, tapping a pointer on the whiteboard. He shook his head at my blank stare. "Get to work, people. You have an hour."

"Brook?" I asked. "You want to work together?"

She nodded without looking up from her notes. It wasn't the most enthusiastic response, but I would take it. Now we needed two more people.

"Hey, Pyper?" Will leaned so far forward his belly hung off the side of his desk. "Can Landen and I work with you and Brooklynn?"

"Sure."

Brooklynn scowled.

Uh-oh.

"Thanks." Will pushed his desk up so it was now next to Brooklynn. "You saved us. Dave was trying to catch my eye. One time I was in a group with him, and I had to do all of the work. I told him no the next time he asked, and he filled my gym locker with shaving cream. You saved my life, really."

"Let's just get started. What occupation should we choose?" Brooklynn looked like she had serious indigestion.

Will went to work suggesting things like NBA players, professional video gamer, and YouTube stars while I went to work trying to figure out what was going on with Brooklynn.

ADVICE COLUMN
Sage Advice

Dear Sage,

My dad says he won't let me date until I'm forty. Mom says he's kidding and I can date when I'm sixteen, but because I'm the youngest, I'm really concerned my dad means what he says. I think he still sees me as a three-year-old with pigtails, making mud pies in the backyard.

My sixteenth birthday is in three weeks, and he's already pulled out all his shotgun cleaning supplies. What should I do if he really won't let me date?

Signed, Desperate to Date

Dear Desperate,

Your dad is right.

Okay, so, forty is a little extreme, but let's be honest: nothing good comes from dating in high school.

My friend, you are young! Just have fun and get to know a lot of different people. You don't actually have to date until later. Did you know that?

Love, Sage

Chapter 10

"Brooklynn?"

Brooklynn jammed things into her backpack like they had mortally offended her. It was the end of class and not the best timing, but I couldn't wait any longer. There wasn't a spare second to talk to her the whole class period. Once we made our assignments, Will spent the rest of the time describing his hook shot in detail.

"Brooklynn?" I tried again.

She finally looked over at me. I opened my mouth to start interrogating her when the bell rang. Of course. This wasn't going to work right now. There was too much noise, and I had to get to second period to help Leah.

"See you at lunch?"

A brief nod was all she gave me before she marched out the door and disappeared into the chaos. That was something, at least. If she was super mad, she would have ignored my existence completely. I gathered my things and headed for the hallway.

"Pyper, wait up!"

Will and Landen scrambled over desks, making more noise than I thought was humanly possible. I stepped out of the way so other students could get by while I waited for them.

"Do you still need help with prom? On the committee thing?" Will whacked Landen in the chest with the back of his hand. "Landen doesn't have a free period, but he said he could come to the meeting after school today."

I glanced at Landen, who nodded. Was Will, like, his spokesman or something?

"Okay, great." I fixed a smile on my face. "Sounds good, Will. Why don't you tell Landen the prom committee will be happy to have him."

They looked at each other in confusion.

Guys were so weird.

"See you after school," I sighed, and headed for the student council room.

Leah waited for me in the doorway. "Pyper! There you are. I was having visions of doing this by myself, and I didn't like them at all. I'm so glad you made it!"

"Come on, Leah." I shook my head. "I'm not going to make you do this alone, even though you threw me under the bus on Friday."

Leah gave me an air hug and walked to the tables in the center of the room. "You would have done the same thing if someone asked you to prom and you had the dress of your dreams waiting."

Ha! The joke was on her. I did have an amazing dress I could wear, but even that wasn't enough to make me want to go to prom.

"Do you know if anyone else is showing up today?"

I dropped my things on an empty chair. "Not specifically, but there were lots of people who said they would be here."

"Oh good." Leah's long, brown hair was pulled into a messy bun with several strands flying around her face like they were running for their lives. Her eyes looked wild behind her oval glasses, and there was glitter all over the back of her neck.

Maybe a little stressed?

"What can I do to help you?" I asked.

"Take my job."

I laughed. "I tried that, remember? You won the election fair and square."

Seeing Leah now, I could be grateful I'd dropped my campaign at the end of last year. I was super glad not to be the student council president. In fact, I could give her a break for wanting to go to prom, she needed something she thought was fun to look forward to after all the work she'd done this year.

"Want to pull all the tissue paper out of the cabinet and organize it by color?"

"On it."

Once the tissue paper was organized, I began stacking coordinating colors into piles so they would be ready when we made the decorative tissue balls. It would have been nice if the school budget would have sprung for tulle; tissue paper was super fragile and harder to work with. Whoever ended up at my station today had better think gentle thoughts.

Within a few minutes, the room was full of students. My station was crazy busy. While some worked with the tissue paper, I gave instructions and carefully committed every person's name to memory with clever tricks, like: Oliver had *all* his teeth covered in braces, and Candy was super sweet.

The time went way too quickly. By the end, I was exhausted, and my voice had gone hoarse from explaining what we were doing so many times. But I couldn't complain when I looked at the colorful rows of tissue balls. We'd gotten a ton done. If I didn't let myself remember that these decorations were for prom, I could almost feel excited.

"Did you survive?" Leah asked, trailing after me as I returned the extra supplies to the cupboard.

"Honestly, that was actually kind of fun." I surprised myself that I meant what I said. There was serious satisfaction in a job well done.

Leah laughed through her nose.

"No, I mean it. The tissue balls were a blast to make. I want to decorate my whole bedroom with them. How did you guys do?" I looked over Leah's shoulder to the other stations.

Shiny cardboard stars were all popped out of their cutout sheets and stacked by size, ready to be mounted on the photo backdrop. The largest stars had been punched with holes and threaded with ribbon so we could hang them from the ceiling along with the streamers.

"Check this out." Leah grinned, her arm waving towards the twinkle light station. "Poor schmucks."

I breathed out a sigh of relief when I saw the strands and strands of twinkle lights neatly wound into circles. I had been dreading untangling those. I was super grateful to whoever ended up with that job.

"It's only Monday" I said, "and we are pretty much done with decorations. You know what, Leah? Despite everything, this might actually turn out to be a pretty amazing prom."

Leah's face relaxed. "Pyper, you are seriously the best. You keep me going when all feels lost."

"What a tribute," I said, putting my hand over my heart. "I want that published in the school paper on my birthday."

"I can make that happen. I sort of have an in with the editor."

I stepped out of the way so Leah could lock the cabinet, and I swung my purse over my head to wear it across my body. I was about to leave when Leah stopped me with a question.

"So, hey. I can't believe we haven't had this conversation yet, but is your boy coming back to take you to prom?" She tucked the keys into her pocket and perched on the end of a table.

"Oh," I smoothed a stray hair into my ponytail. "No. I'm not going."

"What? You have to go, Pyper. You can't put in all this work and not go. That's crazy!"

What was crazy was wanting to go to prom in the first place. I stepped towards the door.

Leah snagged my purse strap to stop me. "There's only one Senior Prom. You'll regret it if you don't go, you know you will. I mean, seriously. How many times in your life will you get to dress up like a princess? Never, that's how many. You can ask my mom how sad that is. She prepared a whole TED Talk about it."

"Honestly, I really don't want to go."

Leah tapped her chin with one finger. "Jason better have a good excuse for not taking you."

I gave a short laugh.

"Hey." She scooted closer. "Just listen, don't say anything until I'm finished. What if you went to prom with a guy that wasn't interested in dating at all? Your boy would be okay with that, right? If there was zero chance of it leading to anything else?" She took a deep breath. "I know someone who doesn't have a date. He's totally safe because he's liked some random girl since middle school. I want him to go to prom. He's super awesome, Pyper. Let me set you up?"

My stomach tied itself into knots. "I'm not really a blind date sort of person."

"I get it. I'm not either. But this guy is different. He's fantastic."

"Thanks, Leah. You're super sweet for thinking about me." I could see the protests working their way out of her mouth again. My brain whirled with ways to get out of the blind date. The idea that came out on top was not my favorite, but I had a hunch it would work.

For sure it was better than going out with some high school guy I didn't even know.

"Hey, how about this. I'll stop by prom for a little while to make sure everything is running smoothly?"

I didn't need a date to do that.

"So," she swung her legs, so they tapped the bottom of the table, "you would go to prom without a date?"

I guess that was essentially what I said. "Yeah."

Leah repeated slowly, "Going to prom without a date..."

She was obviously not talking to me anymore, so I didn't say anything. She stared off into space like she didn't remember I was there. After a while, she blinked and stared at me.

"What are you going to wear?"

I pictured the amazing, glorious prom dress in the back of my closet. It was dreamy and completely perfect.

"I have a dress."

"Like, a real formal? With rhinestones and a skirt so big you can't fit through the door?"

I pressed my lips together to hide a smile. It would only encourage her. "Something like that."

"So, you're dressing up and going to prom. Alone?" Leah stared at me.

"Yeah. I mean, if you think I need to be there." I twirled the end of my ponytail around my finger.

"Pyper!" Leah stood up and clapped her hands. "You are amazing! I want to write a story about you! Pyper's Promenade! It would inspire girls everywhere to live their dreams with or without a date! You are an icon."

"What?"

Leah grabbed my hand and pulled me to sit next to her on the table. "Seriously. People just don't do things like that. I think this will be big!"

Her enthusiasm was suffocating. I scooted back a little and disappeared into my bag, pretending to look for something. What I found was gum. I pulled it out and offered a piece to Leah.

She shook her head, watching me with big eyes and waiting for me to say something.

I folded the stick of gum and put it in my mouth. The cinnamon flavor made my taste buds tingle. "I'm pretty sure I am not the first person in the world to go to prom alone."

"Maybe not, but I still think you would make a great story. If we rushed, we could get it out in Thursday's paper. That would give all those hopeful, date-less girls the option to still go to prom this year."

I zipped my purse closed and patted it. "How about we just concentrate on getting prom finished so there's somewhere for them to go?"

Leah looked around the room at the piles of decorations. Then she sighed. "Fair enough. Plus, I guess there is still the possibility that Jason will change his mind."

"Not likely." I blew a lame bubble and sucked it back into my mouth to try again. "No, it's better this way. I'll be there to make sure the refreshments don't run out like they did last year. I'll keep the teachers from joining in the Macarena, and if any of the twinkle lights fall down, I will get them back in place like that." I snapped my fingers.

"Well, if you change your mind about getting set up, let me know. It would be fun. You could double with Will and I."

"Will Davis?" I asked, grasping the one thing in her sentence that wasn't completely insane. That's right! I forgot she told me Friday that Will asked her. I didn't know Will knew Leah; he'd never mentioned her before. But then, he also hadn't mentioned the fact that he was going to prom at all, so he wasn't a great communicator.

"Yeah, you're already friends. It would be so good!"

"Hard pass. But, thank you. Really."

Leah tried to smile, but part of her mouth sagged. I hated to see her all deflated. There was no way I could take her up on the double date thing, but maybe I could give a little. "How about we get ready together? That part is always way more fun with someone else."

"Deal!" Leah gave me a high five. "Sooooo, do you happen to know any girls who want to go to prom but don't have a date? Now I really want to double with another couple."

I said, "Brooklynn Hall" before I could stop myself. Curse my broken filter! With those two words, I might have just dug our friendship's grave. I wished there was a machine to pull words out of other people's ears and back into my mouth. Brooklynn was either going to be super mad or completely furious. Either way, there was a very real possibility that she would never speak to me again.

Leah gasped. "That is a great idea! She's already friends with Will, so that won't be awkward! Perfect! I'm going to ask her."

"Do you want to check with Will and the other guy first, to make sure it's okay?" I asked carefully. That might work in my favor. If the mystery guy wasn't interested, Brooklynn would never know I volunteered her for a blind double date.

On the other hand, if he wasn't interested in Brooklynn, he was a complete buffoon.

"Nah, I don't need to check with him." Leah waved her hand back and forth. "He'll go with anyone."

Which instantly dissolved all the guilt I felt about rejecting her idea. The last thing I needed this year was a prom date who would go with anybody.

ADVICE COLUMN
Sage Advice

Dear Sage,
I never do things like this, but I really need your advice. There's this guy I really like, but we've always been just friends. Sometimes I think he likes me as more than a friend; other times it's obvious he thinks I'm one of the guys.
Should I just tell him how I feel? What if I do and he doesn't feel the same way?
Sincerely, Out of Patience

Dear Out of Patience,
If you think telling him you like him will put your friendship on the line and is too much of a risk, then take my advice and be content with just being friends.
Love, Sage

Chapter 11

Carly, Brooklynn, and I usually ate lunch at the street taco cart that parked outside the gym. When I got there-a little late thanks to Leah's matchmaking attempts-the usual crazy long line had disappeared, and neither of my friends were in sight.

I had no clue if Carly was even at school. Other than a few texts, pics, and a plethora of emojis, I hadn't talked to her since Friday. I hoped she wasn't sick or hurt or-

"Hey, Pyper."

I glanced over my shoulder. "Oh, hey, Will. Hang on a sec." The taco truck vendor drummed his fingers on the counter while he waited for me to place my order. I asked for two shrimp tacos and a lemonade, paid, then turned back to Will. "Have you seen Brooklynn or Carly?"

"I, uh, have AP English with Brooklynn."

"Right." I knew that. "Any idea where she is right now?"

Will scuffed the toe of his sneaker on the sidewalk. "Uh, no. I mean, usually we walk to lunch together, but she didn't wait for me. Do you have a minute? Uh, I need some advice."

Those were my four most favorite words. "What's up?"

Will's cheeks slowly filled with a faint rosy flush, like one of those painting books where you just add water to make the colors appear. His shoulders drooped and his eyelids hung like they were trying to lift weights that were way too heavy.

"Did you think Brooklynn seems...seemed upset today?"

"Yeah, I did notice that in first period."

He let out a long breath. "She's mad at me. I don't know what to do. What should I do?"

"Will," I said, crossing my arms, "Brooklynn is always mad at you. Why do you need advice about that?"

"This is different. I don't know *why* she's mad. Usually, I know because I make her mad on purpose. But I didn't do anything this time, I swear."

I should have talked to Brooklynn sooner. She was like a volcano. If she didn't get bothersome things out of her head, she stewed and stewed until it was Mount Vesuvius all over the place. I bet she epically erupted on Will. For sure, he did something to deserve it, but I still should have tried to diffuse Brooklynn in first period.

I had to find her; she lived with all guys and always forgot that talking things out was better than punching something.

Or someone.

"Here." I took my order from the food truck and shoved everything into Will's chest, then whirled around. I took the steps two at a time and thanked my brain for choosing flats that morning instead of heels. They would have totally slowed me down.

I cruised through the cafeteria and around the picnic benches outside. I checked the bleachers and the commons. Brooklynn wasn't anywhere. I considered snatching a megaphone from the cheerleading coach to scream Brooklynn's name, but I didn't because that would have mortified her.

Both the coach and Brooklynn, actually.

I made a sharp U-turn, plowed into some guy wearing a plaid shirt, said sorry, and ran to the parking lot. There was only one place left to look.

Sure enough, I found Brooklynn all hunched over in the driver's seat of Moe, reading a book. Or pretending to. No one has ever actually read *The Scarlet Letter* on purpose.

I stopped at Brooklynn's window and knocked. She took forever to look up. I was beginning to think I would be stuck waiting until I wasted away into a very fashionable skeleton.

Finally, she rolled the window down. "Oh, hi."

"What're you doing, cupcake?" I said, leaning on the car's open window frame.

Brooklynn jerked her head to the passenger side. I hurried around the truck and scooted in next to her.

"What's going on, Brookie?"

"Nothing."

"Liar."

"Yeah." She gave me a sidelong look. "I know. But there's no point in talking about it."

When it became obvious that she wasn't going to elaborate, I prompted, "Why not?"

"Because there's nothing you can do to fix it."

Nothing I could do?

Whatever!

I dared any problem to be more than I could figure out.

"Fix what?"

Brooklynn sighed. "Why did you have to say what you said in econ?"

What did I say in econ? I pursed my lips. "You're going to have to help me out here, Brook. I said a lot of things in econ. I have no idea what you're talking about."

"It doesn't matter. Like I said, it's too late anyway." She leaned her head back until it rested on her seat and closed her eyes.

Seriously?

"Brooklynn, have you been watching rom-coms?"

"Why?" she asked without opening her eyes.

I let out a breath. "Because you're acting like we're in one. You know real life doesn't work like that, right? You have to tell people what's going on inside you. People don't just know. It doesn't matter how good of friends we are; I can't read your mind."

After a second, Brooklynn peeked one eye open. "Okay, maybe I've been watching rom-coms. Jeremy's new girlfriend is obsessed with them."

Well, that explained part of what was going on here. "So, what did I say that upset you? You know it wasn't on purpose, right? Whatever it was."

"I know." She picked at the flaking pieces of leather on Moe's steering wheel. "I'm an idiot, Pyper."

I shook my head, even though she was looking the other way and didn't see me. "Why would you say that?"

"I just..." She finally turned her big brown eyes on me. "It's stupid, but I kind of hoped Will would ask me to prom."

I nodded slowly instead of gaping like a guppy, which is what I wanted to do.

She groaned. "I'm stupid! Prom is in, like, four days. But he is a dummy sometimes, you know? I thought maybe he didn't realize how close it was or something."

"I get it." I nodded. "I said that thing about it being too late if you didn't already have a date for prom. That's what you wish I hadn't said?"

"Right." Brooklynn pressed her lips together. "But you're totally right. It is too late. He's not going to ask me now or ever. He told me in English that he's going with Leah."

I tipped my head to the side. "I'm really sorry, Brookie."

And I was sorry. I hated seeing my friends hurt.

Brooklynn rolled her head to the side to look at me. "I'm not mad at you, Pyper. I suddenly realized how hopeless this whole thing was. It was stupid to think Will would ever want to go out with me."

My desire to comfort my friend went to war with my anti-dating convictions. The silence felt as tight as undersized spandex while I battled inside my own head.

"Pyper?"

I pressed my lips together. "Brooklynn, do you really think Will doesn't like you?"

Brooklynn's eyes widened. "Do you think he does?"

I took a deep breath and held it for a second before blowing it out.

Brooklyn sighed. "Forget I asked that. I know I should be content just to be friends, but it's not that easy."

My throat tightened. "Why do you think you should be content to be friends?"

Brooklynn flushed. "Don't laugh, okay? I wrote to the school paper. You know, Sage Advice?"

I tried to nod, but my head got stuck halfway through.

"That's what Sage said to do. If I don't want to risk my friendship, I should be content with just being friends." She peeked sideways at me. "Do you think I'm dumb for writing the paper?"

"Um," I swallowed, "no. I don't think you're dumb. Sage Advice is usually pretty good. Why didn't you talk to me about it, though?"

Brooklynn shrugged. "I don't know. I guess I was embarrassed or something." She looked away. "No, that's not true. I didn't want to talk to you about a guy problem."

My mouth suddenly felt very dry. "Why not?"

"You're just, you know, kind of prejudiced when it comes to guys. I thought you would probably tell me to forget about it because high school guys are super immature." She paused. "Is that what you would have said?"

I had to clear my throat three times before I could get any words out. "Yeah, pretty much word for word."

Brooklynn smiled. "I should have just talked to you about it, though. You're my best friend. Plus, I don't think Sage's advice is going to work. I can't do the friends-only thing. It's already making me bananas. I think I would rather risk telling him and get it all out in the open than always wonder what might have been."

My brain ran at rapid fire speed, trying to shove my own feelings aside so I could see Brooklynn's dilemma more clearly, but there was so much chatter up in there that I had a hard time sifting.

Brooklynn leaned into the seat with her head tipped to look at the ceiling. "I don't know anymore. Just tell me what to do, Pyper."

Now it was my turn to stare out the windshield. I put a lot of effort into producing a realistic thinking face so Brooklynn would know I was working on her problem.

As I thought, the first threads of doubt began weaving slowly through me. Had I done this all wrong? A year ago I thought it was my duty to save others the same heartache I went through, but what if I made a huge mistake? Maybe I didn't actually know anything. What made me think I was wise enough to tell other people what to do?

A horrible question worked its way to the forefront of my mind: Would I have given Brooklynn the advice to be content to be friends with Will if she asked me to my face instead of writing to the paper?

Brooklynn cleared her throat, jolting my thoughts back into her beaten-up truck. I had been silent for way too long.

"That's okay, Pyper. There is no good solution. I already know that."

I turned my body to face Brooklynn without cricking my neck. "Brookie, I'm not going to tell you what to do. I think you should do whatever you feel good about."

"I don't know what I feel good about anymore." She covered her face with her hands.

I took a deep breath. "What did you feel good about before you asked Sage Advice?"

Brooklynn peeked at me through her fingers and then dropped her hands. "I was going to tell him I like him."

"So, why didn't you just do that in the first place?"

"I guess I was...scared? I wanted a dating expert to tell me what would happen if I talked to Will before I actually did it."

"Sage Advice is not an expert!" I blurted, appalled. "It's just a high school newspaper column. She can't tell the future; she doesn't know everything!" Like Kai when he drank a can of soda without stopping, all my words burst out with excess carbonation. "When you have a problem that's weighing you down, you should absolutely talk it out. Ask for advice if you think you need it, but remember that you don't have to do what the person says. No one really knows what's best for you except for you. Gather advice and opinions, but then do what you feel is right."

Brooklynn nodded slowly at first, then more rapidly as my words sank in. "Right. Right! You are totally right!"

"Thanks," I mumbled, still trying to get my emotions back to neutral. I stretched my hands up over my head and imagined peaceful mountain brooks and wildflowers. When that didn't work, I pictured the cardigan display at Juneberry.

That totally did the trick.

"Okay, I'm going to think about this and then, maybe, talk to him. But not today." She shook her head. "Nope. Maybe not until after prom."

"Why not now?"

"Oh," Brooklyn cringed, "I didn't take it very well when he told me he already had a date to prom."

"How in the world did that come up?" It didn't seem like something he would just announce, especially since I was positive that he liked Brooklynn. Why else would he be at her house all the time? Really, her brothers were not that cool.

Brooklynn peeked at me and then looked away.

"Tell me a story." I crossed my arms. "And start with, 'Once upon a time.'"

Silence.

"Brookie!"

"Fine!" She threw her hands up to the roof and thumped it twice. "Fine. Once upon a time, I was walking out of English with Will, and I was still upset about what you said, so I asked Will what he thought about what you said, and he was like, 'What did she say?' and I was like, 'Really? Do you listen at all?' and he said, 'What did you say? Were you talking?' with the dumbest look on his face, so I slugged his arm and he pretended like it hurt, and I asked him if he was coming over Friday for football and fries. Then he looked at me."

Brooklynn closed her eyes again, like she was trying to escape from the memory.

"Yes?"

"His face was all pitiful. No, not like that. I mean, like, full of pity. It was the worst. He said he couldn't because he was going to prom with Leah, and then I punched him for reals and maybe yelled some things. I don't remember. Then I ran away." She brought her hands to rest on the steering wheel and gripped it until her knuckles turned white.

I watched her fingers twist around and around. So many pieces of advice presented themselves, but I couldn't bring myself to say any of them. I wanted to find the thing to say simply as her best friend.

"What?" Brooklynn sighed.

I blinked. "What, what?"

"What do you want to say? I can see it lurking behind your eyes."

I laughed. "Things don't lurk behind my eyes. That's super creepy."

"Come on, just say it." Brooklyn drummed her fingers on her pant leg.

"Okay. I totally think Will would have asked you to go to prom with him if you hadn't told him you didn't want to go."

Brooklynn gasped. "I didn't say that!" She stared at me. "Did I?"

I nodded. "A few weeks ago in econ. You don't remember?"

"I honestly don't. Did I really say that?"

"I believe your exact words were, 'I would rather eat a latrine than wear a dress in public.'"

Brooklynn dropped her head until it reached the steering wheel. If Moe's horn had been working, it would have blared our socks off.

"I did say that. I totally did. I'm such an idiot." She groaned into the steering wheel, her voice muffled.

I nudged her. "You are not!"

"I didn't mean that I didn't want him to ask me to prom when I said that about dresses! I just meant that sports are cooler than girly things. I was trying to be sporty, you know? Appeal to his interests."

"Did you just say, 'Appeal to his interests?'" I raised an eyebrow. "That sounds like cheesy advice from a teen magazine. Have you been reading those, too?"

"Carly lent one to me. I just read the advice columns. The rest of it was so weird." She rolled her head to the side to look at me. "Seriously, why do girls want to tattoo makeup on their faces?"

I kept my face expressionless.

Brooklynn grunted. "Anyway, it doesn't matter now. Will's going to prom with Leah, and I will be spending the evening watching my brothers have a contest to see who can drink the most water without going to the bathroom. Yay." She twirled her finger in the air.

Should I tell her that Leah was looking for her right now to invite her to prom on a blind double date? I opened my mouth and then clamped it shut.

Not my business.

"Okay," Brooklynn said, taking a deep breath. "I got this. I'll talk to Will and tell him how I feel next time I get a chance. Ugh!" She slapped her palm against the steering wheel again. "Dating is the worst! I'm just going to be a nun."

I tipped my head to the side. "I can't really picture that, Brookie."

"Well, start trying because that is my new life goal."

I nodded like I was taking her totally seriously. "So, no more becoming a doctor that cures all the incurable diseases? Good-bye to the Tour de France? Farewell to reading boring old books that no one else gets and has words bigger than my head?" I tapped *The Scarlet Letter* with my fingernail.

"Yep, I'm done with all of that." She flipped the book onto the dashboard. "I can learn new things. Like knitting. I could learn to knit toilet paper for the orphans in Mongolia."

"Cute little!" I said. "You should totally do that!"

Brooklynn looked at me with big, pleading eyes. "And you could come with me."

"To Mongolia?" I clarified.

"Yes."

"To knit toilet paper?"

Brooklynn nodded.

"I'll think about it," I said, as if this was a real conversation we were having about something we were seriously going to do.

Brooklynn sighed. "I know there's no way I'm going to get you to wear a habit."

"Not unless it's pink with sparkles."

"Pyper, I love you."

I reached over for a hug. "I love you too, Brookie. And I was serious. I am sure Will would have asked you to prom if you'd given him a little bit of real encouragement."

Brooklynn reached for her backpack. "Maybe. We should go. I'm sure lunch is almost over by now."

As if on cue, the bell rang.

Dear Sage Advice,

Yesterday, one of my guy friends took me out to lunch so we could talk. He told me he likes my best friend and asked me if she likes him, or what he can do to make her like him. I told him the truth: I don't know. But there's a bigger problem.

I like him. I have for years.

What do I do now?

Signed, Twisted

Dear Twisted,

My advice to you is to talk to your friend. If she doesn't like him, then you could go for it. He might actually like you better anyway...

Dear Twisted,

Wow! That's tough! Do you know how he feels about you? Because he might like you and not realize it...

Dear Twisted,

Well, that stinks! How are you supposed to confess your feelings now that you know he likes your best friend? That's beyond awkward...

Dear Twisted,

Do you have a trusted female adult you could talk to? Maybe she would have some experience with this. I'm just a high school kid that thinks dating in high school is the worst idea ever. I can't help you...

Chapter 12

My stomach was growling like a polar bear.

Alone.

In the winter.

During a famine.

I'd only been in third period for five minutes, but I'd spent the entire three hundred seconds watching the clock move very slowly. I was pretty sure I was starving. All I could think about was the shrimp tacos I'd ordered and left behind.

I had nothing to eat. I'd already checked. Twice. No stale granola bars, no half-eaten bags of almonds. Not even a breath mint. Nothing but lint, and I wasn't desperate enough to eat that.

Yet.

There were eighty-five minutes left in English before I could go to the vending machine and get something completely overpriced and unsatisfying.

I wasn't going to make it.

And that wasn't even my biggest problem. In my backpack was a huge pile of emails I had printed out last night before I went to bed. A huge pile of questions from fellow high school students that I was responsible for answering with Sage Advice.

Unfortunately, I wasn't feeling very sage anymore. That whole experience with Brooklynn had given my confidence a solid shake. I couldn't tell people what to do. What made me think I knew what was best for them? Roxie was right to question me. How many lives had I ruined with bad advice?

I pulled out my phone, not even bothering to hide it. My teacher, Mr. Welling, was retiring this year. We spent every English class watching movies while he dozed at his desk. With minimal risk of my phone being taken away, I sent a text to Leah. I needed some advice.

> Leah, you busy?

Nope. Just hanging out in the student council room.

> Do you have any real classes this semester? :)

Yes! Underwater basket weaving first period and interpretive dance fourth. :P

I smirked.

> Wow, just, wow.

What's up?

> I'm a fraud.

Okay. Computing response.

Need more data.

> The advice column.

> I think I need to resign.

I am screwing it up.

Request denied! Remember freshman year when it was called Secret Advizerer and a different person wrote it every week because no one wanted to do it? That was screwing up lives; you're doing great!

I was afraid she would say something like that.

I'm not so sure. Leah, do you think it's right to tell people what to do?

Absolutely!

No hesitation?

None. Why?

I don't know enough to know what's best for other people.

Waxing philosophical? I like it! As Plato would say…actually, I have no idea. I dropped philosophy after two days. It gave me a migraine. Is that your dilemma? You don't think you're wise enough to give advice?

That's most of it. Maybe it isn't right to give people advice when I don't know who they are or what their back story is, you know? Maybe the advice isn't really helping them.

I get it. No worries. This is just a confidence kink. Every great leader has them. Think of it this way: if you don't advise people, then someone else will. Maybe someone way less thoughtful and caring than you. And it's not like you're telling people what to do; you're just giving advice. People choose to do it or not. What happens next isn't your responsibility.

Is it not? Again, not sure.

Then trust me when I say it's not. Chin up, Pyper! All great writers have their doubts, but those who face their doubts with confidence have courage as well!

I don't think that's how that quote goes. :)

It works, though. Will you have your assignments submitted by the end of the day?

Working on it now.

Thank the lightning bugs. You're the best! I think we're going to get this week's issue out early. Any good questions in that mess of emails?

Mostly people asking for restaurant recs. Where would you say is the best Italian food in town?

Tuscan Tomato, duh. Alright!

Have fun!

Oh wait! Leah?

Yeah?

Did you talk to Brooklynn about that blind double date thing?

Yes! I caught her after lunch. She's going! All is well! She's gonna borrow one of my sister's pageant dresses.

Are you still coming over?

Absolutely! K, back to work!

See ya!

Byeeeeeee!

I glanced at my backpack with all those emails waiting to be sorted, but I didn't put my phone down. There was one more thing I had to do really quick. I opened my text strand with Brooklynn.

You're going to prom?

Why are you texting during class?

Why are you?

I just did it because I knew you'd keep texting until I answered.

True. So, you're going to prom?

How did you find that out so fast? I just talked to Leah.

I know everything.

So, what you're saying is you texted Leah during class, too?

Correct. Question.

Answer.

When it's time to eat that latrine, can I come watch?

I never said I would eat one, just that I would rather.

Right, because those are two totally different things. Now get off your phone and pay attention. Seriously. What is wrong with you, slacker!

Gimme a break.

I glanced at the clock and was glad I did. That blasted inconsistent thing. First it was crawling, now it was flying. I was going to have to hurry if I wanted to answer my pile of emails on time, especially now that I knew Leah would love it if I had them ready for her by the end of the period.

I slipped my phone into my bag so it would stop distracting me, then pulled the stack of emails out of my backpack, along with my favorite pink gel pen. It gave me special powers. I liked to write the advice answers by hand, then type them up. It was easier for me to be brilliantly insightful with a pen in my hand.

Unfortunately, the pen spent a lot of time rolling up and down my desk. One half of my brain pondered Twisted's plight while the other half meandered through my conversation with Brooklynn about Will.

Then, like striking a match on a bale of dry straw, my thoughts took off. I knew exactly what to say to Twisted. I jotted it down, my hand flying across the paper in a blur. Once that hurdle was conquered, it was easy to advise everyone else.

There were only a few minutes left of class by the time I finished—just enough time to skim for spelling errors before I placed the papers into a neat stack. Now I could give all my attention to watching the clock again as it tick-tocked away the last couple seconds.

Let's try that again.

Dear Sage Advice,
Yesterday, one of my guy friends took me out to lunch so we could talk. He told me he likes my best friend and asked me if she likes him, or what he can do to make her like him. I told him the truth: I don't know. But there's a bigger problem.
I like him. I have for years.
What do I do now?
Signed, Twisted

Dear Twisted
This is such a tricky situation, but I think we can figure it out. What I suggest is, before you do anything, decide if telling him you like him is a risk worth taking.
Trust your feelings, and you will know what to do.
Good Luck! I hope it works out.
Love, Sage

ADVICE COLUMN
Sage Advice

Dear Sage Advice,
My best friend's new boyfriend is such a jerk! I don't know why she doesn't see it; it is so obvious. He is totally going to break her heart! How can I tell her to dump him as quickly as possible, but in a nice way? I don't want her to get mad at me.
Please Help.
Suspicious

Dear Suspicious,
I am a huge believer in intuition and am all for protecting your friend. My advice to you is to tell your friend what you suspect, in a kind and gentle way. She deserves to find out what he's really like from someone who cares about her. I'm sure she will be happy to know the truth, even if it's hard to hear.
Love, Sage

Chapter 13

Carly was waiting for me when I walked out of English.

"Pyper!" she screeched, throwing her arms around me. "I haven't seen you in forever! How have you been?"

"Good," I said, hugging her back. "How are you?"

Carly slipped her arm through mine. "I have so much to tell you! Let's walk slowly."

"Yeah?"

"Travis is amazing! Really! You are going to love him. We've been together almost every day since Saturday, and it's been..." She sighed, and my brain went to work filling in the empty space. Dreamy? Magical? A train wreck? "We have been so busy hanging out, I haven't even had a chance to text you! I should have, though. Sorry! But guess what?" She squealed and leaned closer to a whisper, "He asked me to prom!"

The happiness I'd felt when I first saw Carly slid a little. I tried to pull it back in place with a shaky smile as I looked over my shoulder and merged into the flow of students.

Why did it have to be Travis?

"I wish you were going to prom too, Pyper! Then we could get ready together and go to dinner together and ride together. Oh!" She clapped her hands.

I jumped slightly.

"Travis is renting a limo!" She sighed again. "I so, so, so, so, so wish you were coming, Pyper!"

Amid all the so's, I finally found my voice. "I am coming."

Carly gave me a blank look.

"I told Leah I would be there so it wouldn't ruin her date if something goes wrong."

"Oh, that's…" Carly looked like she was pointing out toilet paper on my shoe. "Super. But I wish you were really going, like normal, like with a date, so that we could double."

I filled my mind with sunshine, lollipops, and glittery unicorns to overpower any dark, dank, or dreary thoughts. "Well, we will see each other there. That's something. And we could get ready together. Brooklynn is going now, and Leah Thom. Do you know Leah?"

Carly shrugged, pulling out her phone to check something. I waited for her to finish.

"Well, she's great. I'm sure she won't mind if you come, too. Do you want me to text you her address? It will be super fun." I wished my voice didn't sound so fakey.

"No, that's…wait, did you say Brooklynn is going?" Carly covered her mouth. "Are you serious? In a dress?"

"Well, yeah."

"I have to get a picture. I'm totally bringing my phone now. This is going to be hilarious! If I wasn't going already, I would go just to see Brooklynn in a dress with a date!"

"Carly!" I said, my tone more harsh than I planned. Her words were starting to make my arms itch.

"What?" Carly blinked rapidly. "I'm just saying that she never wears anything other than jeans, yoga pants, and tees. It will be fun to see her branch out. I love Brooklynn, you know that. Who's her date?"

"I don't know," I said, stepping around a person who stooped to tie their shoe. "Leah's setting her up with someone."

"You didn't ask who?"

I shook my head.

"Pyper," Carly gripped my hand. "If Brooklynn's coming, you have to come too. It would make everything perfect if you are there with us!"

"I will be there with you." My smile wavered in the middle like silly putty that was pulled too tight.

Carly let out a breath, "No, I mean, like normal. You know what I mean. Can't you get Jason to come back for Prom?"

I shook my head. "I'm going to go alone."

"Pyper, prom is not an alone dance." Carly's eyes widened. "Prom is a date dance. A romantic date dance."

"I'm not all that interested in romance right now, Car."

Her face got serious, which was kind of weird because I didn't actually know she had a serious face. "I think I know what's going on."

"Yeah?" I seriously doubted it.

"Yeah," Carly sighed and put her hand on my arm. "It must be so hard to be separate from the guy you love. I can't even imagine. Prom makes you miss Jason more, am I right? That's why you don't want to talk about it."

I swung out of her grip. "That's...not...you're...no...Carly." Words bobbed up my throat like beach balls. I tried to hold them back, but part of me didn't want to. I kept thinking about Brooklynn and Will. Maybe Carly needed to know. Maybe I could spare her a lot of pain if I told her the whole story about why I thought Travis was such a jerk.

My stomach clenched.

The whole story meant I had to tell her everything about Jason and prom last year. Carly was right about one thing, I was so not going to talk about that, no way. Last year was dead to me. So, maybe I could just tell her a small part of the whole story.

Ahead, I saw the turn I needed to take to science class. Carly would have to go the opposite direction. There wasn't much time left before we had to part ways.

"I need to talk to you about Travis." I tugged her arm so she would stop walking. I had to get this out now because I wasn't sure when I would get another chance. "I think you rushed this thing with him."

"What do you mean?" Carly's face scrunched up. "I thought you were happy for me?"

"How could you think that?" I blurted. When did I ever make it sound like going out with Travis was a good idea? I couldn't imagine how she misunderstood me so hard.

"Because..." She twisted the strap of her bag through her fingers. "He makes me so happy. I thought that would make you happy."

I sighed. "I do want you to be happy, Car, but I don't think that's possible with Travis. He-"

"Do you even know Travis very well?"

My cheeks stung like she'd smacked me with an open palm. I couldn't get my mouth muscles to form words. I finally got my brain to connect with my mouth, and that's when the words started spewing out.

"I know a lot more than you think I do. Travis is not a nice guy, Carly. I've gone to school with him since the third grade. He was a jerk then, and he's a jerk now."

Carly gasped.

"That's what I've been trying to tell you. He just messes with people. All he thinks about is himself. You don't want to be with someone like Travis. You don't need to be with anyone at all. You have to stop defining yourself by who you date, Carly."

When I saw the look on Carly's face, I had to wonder if I had overstepped. It figures I word vomited all over her, like, five minutes after I vowed to stop giving people such direct advice.

But, then again, Carly was my friend. It was different than anonymous advice. I was just trying to save her from inevitable heartbreak. My intentions were way good.

"I have drama." Carly's voice was void of all emotion. She pointed in the opposite direction.

"Chemistry, this way," I said, trying to brighten the hallway with my tone. "We'll talk later, okay?"

Carly turned away without answering.

I watched her go, feeling a heavy weight settle in my stomach. What had happened to this day? Usually Mondays and I were really good friends.

And then, the bell rang.

Late again.

The Cromer Chronicles

ADVICE COLUMN
Sage Advice

Dear Sage,
This guy I barely know asked me to prom and I said yes because my mom made me, and the guy I really like is going with someone else. Do you think I can still have fun with this other guy?
Sincerely, Reluctant

Dear Reluctant,
Absolutely. I think you can have fun if you decide to have fun. Try and wrap your head around making prom fun no matter what.
Maybe it will help to think how you would want someone to treat you if the situation was reversed.
And, just let me throw this out there: You know, it is possible to go to that dance with someone who is just a friend. It could be more fun that way, actually.
Love, Sage

Chapter 14

I darted down the hall and lunged up two flights of stairs to get to chemistry class. If someone had been close by, they might have heard me mutter a few choice names for the building designers—especially those who thought it was a good idea to put long flights of stairs in a school where students had to get to classrooms from one end of the building to another in less than five minutes.

When I arrived at chemistry, I was totally and completely out of breath. "Sorry, Mr. Raddy."

"Don't let it happen again. Take your seat, Pyper."

I meekly walked to the table I shared with my lab partner. "Hey, Sam," I said, but he didn't look up from his notes.

That was normal. He took science very seriously. I watched him scribble furiously, his curly, brown hair flopping over one eye. I hoped those weren't the notes I missed from Friday. They looked extensive.

I took my seat just as Mr. Raddy turned to face the class. Behind him were a series of equations that made absolutely no sense. I stared at the board with what I hoped was a curious look and not one of pure idiocy. Mr. Raddy rubbed his hands together, causing chalk dust to float lightly to the floor like foundation powder.

"We are in chapter twenty-one, people. Read, answer the unit questions, and finish up your lab conclusion from Friday. If you need something, you know where to find me." He pointed to his desk and then hid behind it.

Lab conclusion? *Monday* was lab day, wasn't it?

"Sam!" I tapped the table between us with my pencil to get his attention. He didn't hear voices very well when he was in the zone. "What did I miss on Friday?"

He just grunted.

I sighed and pulled my notebook out of my bag. I was honest with my mom when I told her I had all A's, but my A in chemistry hung tenaciously by its fingernails, trying desperately not to drop. I knew it would have given up a long time ago, if not for Sam.

I pulled my textbook out and flipped to chapter twenty-one. It was no good. Until I knew what happened Friday, there was no way I could try to figure out what we were doing today.

"Hey, Sam? I need your help! I wasn't here." I perched on the precipice of begging.

"I noticed," he grumbled.

Well, that was better than silence. I tapped my pencil on my book until Sam finally looked at me. Technically, he looked at my pencil. He hated when I did that.

"Fine. I guess we are doing this," he said. Then, with his hands folded together like an evil villain, he rested the tips of his fingers against his chin. I kept waiting for the consequent evil laugh, but it never came.

"Fact! Friday you missed class, and I had to do the lab alone."

I put my pencil down. "We never do labs on Fridays."

"That's funny because I distinctly remember doing a lab completely by myself."

"Why-"

"I'm not finished. Fact! You purposely skipped class because you were miffed about the student council meeting."

"I-. Wait, what?"

Did he just say miffed? I don't think my grandma even said miffed anymore.

"I'm still not done. FACT! You think I'll cover for you while you flitter away your time. You think you can just borrow my notes and all is well, but you can forget about that, missy."

Okay, seriously. Did he just call me missy? What was happening?

"You are going to have to own up to Mr. Raddy that you ditched and figure out how to catch up by yourself." He gave a short laugh, then added, "Good luck with that."

Which I thought was taking it just a little too far.

Sam turned back to his paper, making a show of covering it up with his other arm so I couldn't see anything he was doing. I stared ahead, trying to think of what to say next. It was a little ironic that he was so upset at me about Friday when he was one of the many people who voted against me in the student council meeting. I should have been the one holding grudges.

Except that I couldn't afford to; I really needed his help.

"Sam," I sighed. "I am super sorry that I wasn't here for the lab. We don't usually do labs on Friday, so I thought it would be okay."

Sam snorted.

"I was wrong to, uh, assume you would cover for me. I wasn't trying to take you for granted. So, I'm sorry about that, too."

That made the hunch in his shoulders look slightly less hunchy.

"I'm not trying to excuse what I did, either. Going to the mall instead of class was not the best idea ever, but it was for a good cause."

He snorted again, louder this time. I think that one must have hurt because he followed it with a wince.

"My friend...never mind. It's a long story. Will you forgive me?"

He looked at me finally, but his face was expressionless. "You just want to copy my notes."

"You do have the best notes in school." I said with a winning smile. "You know I'm out of my *element* without you."

Sam's face softened; he was a sucker for science puns. "Don't lose them," he said, gathering a few papers together.

"Thank you, Sam! I won't." He slapped the papers into my palm so hard that the top sheet careened across my desk and onto the floor. I leaned over to pick it up.

"I want those notes back at the end of class, so you better get to work," Sam said, without looking up. "Missy."

I rolled my eyes and opened my notebook to a blank page, ready for note-taking. With exaggerated precision, in case Sam was watching, I smoothed all the notes onto my desk and began to read.

Carboxylic Acid Derivatives.

At least four sighs escaped before I could stop them. I had no idea what that meant, or what it was, or why it was important. An ironic chuckle burst out of my throat.

Most of my problems in life had come about because I totally didn't understand chemistry.

"Are you working?" Sam peered at me over his glasses like the quintessential pinch-lipped librarian.

"Yes."

"You can't laugh and do chemistry at the same time."

Well, that was obvious. I looked around the room. Ain't nobody was laughing. Chemistry had scientifically proven many times that it could suck the fun out of everything.

"I'm working."

"Good."

"Pyper?"

I turned to see Holly leaning toward me. We had been on the freshman cheerleading squad together. I gave it up after sophomore year, but she kept at it, and now she was cheer captain, which just went to prove that 'Victory is always possible for the person who refuses to stop fighting.'

I smiled at her. "Hey!"

"Hey! Are y'all still working on prom decorations?"

I nodded. "Free periods."

Holly stuck her lip into an elaborate pouty face. "I don't have a free period this semester. What else can I do to help?"

"We could use help putting up the decorations Friday after school."

"Fabulous!" Holly clapped. "I'll bring the girls. This will be so fun!"

"Thank you! Leah will love you forever and always."

Holly gave me a thumbs up.

I turned back around with a big smile, which faded quickly when I saw Sam's face.

"What? I'm working." I rustled the papers all around my desk so he could see how diligent I was.

Sam grunted.

I copied definitions and diagrams with all my energy. I can't say with all my heart because that would be a big, fat, hairy lie. I was gradually getting the work done, so that was good.

Then, the little creeper-alert hairs on the back of my neck began to tingle. I peeked over at Sam, who was staring at me without blinking. I formed a question and was just about to ask it when Sam opened his mouth.

"Pyper, would you go to prom with me?"

I stared at him, wondering if I was hallucinating or something. I've heard this can happen to a teenage girl if she goes a long time without eating chocolate. I hadn't had any since yesterday. Come to think of it, I talked to Carly between classes instead of hitting the vending machine, so I still hadn't eaten anything at all since breakfast. Maybe I was having a low-blood-sugar episode.

"What?" I blinked.

Sam sighed with more exasperation than I thought his body was capable of holding, and he reached for his notes. "Did you finish? I need those back now. Class is almost over."

Was it really? I glanced down at my watch and saw that Sam was right. We were only a few minutes from the end of the day. That went fast. I had just copied pages of notes and reviewed the lab from Friday, and I hadn't remembered any of it. That was so not good. I began to feel a little dizzy.

Sam clicked his tongue impatiently until I placed his notes safely in his open palm.

"So?" he said, not looking at me because he was too busy checking to make sure I hadn't stolen any of his hard work. I could tell by the way his eyes shifted back and forth from me to the notes that his eyebrows were heavy with suspicion.

"So, what?"

Sam heaved another end-of-the-world sigh and crossed his arms, causing his papers to tap against the desk. "So, are you going to prom with me, or what?"

"Wow." I couldn't think of anything else to say. That was probably the most bizarro way anyone had ever asked a girl to prom.

Ever.

At least he had asked, right? Jason hadn't even done that.

The bell rang, interrupting the silence that stretched between us.

"Well? I have to go catch my bus. Are you going to go with me, or not?" Sam snapped his fingers in front of my face.

I moved my head away from his fingers, irritation clouding the corners of my vision. "Sheesh, Sam, you really know how to sweep a girl off her feet. Are you sure you want to go to prom with me? Because right now I feel like something on your lab worksheet. Like, bunson burner on? Check. Ask Pyper to prom? Check."

Sam sank into his chair so that only his eyes were visible above the top of his desk. The classroom was pretty much empty now except for the two of us and Mr. Raddy.

"Sorry," he mumbled. "I wasn't trying to make you feel bad."

"What were you trying to do?" I was genuinely curious.

"Ask you out," he said, sinking lower. The wrinkles in his forehead were all I could see.

"Sam, look at me." I waited for him to sit up straight. "Do you really want to take me to prom? I haven't made it a secret that I hate prom, and I sort of got the impression that you think I'm super annoying."

"And you have a boyfriend. But…" Sam pursed his lips and straightened his shoulders. I knew that look; I saw it every lab day as he was preparing an experiment.

"What would you say if I told you I've never been on a date?" His face hardened, preparing himself for raucous laughter and finger pointing.

"Good for you." I applauded lightly.

Sam's head tipped to the side, then the lines in his face smoothed out. "That doesn't sound weird to you?"

"Nope. I think dating is stupid."

"Ironic coming from the girl with the perfect college boyfriend." Sam studied me for a moment, then went on. "Well, anyway, I have never been on a date, and it occurred to me that I should clear some room in my schedule for opportunities as they arise. That's why I didn't vote for your prom cancellation idea. My older brother says prom is dating insurance. Girls want to attend so badly that they will go with anyone."

I opened my mouth to protest, but Sam examined the ceiling and just kept talking.

"Obviously I can't go without an upperclassman until my junior year. I am not comfortable doing things without practicing first." He held out his hands as if they were going to explain everything for him. "You're a girl that I am marginally at ease with, so I thought you would be someone I could practice asking out."

I gave myself a headache trying not to roll my eyes. "So, you were just practicing? You weren't really asking me to prom?"

He pushed his glasses back up his nose. "Yes, however, if you say yes, then we can go. That would be adequate practice as well."

"What about the boyfriend?"

Sam paused. "Is he going to kill me?"

I shook my head. "You're safe. But what about the fact that I don't like prom. Or, you know, hate it with a fiery passion? What about that?"

"Yes, well," Sam said as he shook his head, "that is a stumbling block, but I had to try. I can't think of another female in this school to broach such a question without feeling inferior." He sighed. "Every great one has their Achilles' heel."

Good thing I'd memorized the famous Eleanor Roosevelt quote, so I knew no one can make me feel inferior without my permission, or I would have been totally offended.

Okay, I was still offended.

A little.

I spread my palms on the table. "Can I give you some advice, Sam?"

I waited for him to nod before I went on. "If you are going to practice asking a girl out, then you should tell her beforehand, so she knows she's a lab experiment. You wouldn't want her to agree to go with you and then not be willing to take her, right? Dating 101: be sensitive to your date's feelings." I slid my things back into my bag as I talked. The day was catching up to me. I could feel the biggest slump of all time tingling in my pinkie toe. It was just a matter of time until it spread.

"That's good advice." Sam tapped his chin. "Do you have any more advice? For dating?"

"Oh, tons," I said flippantly.

"Then how about we actually go to prom? I could practice dating, and you could give me advice." Sam stuck out his hand. "What say you?"

I stared at his hand. My first instinct was something along the lines of absolutely not. I was done with dating selfish jerks.

Then again, Sam was not a jerk, although he was totally condescending. He was just young and doing his best to figure all of this out.

And really, weren't we all?

Sam's hand wiggled in front of my eyes as he waited for me to take it. Then it dropped to his side and hung limply.

"During that long silence, something occurred to me. There's no scenario in which a girl like you would go out with a guy like me."

"What is that supposed to mean?" My voice was shrill enough to make my own ears ring.

"Look at you." He waved his hands like he was trying to fling some disgusting, sticky substance onto my shirt. "And look at me." His hands fell gracefully to his sides. "A fish won't date a bird; a senior won't date a freshman; a hottie won't date a nerd."

Hottie? That was the closest Sam had ever come to sounding like the typical teenage boy. I wasn't sure how to respond. He was right that I didn't want to go to prom with him, but he wasn't right about the reason. How could I make him understand? The dude was all facts and figures, experimentation, and proof.

I thought hard. Words came into my mind as pre-formed ideas, like someone had just sent an email directly to my brain. I knew the right thing to do, and I was going to do it because Sam needed this, and because I was going to prove to myself that not all dating was about being self-centered.

"Sam?"

He looked up, peering at me through his glasses the way he looked at the temperature gauge during an especially difficult experiment.

"I would love to go to prom with you."

ADVICE COLUMN
Sage Advice

Dear Sage,
What do you do when you're on a date that is really not working out? I haven't had that happen yet, but other people have, and I want to be prepared so I'm not stuck doing something I don't want to do with someone I don't want be with anymore. Does that make sense?
Sincerely, Planning Ahead

Dear Planning Ahead,
Good for you for thinking ahead. My dad always says that if you make a decision ahead of time, you don't have to make it when you're in the middle of it. Meaning, you can think more clearly and plan better when you aren't in the thick of something stressful.
So, my advice is simple: get to know guys as friends before you go out with them. Then you'll know which qualities to avoid. Decide ahead of time what you will and will not put up with, and if something or someone crosses the line, then always keep your cell phone handy!
Listen to my mom on this one: plan for the worst but hope for the best!
Love, Sage

Chapter 15

I stumbled into the auditorium ten minutes late and totally flustered. The committee members were already assembled and just about hanging from the rafters. I guess it was too much to expect that the guys would wait calmly in chairs.

I dropped my bag and books into the aisle and gave a piercing whistle that echoed beautifully thanks to the phenomenal auditorium acoustics. The noises died abruptly, and everyone looked at me.

With as much dignity as I could muster, I gathered my things and walked the rest of the way to the stage. I took an extra minute to smooth my shirt and redo my ponytail before I turned to face everyone.

"Thank you for waiting. I'm really sorry I'm late."

There were way more people there than those on the committee. John and Brant sat in a middle row with their feet on the seats, trying to gross Nova out with something green and sticky.

I totally didn't want to know.

Abby sat between Juan and Tyson; all three earned bonus points for actually paying attention to me. Will and Landen earned those points, too.

But not Travis.

What was he doing there, pretending to be all attentive and ready to help? Like I didn't know what kind of person he was. Ten to one he was finding out what we were going to do so he could sabotage it.

I put my hands on my hips. "We don't have time to mess around, people. Prom is only a few days away, and the student council is determined to do it even though our original venue flooded and Kathy has mono. So, stick with me." I jabbed these words at John and Brant. "I don't want to be here all night."

I flipped through the notes that Kathy's mom had dropped off at the school that morning, but I was interrupted when I heard a loud roaring sound that echoed around the auditorium.

What was that?

Then it came again, and I looked down, expecting to see an alien trying to emerge from my belly. My stomach growled for a third time. Apparently, it was done waiting for me to do something about feeding it, and it took matters into its own hands.

I mean, if it had hands.

"Was that you?" John sputtered, as he fell back into his seat, laughing.

"I skipped lunch." My cheeks burned as I pawed through my bag for something edible. I already knew there was nothing there, but I had to try.

"Oh, yeah. Those tacos were awesome. Thanks."

"Will! You ate her lunch?" Abby's voice was stern. "Pyper, you shouldn't skip meals."

"I know. I just got busy."

"Well, then, you *really* need to eat three meals, maybe more. All the stuff you do uses energy-"

Despite her good intentions, I tuned out Abby's voice. She was giving me flashbacks to middle school health and nutrition class.

"Here."

I looked over to see two protein bars sitting in someone's hand. My eyes followed the hand up the arm to the face. It was Landen. "Take them," he insisted.

"Thank you." I unwrapped one with a shaky hand and immediately took a bite. The instant I swallowed my stomach was appeased. The growling stopped, but I went ahead and finished both bars.

That felt so much better.

"Okay, guys, listen up. We have three and a half days to make the best prom ever. This paper from Kathy says Nova, you're in charge of the photographer. Kathy was in charge of refreshments. We don't have a D.J. yet and...what am I missing?"

Travis raised his hand. I tried to ignore him, but so many people were looking at him that I couldn't move on without being a total jerk.

"Travis?" I sighed.

"Carly said her parents could cater the refreshments. We just need to let them know how many people and if there are allergies."

Hearing Carly's name made my stomach squirm. I squinted at him over the papers in my hand. "Are you sure?"

He nodded. "Carly told me. She would have come to this meeting, but she had twirl practice."

I made a mark next to refreshments. I would for sure check his facts before I assumed that was all true. But if it was, I owed Carly. Having refreshments taken care of was a huge relief.

"Also," Travis waited for me to look at him again, "I know someone who can DJ."

"That's really awesome!" Abby smiled. "No, really. That means we don't have to listen to the teacher's nineties playlists again this year! And that also means the committee doesn't have anything else to do except confirm with the photographer and help Leah with decorations."

"Travis," Brant snorted. "Suck-up."

"Right? Overachiever." John threw a crumbled piece of paper at Travis' head.

Travis caught it and threw it back.

"Make sure you guys pick all that up before you leave," I said in a tight voice.

"So," Juan started to stand, "are we done, then?"

I shook my head. "How much does your DJ charge, Travis? We need to make sure that's going to fit in the budget. Also, how much do the Jenson's want for refreshments?"

Travis spread his hands out to the sides. "All free."

"What?" Tyson sputtered. "None of them are charging anything?"

"Nope."

I shifted to my other foot. "I'm not okay with that. We have the budget; we can pay them."

"No, really." Travis leaned forward to rest his arms on the seat in front of him. "They want to do it for free. We can use that prom money towards an awesome Senior gift."

"Dude, that's lit." Tyson grinned.

I refused to agree. "Okay, so, we just...Abby?"

"Yeah?"

"Can you check in with the Jensons and with Travis' DJ friend, and make sure it's all on the up and up?"

Travis raised an eyebrow. "You don't trust me?"

I stared at him, refusing to blink. My eyes watered, but I willed them to get over it. Of course I didn't trust Travis. There was no way I was leaving the fate of the dance in his grubby hands.

"It's not that," Abby answered for me. "It's good leadership. You always have back-ups and double checks. I'm on it, Pyper. I'll text you tomorrow."

"Thank you." I gave her a small smile.

"So, we're done?" Juan slung his bag over his shoulder.

I nodded and reached for my water bottle. Noise filled the air as people gathered their things and left. I sipped water and seriously contemplated spreading out for a nap on the auditorium chairs. I was suddenly bone tired.

Will and Landen walked over to me and waited until I swallowed.

"So," Will dragged the word out like it made its own sentence. "You just need help putting up decorations?"

I nodded. "If you can come Friday right after school."

Will glanced at Landen. "Are you going to be there, Pyper?"

"To decorate? I'm planning on it."

"What about prom?" Will scuffed the toe of his sneaker on the carpet.

"Yeah," I sighed. "I'm going."

"You are?" Landen peered at me.

I nodded, again. "I wasn't going to, but then, a friend asked me to go as a favor, and I agreed."

"Cool." Will grinned. "Cool. Well, see you there."

I raised an eyebrow. "Also, I'll see you at econ tomorrow."

"Yeah, that too." Will nudged Landen and turned to go.

I followed them out of the school.

Finally.

Longest. Day. Ever.

ADVICE COLUMN
Sage Advice

Dear Sage Advice,
My best friend hates my boyfriend. What do I do?
Signed, Stuck in the Middle.

Dear Stuck in the Middle,
Try to remember that you will probably date a lot of guys throughout your high school career, but your friendships have the possibility of lasting forever. Just a little perspective for you.
Love, Sage

Chapter 16

I purposely waited until the next morning before school to check my phone messages. I knew there would be millions, and I seriously needed a break. When I was sitting in Beauty, ready to drive to school, I finally pulled out my phone.

Carly had still not answered my text. Most likely it got marked as spam or something weird. I resent my message from the day before, thanking her and her parents for helping with prom and asking if she wanted to talk. Then I opened the group text to Leah and Brooklynn and reread the text I sent them the night before.

Going to prom with Sam.

Okay if we triple?

What?

That was from Brooklynn.

Yay! Pyper!

That one came from Leah.
Then Brooklynn went kind of nuts.

Sam who?

Do you know any Sams?

Are you messing around?

You hate prom.

Why aren't you answering your phone?

The only Sam I know is Sam Pederson.

The freshman? You have a class with him, right?

I can't believe he asked you to prom! He's so shy.

I need more details.

Where are you?

And then Leah.

I am so flipping excited!

I decided not to answer their texts right away. I would be at school in five minutes; it would be so much easier to explain everything face to face.

As I was driving, my phone rang with the Dora the Explorer theme song. I should have known Brooklynn wouldn't be able to wait that long.

It was no surprise that Brooklynn stood on the yellow bumper blocker thing at the head of my parking space when I pulled up. I hadn't even gotten out of my car when she started talking. I propped the door open with my foot so I could hear her while I got my things out.

"You're going to prom with Sam? When did this happen? Why didn't you tell me? Why are you going? This doesn't make any sense! I want you to go, of course. I would be miserable without you. It isn't about that. I mean, do you really want to go? Something is up. Why would you change your mind suddenly? You better start talking, quick!"

"Or what?" I smiled, closing Beauty's door with my hip. Lately the latch had been having a hard time sticking. I breathed out a small sigh of relief when it stayed put.

"Pyper!"

I looked at Brooklynn with her adorable pixie haircut, wearing her brother Hugh's old football jersey over a long-sleeve white tee. She was so adorable, even when she was irritated with me.

"Yes?" I dragged the word out until it sounded like I had a rocking awesome lisp.

Brooklynn laid across Beauty's hood, clutching her backpack to her chest. "Please tell me. I can't stand the suspense a second longer. It would be more bearable if I could make a tiny bit of sense out of this, but I can't, and my head hurts."

I dropped my bag on the asphalt and laid on the hood next to her. Beauty groaned, but I ignored it. I knew she could handle our weight. She was just being whiney.

"I don't have a super good explanation, Brookie. Sam asked me as an experiment. One minute, I had every intention of saying no, and the next minute I was saying I would love to go."

Brooklynn rolled her eyes and waved a hand in the air. "Start at the beginning."

So, I did. I told Brooklynn every single detail to the best of my ability. Not to brag, but I did an impressive impersonation of Sam. That wasn't going to win me an Oscar, but it made me feel pretty good deep down inside that I could accurately nail his puppy face and that slight nasal way he said his B's.

"Okay," Brooklynn nodded. "Okay, the world makes sense again. You were just being Pyper." She breathed out deeply and sat up, making the metal on Beauty's hood shriek.

I slid off the hood, and we began the short walk to the school's front door. "What did you mean I was just being Pyper?"

"Oh." Brooklynn stepped sideways to let a particularly large group of boys get by. They were too busy looking at their phones to notice that they had almost plowed her over. "Going to prom with Sam, that's totally you."

"What? Getting guilted into doing something I don't want to do?"

"No, dummy. Doing something you don't want to do to help someone else. That is so Pyper."

That sounded way better than what I said.

But it made me wonder. Was that true? Did I do things to make others happy? I thought about this as we walked to econ together. I came up with two ways of looking at it.

On one hand, I could be bitter that I was going to prom when I really didn't want to, but on the other hand, I could be excited that I was helping Sam and being selfless. Was everything in life this way? Two-sided? Did something feel like the worst thing ever just because that's how I thought about it? And if so, did that mean I could change how I felt about a situation just by thinking about it differently?

Now that was a thought and a half! Like, I wanted to mime an explosion coming out of my head. Because if that were true, that I could change any situation just by thinking about it differently, and that meant I could change my world!

Better yet, I could change my past.

"Hey," Will said, as he took his seat. "Did you get your assignments done?"

"What do you think, Einstein?" Brooklynn rolled her eyes. "Did you get yours done?"

"What do you think, Einstein?" Will mimicked Brooklynn's voice, waving a stapled stack of papers in her face. She pushed the papers away with a little too much force, almost propelling herself into Will's lap. He laughed as he grabbed Brooklynn's wrists to steady her until she got her balance back.

I turned my eyes away from her flaming cheeks and tossed a pink folder at Will so he wouldn't make fun of her. "Done and done."

Will opened it, but instead of looking at my work, he gave me a wicked grin. "Are you though? Are you done? What if I look through this and find a gross error and you have to do it all over?"

"Not worried."

"Maybe you should be."

I shook my head. "Walt Disney said not to worry, and that's good enough for me."

Will stopped flipping pages to give me a confused look.

I pointed to the whiteboard. "Quote of the day two weeks ago. 'If you've done the very best you can, worrying won't make it any better.'"

Will glanced at my papers. "But have you done the *very* best you can?"

Brooklynn blew out a huff of air. "Quit bugging Pyper, already. You are always bugging, seriously."

Will opened his mouth to respond but got distracted by Landen and the loud thump his bag made when it dropped to the floor.

I smiled as Landen slid into his seat behind me. He smiled back, nodded at Brooklynn, and then busied himself with getting his stuff out and organized.

Will finally gave my paper the attention it deserved. "Pyper, really?" He held up my folder. "You chose to be a psychiatrist? Do you really think that's a good idea?"

I opened my mouth to answer but didn't get a chance.

Brooklynn huffed. "It's a perfect fit. Pyper loves fixing people. She's always trying to solve everybody's problems. You know that, Will. Don't be a doofus."

"Yeah, I've been on the receiving end of her advice enough times." Will whistled the theme to *Jaws*.

"Why are you doing that?" Brooklynn slapped her hand with her portion of our group project onto Will's desk.

"Why not?" he grinned.

"Idiot." Brooklynn mumbled, turning around again.

Watching them made me feel the same way I do when I see a big nasty bug, especially a spider, in my bedroom. Part of me is so disgusted I want to squish it flat with my thickest shoes, but the other part of me feels sorry for it. It's not like it's hideous and creepy on purpose.

Except in this case, it was like one part of me wanted Brooklynn to go ahead and snark attack Will because he was a booger and had been since fifth grade when he would mash up all of his food and make us watch him eat it. But then there was the Sage part of me that wanted Brooklynn to be more kind to Will so they could live happily ever after.

I guess that meant I would never get too bitter or jaded to want everyone else to have a happy ending.

That might be good news.

"Sounds good?" Will said.

I nodded automatically except that I hadn't been listening to what was going on around me, so I had no idea what I was agreeing sounded good.

"Okay, cool. Landen and I will pick you girls up at six."

Wait, what?

I looked at Brooklynn, who was looking at me with what I am sure was an identical confused face. I opened my mouth just as Mr. Rypkema welcomed the class and gave announcements. I couldn't concentrate on any of it. Why did Will look at me when he said that about picking girls up? What was he even talking about? Pick us up for where? I shifted through my brain for something that would clue me in on what he was talking about, but it came up blank.

I stared at Mr. Rypkema, waiting for him to stop talking. All I heard was a wonky, distorted version of his voice, which sounded a bit like the grownups on the old Charlie Brown cartoons.

Finally, Mr. Rypkema gave us time to work in our groups, and we all moved our desks together. As soon as the scraping and banging stopped, I leaned forward, fixing Will with my most penetrating look.

"What did you mean you and Landen will pick us girls up?"

"What did it sound like? This is econ, not Spanish."

I cut him off before he could mock me a second time. Or was it the third time now? It didn't matter. The mocking pretty much never stopped with Will.

"I heard the words, sassafras. They didn't make sense, though."

"Let. Me. Break. It. Down. For. You," Will began in a slow, robot voice.

Landen threw a wadded piece of paper at him. "Answer her question, Will. Don't be a punk."

I smiled at Landen. "Thank you."

Will huffed. "I would if I knew what the heck she was asking me. I thought it was pretty clear the first time I said it."

Up to this moment, Brooklynn had been quietly listening, but I knew that wasn't going to last. Her tolerance meter for Will's nonsense was very low. Sure enough, Brooklyn wadded up another piece of paper and threw it at his head. "You said you and Landen will be picking up us girls. What for?"

"Prom! Duh."

"Okay, but you said that to Pyper."

"Yeah?" Will shook his head impatiently.

Brooklynn scowled at him. "And Pyper isn't going to prom with you."

"I am aware." He rolled his eyes.

"And she isn't going with Landen, either. I am going with Landen, so what were you talking about?" Brooklynn spoke slowly like she was explaining the plot of *Finding Nemo* to a preschooler.

"Wait." Will sat up. "You're going with Landen?"

"To prom?" I swiveled my gaze to Brooklynn.

"Yeah." She looked at me strangely. "You knew this. Leah set me up, remember?"

Will's eyes flew around at each of our faces. "Wait," he said again.

Landen shifted forward to block Will with his shoulder. His voice was suddenly extremely loud. "Quiet, Will. You knew that, too. Leah set me and Brooklynn up for prom." He was talking so quickly that his words sounded the way a blurry picture looks. "She wanted to double so she wouldn't have to be alone with you."

"Oh, ha, ha." Will pushed Landen back. "I'm not the stupid one here. We thought the girl Leah set you up with was—"

"Pyper!"

I turned around. "Hey, Richie!" I smiled super big.

Landen leaned over and whispered to Will, creating a distracting buzz behind me.

"Hey," Richie flipped his hair out of his eyes. "Holly said you need help with decorations Friday?"

"Yes!" My friendly smile morphed into a grin. "We have a bunch of lights that we need to hang across the ceiling."

"Me and the team are on it," he smiled.

"Really? Oh, my goodness! You're the best!"

When I turned back around, Brooklynn, Will, and Landen were staring at me like I had green hair. Or maybe they were still as confused as I was about our previous conversation and were trying to sort it out.

Will rolled his eyes with so much energy that all the people in our high school could probably feel it and were getting vertigo. "This is weird, so I'm going to change the subject now. Pyper, are you excited for prom?"

I gave him a look. "That's not really changing the subject, Will."

"That's a change of syntax, not subject," Brooklynn said.

"Thank you, professor encyclopedia." Will glared at her. His eyes darted to Landen's face, which had gotten very tight. "I'm asking Pyper a question, so she should answer it."

"Sure, I'm excited," I said carefully, not really sure what was going on.

Will scooted his chair closer, shaking his head. "What I meant was, are you excited to go to prom with-"

"Fireman!" Landen said loudly, drowning out Will's last few words.

"Dude!" Will protested.

Landen glared at him and mouthed something I didn't see, then turned to the group. "I think a fireman would be an interesting career, and I have an uncle we can interview."

"What in the world is going on here?"

Neither one of the boys answered Brooklynn. The conversation happening between their eyes was apparently much more interesting. Finally, Will tore his gaze away from Landen.

"This is ridiculous. Pyper, who are you going to prom with?"

I opened my mouth to answer, but then closed it. Both Landen and Will sat on the edge of their chairs. For some reason I couldn't fathom, I felt like whatever answer I gave to that question had the power to change the course of history.

That was a lot of pressure.

Brooklynn's head slowly moved back and forth from Landen to Will. She watched them with a calculating look, the kind she used when she was trying to solve an especially difficult equation. When she turned to me, her face was wrinkled in confusion.

She shrugged.

"Sam Pederson," I said finally.

"Wait." Will leaned forward, but Landen pushed him back in his chair.

"Sam's a nice guy," Landen asked.

"Sam Pederson? He's a freshman!" Will's face twisted first with disgust and then with pain as Brooklynn kicked him under the desk.

"So were you once, bucko. It isn't a permanent condition."

"No, it's just—. I'm just surprised." Will stammered under Brooklynn's glare, a flush spreading to his ears. He glanced at Landen, who was still and as stone-faced as a statue. I wondered if he was even breathing. Will grabbed his arm and pulled Landen away from us, his chair squealed obnoxiously across the floor.

"Pyper?" Brooklynn whispered, leaning toward me.

With another glance at Landen, I turned my attention to Brooklynn. "Yeah?"

"Do you think I'm being too mean?"

"What?" There were, like, three unresolved conversations happening here at our little group of huddled desks. I was having a difficult time adjusting. My brain needed resolution before it could move on something else. As I tried to focus on Brooklynn's question, I could feel my attention split like an over-spliced atom, and all that was left was a pile of goo.

"Am I overcompensating? I just realized that I've been hard on Will cause I'm all sensitive that you know I like him. It's making me feel weird. Am I overdoing it? Is he going to think I detest him?"

"Um," I thought, gathering the scattered thoughts together. "You could probably be nicer. It does kind of come off like you think he's a moron."

"Well, he is, but I still like him. How do I come across that way?"

I glanced at the boys, who were still whispering together. I wondered what they were saying. Then I wondered if they were wondering what we were saying.

I sighed. "Just be you, Brooklynn. Do what you feel best about. But, you know, don't overthink it."

She nodded, chewing on her lip thoughtfully.

"All right!" Will bellowed, causing half of the class to look at our group. "Our project looks really good. We should review this. Right now." He always spoke louder than most people, but his volume was suddenly overpowering, as if he was trying to drown out the very memory of our previous conversation. It was kind of working. He was totally in my head.

"Will?" Brooklynn whispered.

He didn't answer her. Instead, he put the folders and pages we'd given him earlier in the center of our desks so everyone could see them clearly. "I think we just need to decide which career to present to the class."

"Will!" Brooklynn said louder.

His eyes reluctantly slid to her face. "What, Brooklynn? We don't have time to mess around. We have to get this project figured out today so we can get a good grade."

Which is just ironic, really. In all the time I'd known Will, I had never heard him string that combination of words together. It was like he and Brooklynn had switched personalities.

Brooklynn nodded. "Yeah, but this will just take a sec."

Will raised his eyebrows at her, tapping his pencil as he waited.

Brooklynn gulped. "Stop doing that. I can't even think with that noise."

"Just say what you're going to say. We're running out of time."

"I'm trying. Stop tapping your pencil."

"Fine. I stopped. What?"

"I love you." Brooklynn blurted and then covered her mouth with both hands.

Very slowly, all eyes turned to Brooklynn. I wish I could say it was just the eyes of the people in our group, but Brooklynn's voice had been louder than normal as she tried to speak over Will and his boombox voice. The whole class now watched the four of us. I could just imagine what we looked like: me with my lips pressed together, Landen with his eyes wide, Brooklynn sliding further down in her seat, and Will with his mouth hanging open.

Mr. Rypkema took a step toward our desks.

I had to do something.

So I stood up.

And applauded.

"Brooklynn! What a great audition! So much feeling. I totally think you nailed it. That part is yours. No one else stands a chance."

Mr. Rypkema stopped, looking at us quizzically.

Landen leapt to his feet and began clapping with me. "The drama club doesn't know what it's missing. You are amazing!"

Once again, I smiled at Landen, this time for backing me up. He smiled back, but it didn't quite reach his eyes.

The class joined in our applause for a few moments, shouting out catcalls and congratulations to Brooklynn, who was still trying to disappear. Mr. Rypkema waited for the clatter to stop before he walked over to us and leaned his knuckles on my desk.

"I don't know what is going on in this group, but here we do economics, not drama. Understood?"

We all nodded. Landen and I took our seats quietly, and the four of us got to work, our heads bent over our individual desks, not one of us daring to look up. It was probably the most awkward fifty-five minutes I had ever sat through.

So much for being done with drama.

The
Cromer Chronicles

ADVICE COLUMN
Sage Advice

Dear Sage,
So, it turns out my whole life is a lie. There's this guy I have known forever. I thought he was a certain way, but I just found out he isn't. And the thing is, if I had known that, I would have done things very, very differently. Tell me, Sage. What should a person do when they find out they are really, really wrong about another person?
Sincerely, Stumped

Dear Stumped,
Well, I'm going to give you a gold star for being the vaguest question I've ever had! Without knowing more details, it's difficult for me to give you specific advice, but I will do my best to inspire you to a solution.
In my experience, it is impossible to know how a person thinks and feels all time, no matter how close we are to them. I don't think we even know how we think and feel all the time.
You can't change how you acted or how thinys were in the past, but you can totally do things differently now and in the future. Consider the possibilities.
Love, Sage

Chapter 17

I walked into the newspaper room, feeling squished by the weight of a thousand unanswered questions. Usually this feeling motivated me, but today I just felt gloomy.

"Why so down?" Leah asked, noting my slumpy shoulders and flappy walk.

I sighed and set my bag on the table next to my computer, which was covered in multicolored sparkle star stickers. That almost made me feel better.

"Nothing, really," I sighed. "There was this thing in my last class, with these guys-"

"Oooooooh," Leah wiggled her eyebrows. "Guys!"

"Yeah, no." That was definitely not what I meant. "I'm not even sure what happened. I've been trying to sort it out for, like, the last hour, and I have no idea what to make of it."

Leah tapped her front teeth with a pencil. "Maybe I can help. What happened?"

"Long story."

"Hmmm." Leah looked at the clock with an exaggerated frown and then turned to show me her smile. "We've got time!" She closed her laptop and rested her chin on the tops of her hands. In full range of her unwavering gaze, I slid onto my desk and let my legs swing a few times as I considered where to start. Because Leah was going to prom with Will, I would have to be very careful with what I said.

And didn't say.

"Okay, so here's the thing. I have econ first period-"

"You have econ first period?" She sat up a little straighter.

175

I wrinkled my brow. "Yeah."

"Okay. Go on."

"So, I am in a group with Brooklynn, Will, and Landen, um…" I suddenly realized I didn't know his last name. But that probably didn't matter. Leah must know it, since she was the one who set him up with Brooklynn.

"Anyway, Will told me that he and Landen were going to pick 'you girls' up for prom at a certain time, and he looked at me. I tried to get him to explain, but he never really gave me a straight answer."

"Sounds like Will," Leah laughed.

"Yeah." I looked at her intently. "How well do you know him?"

"Pretty well," Leah shrugged. "He's a good friend, when he's not being a punk."

I shook my head. "I mean, are you two together?"

"No way!"

"How did he end up asking you to prom, then?"

"Oh, that!" Leah adjusted one of her earrings. "I asked him."

"Wait, the other day you told me he texted you and asked you to prom."

"He did," Leah shrugged. "I realized that I'd been working so hard on organizing prom that I hadn't put in the energy to flirt my way into a date. So, I called Will and asked him to ask me to prom. Then he texted me the question."

My temples throbbed.

"That was right after I found the perfect dress. Really, it would have been a travesty not to wear it. But," Leah went on, "what I don't get is why Will thought he was picking you up. I haven't told him that you and Sam are coming with us yet. So, that doesn't make any sense at all. I wonder if he heard it from someone else. Maybe Brooklynn told him?"

"I don't-" I began.

"Oh no!" Leah stood up suddenly. "Wait! Oh no! Oh flapjacks!" She began pacing, mumbling to herself. I watched in confusion as she walked and exclaimed over every part of a pancake breakfast.

"Oh, sliced bananas! Oh, whipping cream! Oh, maple syrup!"

It was kind of making me hungry.

Finally, Leah sank into her chair and groaned. "Oh no!"

"What's wrong, exactly?" I asked.

"I had no idea! He never said... If I had known, I never would have..."

"Wait, slow down and finish a sentence!" I laughed. "I totally can't keep up with what you are saying!"

Leah looked at me with big eyes. "I am a serious doofus. I messed everything up."

It was like our conversation started out on parallel train tracks and then one of the trains suddenly veered sharply to the right. Leah was pacing the room again, waving her hands wildly as she talked.

"Wonkadoodle ding dong! This is such a mess. He is going to kill me!" Leah stopped walking and stood right in front of me, her eyes slightly wild. "I totally didn't know! I swear! But I should have! I should have figured it out sooner!" Her eyebrows raised expectantly, but I didn't know how she expected me to respond to that.

"I have no idea what we're talking about, Leah," I reminded her.

Leah sat down again and closed her eyes. I waited patiently, only slightly tapping my foot incessantly on the floor.

When Leah opened her eyes, she looked much calmer. "Okay, here's the thing. Remember how I wanted to set you up with a guy for prom?"

"Yeah, but you set him up with Brooklynn instead," I said. I didn't want to hear what I already knew; I wanted her to explain what in the world was going on inside her noggin.

Leah just nodded, looking a little overwhelmed.

"Landen, right?" I said, prompting her to continue.

She looked at me sharply, maybe even a little suspiciously. I didn't know if that was the right way to describe it, but I suddenly felt like I was under a bright lamp at the police station.

Leah narrowed her eyes. "Did you know it was him? Is that why you said no?"

"No!" I said, raising my eyebrows. "Of course not, Leah! Seriously?"

"I didn't think that would be something you would do," she said softly, more to herself than to me.

"I really was planning on going alone." I hurried to fill her in on how the whole thing with Sam came about.

Leah nodded. "That makes sense. But it is still a mess. I wish Landen wasn't so stinking private about this. Usually, he doesn't have a problem saying things like they are. If he had just told me-." She stopped and looked at me with big eyes. "Well, anyway, none of this would have happened."

"So, what happened exactly?" I asked, sliding off my desk and into the chair. I needed back support.

Leah rubbed her temples. "Okay. I'm going to just think out loud here. It will help me figure out what to do."

But she didn't talk for a very, very long time. I could almost see her sifting words, choosing carefully what she would and would not say to me. That was very familiar. I'd just done the same thing when trying to explain what happened in econ. I wondered what it was she was trying to not tell me.

And who she was protecting.

Leah pulled a chair over to my desk and sat across from me. We looked like something from an old detective movie; she just needed a hat with a veil and a tissue to wipe her tragic tears. But then that would mean I needed a bowler hat, a trench coat, and a cigar.

Gross.

"Okay, so, here's the story. I knew I would have to be stealthy about setting Landen up, or he would never go through with a blind date. He thinks blind dates are right around the same neighborhood as shark attacks and bee stings."

That sounded about right to me. Except, "I thought you said he would go to prom with anyone?"

"Did I say that? I don't remember. Anyway, I saw him at lunch time yesterday. We sat with some other people from track—Dawn and some others. Will sat with us, too- Anyway, I told everyone that I had a friend who needed a last-minute date to prom."

I nodded, more to encourage her to keep talking than to show that I was following her story.

"I knew if I told Landen straight out that I wanted him to double with Will and I, he would just laugh and be like, whatever. Because that's what he did the last two times I begged him to double date with me. I mean, Will is great and all, but one-on-one dates are so awkward. You know? Anyway, I was appealing to Landen's Superhero Syndrome."

"Did you just make that up?"

"No. It's totally real, I swear. Guys like to swoop in and rescue people, you know, save the world."

I pursed my lips, considering. Okay, maybe that was a thing. "Go on."

"So, Will, being obnoxious, said he was taken, obviously, or he would help out, but Landen wasn't going with anyone. I put on this big show scoffing and waving my hands around, saying Landen would never, ever go to prom in a zillion years. I asked everyone else if they knew of anyone because Landen was obviously out. Will got all surprised and asked Landen why he would never go in a zillion years, and Landen didn't answer. Will kept bugging him until Landen had to punch him and tell him to lay off. Will asked who the girl was. I told him it was a really great girl who doesn't date all that much but really, really needs to go to prom. Then, Landen said he would do it. Just like that. I was shocked, but I took him up on it before he could change his mind."

"Hm." I chewed my lip thoughtfully, trying to smoosh the pieces of her story into places that would make sense with what I knew.

Or thought I knew.

"I never said Brooklynn's name." Leah shifted in her seat. "So, um, Pyper, this is a safe space, right? I mean, this stays here?"

"Of course," I said, surprised at how uncomfortable she looked.

"Because I kind of, sort of, totally think..." she took a deep breath, "Landen thought I was talking about you."

I pressed my lips together. "What's that word you said?"

"When?"

"When you were ranting."

"Wonkadoodles?"

"That's it. Wonkadoodles," I said, leaning back in my chair. I see why she chose that word; it instantly made me feel better when I said it.

"I'm so sorry, Pyper," Leah said. "I'm not sure how we all got so thoroughly confused or how you ended up in the middle of it, but I am really, really sorry!"

"It's okay, Leah. It's just a weird misunderstanding." I leaned forward with my hands on my knees. "I don't know what to do now, though. Do you think Landen thinks we were messing with him? Will he be mad?"

Leah tapped the desk thoughtfully. "What did he do in class when he realized Brooklynn was his date?"

I tried to remember. "I think he just tried to get Will to be quiet. And his face got really tight."

"He's not mad then," Leah nodded. "If he was mad, he would have switched classes."

"Nuh-uh! There's only, like, five weeks left of school!"

"Right. When Landen is mad, he does dumb things. That would be a dumb thing. He's not mad. He's probably super confused."

"Fair enough." I thought about that. "I am, too."

Leah laughed shortly. "Aren't we all?"

We sat in silence for a few minutes, me thinking disjointed thoughts and Leah twirling a pencil through her fingers like a baton.

All my encounters with Landen were so dysfunctional.

"Okay, Pyper." Leah sat up straight in her chair. "I've been through this in my brain about fifteen different ways. I really don't think this is fatal. I'll just explain the whole thing to him, and it will be fine. Landen is a logical guy. My mom loves to tell the story of when we were, like, two and found an ant hill. Landen kept walking around it, looking at the ants and watching them. My mom always says he would have stood there for hours observing, but then I came running up, right to the center of the big old ant hill, and started stomping on it until ants crawled up my legs and bit me. He's super slow and quiet and methodical. It drives me nuts. But because he is, he's super understanding." Leah nodded at me, like she had just proved an important point.

Wait, what?

"How does your mom know Landen so well?" I asked.

She blinked in surprise. "Pyper! He's my twin brother."

ADVICE COLUMN
Sage Advice

Dear Sage,
So, have you seen Pride and Prejudice? Or read the book? I have a total Mr. Darcy thing going on. This guy I work with seemed like the biggest jerk, so naturally I retaliated by treating him like one. But as I've gotten to know him better, I realize he isn't a jerk at all. He's amazing. I think I've fallen for him hard. The problem is, I don't know how to show him that my feelings have changed. Please help, Sage! You are my only hope!
Signed, Not Proud of Being Prejudice

Dear Not Proud,
It's good you realized the truth universally acknowledged, that people are not always what they seem. But what to do with that knowledge? My advice? The golden rule. Treat him how you want him to treat you. He will know your feelings have changed based on the way you treat him. Then, I think all the confusion will melt away, and you two will understand each other perfectly. It could be the best love story ever!
Love, Sage

Chapter 18

I don't know if this is a common thing for other people, but sometimes I'll wake up in the morning totally stressed out for no good reason. It will usually take me a while to figure out why, and it almost always has to do with either something that happened recently or something I was worried about before I went to sleep.

On Wednesday morning, I rolled onto my back and pulled the pillow over my face. There was no gradual awareness as I rolled back to consciousness. My conversation with Leah the day before slapped me in the face the second I had a coherent thought.

I couldn't believe I didn't know Landen and Leah were twins! How could I have missed that obvious detail? Even though they weren't identical, they definitely looked related. The more I thought about it, the more idiotic I felt for not making the connection sooner.

Forget twins, I didn't even know they were siblings!

How?

A barrage of thoughts peppered me like a pellet gun. I wanted a massive do-over. Maybe if I closed my eyes really tight, clicked my heels together three times, and wished harder than hard, I could wake up on Tuesday morning and start the whole day over.

No, I would go back to Monday morning and redo both days.

No, no, no. Friday for sure, and I would remember Landen's name this time.

Actually, I think I needed to go back to this time last year and re-do the whole Jason thing.

And if I really could do that, I needed to start at the very beginning and see Jason for what he was instead of what I thought he was.

My phone alarm beeped as the snooze reminder went off for the third or fourth time. I didn't need to look to know that if I didn't get going soon, I was going to be late for school. I needed a plan, and I needed one fast. I wiggled under my blankets to the fluffiest, coziest spot where I can do my best thinking. What were my options?

I could pretend like none of it ever happened.

This plan would make Brooklynn very happy. She texted me last with those very words: everything that happened in econ that day never happened. She was just going to go forward in blatant ignorance until Will decided to bring it up with her. If ever.

But would this work for me? I kneaded my fingers through an afghan my grandma made when I was a baby. The yarn was so worn and faded now that it looked more white than yellow, but I still loved it. All those crocheted holes were the best for contemplating the universe.

I couldn't pretend like it never happened. That would be too weird. I'd already apologized to Leah a kazillion times from the depths of my sincerest heart. If I saw her today and was all like, I totally knew you were twins, it would be the fakest thing ever.

So that was out. What else?

I could just get over it.

This plan would make my mom super happy. It was her philosophy of life; well, one of them. She actually had, like, an infinity of happy-life philosophies. But 'face it', 'resolve it', and 'let it go' were her favorites. That's why she got so excited when the movie *Frozen* came out.

So, I faced it already by owning my mistake to Leah. I resolved it by apologizing, and now I could let it go, right?

I just felt so awful.

And, even weirder, I felt awful that I felt so awful? It was a dumb thing to forget someone's name and not knowing their family ties, but it's not, like, the worst thing a person could do. No one was going to hate my guts forever over something like that. Leah already, once she got over the initial surprise, told me not to feel bad, that it was no big deal. So why did I still feel so bad? All wrapped up in a guilt burrito smothered in shame salsa.

Why was this bothering me so much?

My mom would probably ask me if that was really it. Was that what was *really* bothering me, or was that just the safe thing that I could focus on instead of facing the thing that was really, really bothering me?

I threw my blankets back and jumped out of bed. I had to get ready for school; there wasn't time to figure it out now. I would think about it later.

Maybe.

I reached for my phone and unlocked the screen. I'd missed a phone call. I was so happy for the distraction that my heart did a little tap dance in my chest. My mind grasped onto the mystery of who it was and why they were calling this early in the morning like I was grasping a life preserver. I pushed the message button and held my phone to my ear.

"Hi, Pyper. This is Natashia Thom. I am an owner of Greedy Cow in the mall. I looked over your application, and I would love to meet with you to discuss the possibility of you working for us as soon as possible. Please give me a call back."

My mouth dropped to the floor, not even caring about dust bunnies and rogue spiders.

A job!

With fumbling fingers, I hit the redial button. No way I was waiting ten more seconds. I cleared my throat and ran my fingers through my hair. Ew! Maybe I should have gotten ready first. This wasn't the first time I was grateful people couldn't see me through the phone.

"Hello?"

"Hi! Is this Natashia? I'm Pyper Lewis! Sorry I just missed your call."

"Oh, yes! Hello, Pyper."

"Hi," I said again and then wished I could suck the word back into my mouth like a super long spaghetti noodle. I sounded overeager.

"It's very nice to meet you. Let me just grab your file really quick. Alright, here you are."

I could hear pages fluttering through the phone.

"I have to tell you, you received a very high recommendation from one of our employees. He was very impressed with you."

Landen?

He was the only employee I'd ever noticed working there, so it must have been him. The surprise I felt was so tangible that I looked around to see if it was floating in the air around me like dust particles.

I didn't know what to say. Various words slipped over my tongue. Cool? Thanks? That's nice? None felt quite right. Luckily Natashia had pity on me and picked the conversation right up like I hadn't just turned it awkward with a long silence.

"I would love to meet with you. Are you available tomorrow after school?"

"Sure," I said. "When is a good time for you?"

"How about four o'clock? Does that give you enough time?"

"Yes! That's perfect."

"Lovely. I will see you at four."

"Sounds great. Thank you!"

"Thank you, Pyper. See you soon."

I hung up the phone and tossed it on my nightstand. Roxie poked her head out of my closet.

"Was that Greedy Cow?"

"Sequined tulle, Roxie! You scared me." I took a deep breath. "What are you doing in my closet?"

"Eavesdropping, duh. Was it?"

"Yes."

"And?"

"And I have a job interview tomorrow."

Roxie screamed, ran across the room, and collapsed on my bed with her arms stretched out to the sides.

"Roxie!" Mom rushed into my room, her eyes huge. "Was that you? Pyper, are you okay?"

"Better than okay!" Roxie jumped up and twirled, then waved her arms in my direction. "You are looking at the newest interviewee for a job at Greedy Cow!"

My mom clutched her heart like an old lady and sagged into the door frame. Gavin peeked out from behind her.

"I am either really glad you are okay, or I'm going to throw you both out the window. I haven't decided which. Roxie, don't you ever scream like that again unless you are seriously hurt!"

"Or the house is on fire," Gavin whispered through his fingers.

"Or you accidentally shaved your head bald," I said, flipping a piece of her hair.

"Or you found a really cool toy in the cereal."

I peeked under my bed, looking for the voice. "What are you doing, Kai?"

"Spying." He answered in a tone that made it seem like I had just asked a dumb question.

"How long have you been under there?" I pulled him out by the wrists. "Never mind, I don't want to know." I lightly shoved him out of my room and waved my hands at everyone else. "All right people, I have to get ready for school! Shoo, shoo!"

Mom stepped closer to give me a one-armed hug before she left my room. "I really am excited for you, honey." Then she wrapped her arm around Roxie and leaned in as they marched out of my room. "If you scream like that again, you are grounded for the rest of your life."

I closed my bedroom door, checking the knob to make sure it locked.

This was my first real job interview. And yes, it was just an ice cream shop in a mall, but I wanted to rock this. It felt important. Like, maybe I needed to prove to myself that I could do something on my own. I could be someone without...

Well, without help.

I had a few precious minutes to find the perfect job interview outfit. If I didn't do it now, I would spend all day thinking about it and be totally worthless at school. My clock glared at me from the nightstand, but I purposefully turned my back. It was better to be late than worthless.

I threw open my closet door. On Saturday when I went to the mall for applications, I dressed to look responsible, but with an interview pending, I needed a different tactic. I wanted to wow their socks off with my enthusiasm. My goal became a chant in my head as I flipped through hangers of clothes.

Dress to impress. Dress to impress. Dress to impress.

A flash of color from the back of the closet caught my eye, and just like that, I knew what I was going to wear. It was meant to be; there was no other explanation. This particular dress was nestled comfortably with the fall and winter clothes, and normally would have been out of bounds for the spring. But when I pulled it out by the hanger, my heart fluttered with excitement. I felt it deep in my pinkie toe. This dress was the one.

Suddenly, I was a changed person, enlightened even. No more would I categorize my clothing by color scheme, regulating out-of-season outfits to the dark corners of my closet. From now on, I vowed to be open-minded to all shirts, pants, dresses, and skirts no matter what color they were and no matter what time of year it was. This flowy, knee-length, flowered dress of ivory, rose pink, and brown had taught me a great lesson.

I laid the dress across my desk chair and added a pale pink woven belt, tall cowboy boots that had never seen cows, and debated on a cardigan but decided that I liked the loose elbow sleeves too much to cover them up. As for my hair, I would leave it down this time, curling it into loose waves.

With all those important decisions made for the next day, I was ready to face the day I was in. I pulled on a pair of lime-colored capris and added one of my favorite white and purple flowered tops. The leaves were shades of green that just barely picked up the same tint as my pants. It was so subtle, I loved it.

With a cheeky wink to myself in the mirror, I smiled and left.

It wasn't until I was walking from my locker to economics that I remembered I forgot to make a plan for econ. It was going to be all kinds of awkward in there after yesterday. Surely by now Leah had told Landen that I didn't know they were twins, or even related. That was almost as bad as not knowing his name. My steps faltered just enough to connect with the uncertainty I felt, but not enough for anyone around me to know it. I was still smiles and sunshine despite the impending hurricane.

Honesty was best, right? I could just fess up and apologize for being a knucklehead.

Or maybe aloofness. Maybe I wouldn't talk to Landen at all.

That didn't seem right.

What was I going to do?

I reached the door to economics, wondering if I could get away with not going in. About three seconds later, the tardy bell rang. I scooted through the doorway when it reached a crescendo, announcing my presence like a trumpet.

The first thing I noticed was Landen's seat.

Empty.

And the second was Will, leaving Mr. Rypkema's desk with a pink slip in his hand. He walked by me without meeting my eyes.

I took my seat with a sigh of relief.

"I know, right?" Brooklynn whispered.

And just like that, economics became my favorite class of the day.

With that weight off my mind, I was free to think about my interview. And I did all day. During free period, I daydreamed about cookies and sprinkles while I made more tissue ball decorations and answered the few new requests for advice. Now that prom was two days away, the emails had slowed.

During lunch, I talked Brooklynn's ear off, replaying over and over my conversation with Natashia. During English, I imagined Natashia and I hitting it off and becoming the best of work besties. Before I knew it, I was taking my seat in chemistry, the last class of the day.

ADVICE COLUMN
Sage Advice

Dear Sage,

I'm interviewing for my first job this weekend, and I am super nervous. What if I say something idiotic? What if I babble about random things? I'm a mess. I don't think I can do this, but I really want the job. Can you give me some tips?
Signed, Worried

Dear Worried,

Just be yourself! You can do this. If you say something you didn't mean to, laugh it off and explain what you meant.
If you don't get this job, then there will be something else for you, something amazing. Just have fun with it. Try not to worry and always, always, always remember to smile! That's how the West was won!
Okay, not really, but you know what I'm saying.
Love, Sage

Chapter 19

I sat back in my seat in the food court outside Greedy Cow and breathed a heavy sigh. My interview was over. I'd just said goodbye to Natashia, my new boss who was also Landen and Leah's mom, and now I felt like a wrung-out towel hanging over the back of a chair.

The last twenty-four hours had passed in a complete and total blur. I could barely remember what happened at school that day. I'd worked on projects and decorations, and had done everything else in a foggy sort of way as I anticipated this interview.

In fact, it was a good thing I'd had the foresight to pick out my clothes the day before, when I wasn't mondo distracted, or I might have shown up to meet Natashia wearing my swimsuit, a tutu, and flip flops.

I closed my eyes for a second, reliving the last half hour. It had been exhausting but so, so super awesome. I nailed that interview.

I just got a job on my own.

"Pyper?"

I opened my eyes. "Oh, hey, Landen."

I didn't mean to cringe, but it happened before I could stop it.

He gave me a pained smile and slid into the seat across from me. I tried to find something to do with my hands, which felt like dolphin flippers. I wished I could think of some brilliant words to clear the foggy space between us.

"So, hey. Leah told me you didn't know we were twins."

I sat up.

Way to go, Landen. Straight to the point. I decided to try it, too.

"Yeah, so, Leah told me you thought you were taking me to prom instead of Brooklynn."

Landen leaned back, obviously surprised. It took him several minutes to formulate his next sentence. He obviously did not expect me to counter-attack.

"That's true," he said, looking at me squarely. The corner of his mouth twitched just a bit. "I did think that. It threw me off when you said you were going with Sam."

"I noticed."

Landen moved his hands across the table in a way that made it feel like he was manually turning the tide. Starting over. "So, you really didn't know that Leah is my sister?"

"Come on, Landen. Like a week ago I didn't even know your name. How am I supposed to know who your sister is?"

Landen shook his head. "Hey, what do you say we do something crazy?"

"How crazy?" I asked, trying to read his face. Not a quirk of the eyebrow, not a twitch of the chin. I wasn't getting any information from there. He was going to have to explain that idea some more before I committed. I was not about to pierce something or get a tattoo.

"Not a ton, just a little crazy. What do you think about you and me starting over? Let's pretend like we don't even know each other." He pushed his chair back and stood. "Come on. This should be really easy for you."

His snarky grin was what convinced me. A do-over sounded fantastic.

I pulled my purse over my shoulder and, without looking back at him, walked out of the food court. I waited a few minutes to give Landen a chance to walk behind the counter of Greedy Cow and then strolled through the entrance.

"Hello, worker person I have never seen before." I raised my hand high and moved it in a large circle with my palm facing him the whole time.

Landen crossed his arms and rested on the high counter that kept people from breathing on the ice cream. "Wow, you are really bad at this."

"Judgey!" I shooed away his negativity. "Plus, also, you're totally break-ing character."

He cleared his throat. "Sorry. Okay. Hello, customer who is always right. Welcome to Greedy Cow. My name is Landen Thom. What can I do for you?"

I leaned an elbow on the counter with my cheek resting in the palm of my hand. "Well, obviously I need ice cream because I just came to an ice cream place."

"What flavor do you want?"

"Oh, I don't know. What do you recommend?" I fluttered my eyelashes just because I could. It seemed like the right thing to do.

"That depends," Landen said as he turned to the menu board, "on what you are in the mood for."

My stomach lurched, making me be the one to break character this time. "Oh, ugh! Never mind. I totally don't want ice cream."

"What?" Landen's eyebrows lifted.

"I know! I never would have thought it was possible, but I think I actually OD'd on ice cream this week!"

Landen took a step backward. "Impossible!"

"I ate so much. Your mom ordered for me, and I didn't want to waste it."

"Right, the Hullabaloo. And how was it?"

I shook my head. "I hate to say this, but you were so right. What was Leah thinking? It was completely ridiculous. So good and so disgusting at the same time."

"I tried to warn you." He pressed his lips together, making a dimple appear in his left cheek.

"I should have listened. Where were we with this whole starting over thing?"

Landen shook his head. "I can't remember. All I can think about is you shoveling ice cream and marshmallows into your face."

"Stop," I slapped my palm on the counter. "Don't talk about food anymore."

"I think we need to do-over our do-over. I'm Landen Thom." He extended his hand over the counter.

"Pyper Lewis." I took his hand, which was totally freezing cold. It made me want to rub his hand between both of mine to warm him up. I looked up and, meeting Landen's eyes, totally wished I hadn't. I suddenly felt exposed, like I'd caught him reading my diary. I pulled my hand away from his.

"It's so nice to meet you, Landen," I said with a big, cheery flip of my hair. "I can promise you that I will never forget your name, ever."

Landen crossed his arms on the counter and leaned forward. "I don't believe you."

The look on his face did something to my stomach. No, it was just the ice cream. I'd eaten too much, that was all.

"So, yeah, good start over. I'm proud of us. We're all fixed now, right?" I asked. The back of my neck felt warm. I couldn't really explain why. It definitely wasn't hot in there. For some reason I've never understood, places that sell ice cream are always ridiculously cold. Not great marketing. If they wanted my advice, they should crank the heater. That would entice people to eat more ice cream.

Then again, that might melt the ice cream.

"I'm good. You?" Landen stood up straight. When he moved, his thumb brushed across the top of my hand. I couldn't tell if it was an accident as he shifted, or if he did it on purpose. But why would he?

The heat crept to my cheeks, forcing me to take action. I have the worst blush in the world; it gets all splotchy like I have a rare skin disease. Who are those girls in movies who get to blush attractively? That's the gene I'm going to request in my next life.

I slid backwards. I didn't want it to be weird, so I adjusted the strap on my purse and pretended to look for lip gloss. When I found it, I put it on even though my lips weren't dry. My mouth was; my tongue felt like an old sponge, but lip gloss wasn't going to help with that.

I looked up. "Sorry, what did you say?"

"You good? With our do-over?" He took a rag and started wiping the counter where he'd been leaning. Every so often, his eyes flickered to my face and then away again.

I cleared my throat. "I'm totally good. I think with a do-over like this, we are destined to be best friends for life."

Landen stopped working and looked at me. I mean, really looked at me. If I thought I was squirming before, I was totally under-educated in what squirming meant. I felt like every thought I had ever thought was on display. Like he could see beyond what I looked like on the outside to who I was deep inside.

I couldn't remember ever feeling this...this *seen* in my entire life. I had to do something. Something big and distracting.

So, I knocked over the sample spoon display accidentally.

On purpose.

An orchestra of tings danced all over the counter and floor.

"I'm sorry! Clumsy! Do you want me to pay for those?" I stooped to pick up the little spoons that had clattered onto my side of the counter while Landen scooped up all those that had fallen onto his side. He threw the spoons into the trash and held up the trash can for me. I opened my hands and let all the spoons fall inside.

"Nah, it's okay." He took the trash back and ducked out of sight to grab some of the more ambitious spoons. "Happens all the time."

"Really?" I looked at him.

Landen stood up. "No, but you don't have to pay for them. Dad buys them in bulk, so they are, like, a penny each."

"How many dollars is a million pennies?" I asked, looking at the pink interior of the trashcan. I really hadn't meant to make such a big mess or waste so many spoons. It was sort of a reflex thing.

I wished I'd thought that through better.

"Really, it's not a big deal."

"Are you sure?"

"Positive." Landen stood up straight again and gave a smile that crinkled the corners of his eyes.

I sighed.

"What?"

"What, what?"

"Why did you breathe out like that?"

"Like this?" I sighed again and leaned on the counter before I remembered that Landen had just wiped it clean. Too late now. "Have you noticed that you and I are a disaster together?"

"Together?" he said slowly.

"Yes. I mean, every time we're together, one of us does or says something stupid, or we have a big misunderstanding. I don't think starting over can fix whatever is going on with us. Do you?"

"I think-" Landen's eyes moved over my head. "Can I help you?"

I turned to see an older couple, like my grandparents' ages, standing behind me, looking up at the menu board. I quickly stepped to the side.

"Oh, go ahead. I'm not in line."

They smiled at me and moved up to place their orders. I stared off into space while Landen got them soft serve cones. I was reminded how super tired I felt. After all the anticipation of my interview and all the extra student council work the last couple of days, I just needed a rest. That was all. Like a nap or a sappy chick flick in my pajamas.

Actually, option two.

A good cry also sounded awesome.

When the couple had paid and left Landen turned to me with an apologetic smile. "Sorry about that. Occupational hazard."

"No, it's fine." I waved my hand through the air. "I should probably let you get back to work. Are you the only one here?"

Landen nodded. "Leah's too busy, and our younger brother isn't old enough to work yet. Everyone else is moved out and working somewhere else. That's why I'm so excited we just hired a new employee. Congratulations, by the way." The corner of his mouth tweaked up.

"Thank you. I'm excited."

"Are you?" He sounded doubtful. "I was really surprised you filled out the application. Don't you always work at the Myler's climbing wall?"

My left eye twitched. "I did."

"Not this year?"

My eye twitch turned into spasms that I covered up by rubbing my eyes. "Nope."

Landen's words came out, sounding like Beauty when she stalls at a stoplight. "Is it...because...Jason...?"

I closed my eyes, then opened them so I could look directly at Landen. "No."

"No, it makes sense." He looked away. "It's gotta be weird to work there without your boyfriend."

"He's *not* my boyfriend!" I clamped my mouth shut. I did not mean to say that, and definitely not so loud. The words just flew out like they were tired of being caged. Which, come to think of it, was the exact truth. I took a couple deep breaths to calm myself down.

Landen cleared his throat. "No?"

I leaned my elbows on the counter and slumped forward, "No."

"Everyone at school--"

"I know," I sighed. "I know what everyone thinks and what everyone says but none of it is true. Jason and I broke up after prom last year. I just let everyone keep thinking we're together."

"Why did you do that?" Landen's voice was low.

I shrugged, which brought on a wave of weariness. "Actually, that's not true. Landen, can I be real?"

"Absolutely."

I couldn't believe I was telling him this, but now that I was, I couldn't imagine not telling him. I was so tired of carrying this all by myself. I wanted someone else to know why I was the way I was.

"I let everyone go on believing Jason and I were a thing so that guys would leave me alone."

"I don't follow." Landen stared at me intently, like he really wanted to understand.

I smoothed my hair away from my face. "Guys are biologically flawed to be selfish and heartless. I mean, even though you seem like you're all nice and thoughtful, deep down, you only care about yourself. It's okay; you can't help it. Some girls can overlook it. Personally, I don't want anything to do with that noise until your brains connect."

"My brain connects?"

"Not you specifically." I waved my hands around the air. "Like the royal you. All y'alls brains."

"And girls are different?"

I paused. "Yeah, I think so. We're hardwired to be more sensitive, so I don't think it's the same for girls."

"That's pretty bold," Landen said in an even voice, "to lump so many people into just two categories. Are you sure you have it right? Maybe some people aren't like that."

"Maybe not." I shrugged. I didn't want to talk about it anymore. "How often do you work here?"

Landen's eyes took their time moving away from me. He glanced at the clock behind him. "All the time. Pyper-"

I raised my voice to drown him out. Didn't he know a subject change when he saw one? "For reals? You're always here? Like, always, always?"

Landen sighed with so much resignation I saw the words in the air around him. "I do prep in the morning before school. I have on-the-job second period, then I come straight here after school and work until close. Most of the day Saturday. Lucky for me, we're closed Sundays. So, yeah, I'm always here."

"Cool," I said, stopping a grin from spreading.

Landen cocked his head. "Are you trying to be punny?"

"No, really." I shook my head. "I think you have the best job."

"You do?" He narrowed his eyes at me, as if waiting for the punchline.

"Everyone who comes here is excited because they are about to have ice cream. And everyone who leaves here is happy because they now have ice cream, or just ate it. This is, like, the happiest place on earth!"

"Not Disneyland?"

"Totally better."

"Pyper, you are-"

I didn't get to hear what I was. Maybe that was good. Sometimes it's better not to hear what people think you are.

Landon was cut off when the phone rang with Landen's dad on the other end wanting to know if it was very busy at the store. Yes, I shamelessly eavesdropped, but it wasn't totally my fault. His dad's voice was as loud as Will's and reached far outside the confines of the phone. I would have heard everything he said even if I hadn't been trying to.

"I think we should close early and do a thorough clean."

"And, by 'we' you mean me?" Landen said, his voice light.

"Well, son, I gotta be at Beau's game. Leah has her prom thing and Mom's helping her. I can call some of your other sisters and see what they're doing tonight if you want."

"No, no. I'll take care of it. No worries. See ya, Dad." Landen hung up and turned to me. "Miss, this store is closed. I'm going to have to ask you to leave."

I pulled my purse further up my shoulder. "How many sisters do you have?"

"Including Leah?"

I nodded.

"Six."

"Wow, that's...math-"

"Eight." Landen laughed as cleared the counter. "Six girls and two boys."

"And I thought my house was nuts with four!"

Landen chuckled as he worked. My purse weighed my shoulder down, so I set it on a stool.

"Do you want help?"

He froze. "Are you serious?"

The intensity of his stare made me squirm. "Yeah. I mean, I don't officially start until Saturday morning, but I'm here and could totally help."

Landen's face melted into a smile. "That would be great, Pyper. Thanks."

My slumpiness melted away. "What do we have to do?" I stashed my purse behind the counter and looked around, my hands resting on my hips.

"Let's start by sanitizing all the tables and chairs. Then we can clean the windows, counters, and display. Dad probably wants me to clean the machines, but let's see how long everything else takes. Then we'll need to sweep and mop. Are you sure you want to do this?" His voice sounded skeptical.

I took that as a personal insult.

"Don't think that just because I am super gorgeous I don't know how to work." I pointed at him, trying to keep a straight face.

Landen coughed.

"Throw me a rag and disinfector, or whatever. I've got this." I lifted my hand and caught the rag easily. Landen, thankfully, didn't toss the squirt bottle of cleaner. It was a miracle I caught the rag; the bottle would have ended up in a puddle on the ground.

It really was kind of fun wiping down the cute little parlor tables while Landen closed out the register. I glanced over at him a couple of times and got distracted by the way his lips moved soundlessly while he counted inside his head. Kai did that, too. It was kind of adorable.

When he finished, he locked the register and stashed the cash in a safe under the counter.

"So, what did you think of your interview?" Landen asked when he stood up.

"Oh, I'm so glad you asked," I said, slapping the rag against the shining tabletop I just finished. "It was fantastic! Your mom is really great. I've never done a real interview before, but if all of them were like this one, I would do it every day. We just talked for most of it. Like, did you know she's a black belt and she grew up in New York City? Like the Empire State Building and Broadway, New York City. That New York City? It was really the best interview ever."

I looked over at Landen to see his shoulders shaking while he scrubbed the countertop.

I narrowed my eyes. "I think you're missing some spots."

Landen shook his head. "I have never heard someone talk that much without a breath."

"Whatever." I joined him at the counter. The furniture was gleaming. "I'm sure that's not true. You have sisters."

"That's right. I do. I almost forgot that. I must be turning into you." Landen smirked.

I tossed the nasty, sopping rag at Landen's head. He caught it with one hand, which was both cool and anticlimactic. I thought it would at least slap him in the face, maybe drip down the side of his head and land in a heap at his feet. That would have been beautiful karma to his teasing.

"Nice try. I've been catching soggy rags since before I was born," he said, tossing the rag into a wicker basket they must use for laundry stuff. "Remember, I have sisters."

"Ah," I said, realizing. "You are to Leah what my brother Kai is to me. Except he is almost six years younger than me. That must mean you act like an eleven-year-old."

Landen rolled his eyes. "Why don't you stack the chairs so we can sweep and mop. I'm going to clean out the soft serve machine."

Bossy.

I marched to the nearest table and picked up a chair. I flipped it upside down and set it on the tabletop, then moved to the next chair.

"Oh, crap!"

I turned just in time to see Landen fall on his rear under the soft serve machine, which was now spewing ice cream all over the floor. I dropped the broom and dashed behind the counter.

"What happened?" I lifted Landen's arm, but it was like the floor had turned into an ice rink. He couldn't get his feet under him.

"I hit the self-clean button by accident! You're only supposed to do that when the machine is empty." He slipped and fell, almost taking me with him. "It's not."

"What do we do?" I leaned on the counter to get some leverage as I tried to help Landen to his feet.

He climbed to his knees, grumbling. "Why do they put that dumb button right by the power button?" When he tried to get his feet under him, he slipped and landed on his back.

I gave up on getting Landen up and slid to the machine. An especially explosive round of vanilla slop splattered all over my legs, oozing down into my boots. I kicked them off and moved to the side of the machine in my socks.

"Which button turns this thing off?" I don't know why I was yelling; it's not like the machine was super loud. The whole moment felt frantic, like a raised-voices-and-wild-eyes kind of moment.

"The little yellow one," Landen sputtered, gripping the counter as he inched himself closer to where I was standing.

My fingers flew across the cool metal until I felt the rough texture of a button. I double checked it three times to make sure it was, in fact, yellow. When I was certain, I punched it with my finger, and the whole machine shuddered to a stop.

Landen sank to the floor, leaning his back against the cabinets. Melted ice cream seeped through my socks, between my toes, and dripped off the hem of my super cute dress. One of my boots lay to the side, half buried in melting soft serve. With a sigh, I dropped next to Landen. It was like sitting in a freezing kiddy pool, but I didn't even care.

"Why in the world is the off button all tiny when the self-clean button is enormous, red, and right in front?"

Landen shook his head. "Engineers. They probably think it's funny."

"I'm not laughing."

We sat in silence. I don't know about Landen, but I was just trying to process what had happened. It didn't seem like we were sitting there for very long, but it must have been some time. I moved my leg to scratch an itch on my calf and came back with a fingernail full of dried ice cream.

"Landen?"

"Yeah?"

"If we don't get up now, I think we're going to be cemented to the floor."

"Okay, let's clean this up." Landen stood up slowly, leaning heavily on the counter, then reached his hand down for me.

"Where do we start?" I asked as I smoothed my dress, trying not to look at the disaster all around us.

Landen took a deep breath. "I'll get some spoons. I think we're going to have to eat through it."

I stared at him, waiting for a break in his expressionless face. He wasn't serious, was he? I mean, I could eat ice cream, no problem, but eating ice cream that was drying all over the floor and under my heinie was not super appetizing.

"You should see the look on your face."

"It's awesome, right?" I said, relief loosening all the knots in my shoulders.

"Totally. If I had my phone, I would take a picture and cherish it always."

I flicked ice cream off the ends of my fingers into his face. "You're funny. For reals, where do we start?"

Landen pointed to a drain in the floor between us. "Unfortunately, this is not the first time this has happened."

"So, we are literally going to hose everything down?" I laughed because that was funny.

"Literally." Landen stepped around me and opened a door to a small closet filled with cleaning tools, supplies, and a long hose that snaked around a hook on the wall. I propped myself up to sit on the counter so I would be out of the way as Landen sprayed water on the cabinets, and the soft serve machine. It was mesmerizing to watch the ice cream thin and swirl down the drain.

"All right, your turn." Landen gestured with the hose.

I shook my head, clinging to the counter. "You have got to be kidding me."

"Do you want to walk through the mall to your car like that?" He gestured to my crusted dress and white streaked legs.

"Ew, no!"

Landen swung the hose in my direction. "So then…"

I bit my lip.

Sticky or wet.

Choices, choices.

I scooted off the counter and held out my hand. "Fine. But I am not going to let you hose me down. I'll do it myself, thank you."

Landen handed me the hose. "You sure? I don't mind."

I scrunched my nose at him.

He grinned as I held the hose directly over my head. The water wasn't cold, thank goodness, and went straight after the crunchy strands of hair around my face until they smoothed into a stream. I moved to my arms, then dress and legs. It wasn't until I looked up and realized that Landen was watching me that I felt completely self-conscious.

I laughed to cover it up. "Drowned rat, right?"

The corner of his mouth quirked up slightly. "That was not what I was thinking."

I sprayed a mist of water into his face and tossed him the hose. "Your turn." While he sprayed off his clothes, I dried off with four hand towels I found in one of the drawers and a handful of napkins from the countertop. When Landen was done, and the hose was safely back in the closet, he faced me with his hands on his hips.

"I really don't think we should ever see each other ever again," he said.

By now I was getting used to his sense of humor. I nodded in agreement. "I told you. We're a mess, you and me."

"We have to act fast, before our group project in econ either implodes or is hit by a meteor. Do you want to drop out of school, or should I?"

I pretended to give his question serious thought. "I will. I was planning on it anyway. The circus is in town, and I've always wanted to train elephants."

"Perfect. Because I want to finish school, so I can go to college and do something other than douse people in ice cream at the end of the day."

I laughed, extending my hand. "Deal."

Landen looked at my hand for a long time before he took it, and when he did, he moved ever so slowly, sliding his palm into place against mine.

"Pyper?"

Something unnatural was happening to my arm. I looked around for an outlet because there was a distinct surge of electricity all the way up my shoulder.

"What?" One of my lips twitched without my permission.

Landen noticed and smiled in a way that made my stomach flip-flop. "Do you think-?"

"I should go," I interrupted. "My mom is probably wondering where I am, and I should really not be in public looking like this." I tried to laugh, but it sounded wrong.

Landen took a step forward, his eyes never leaving mine. "There's nothing wrong with the way you look, Pyper."

I got lost in the beautiful, deep brown of his eyes. It was like swimming in the Chocolate Coma shake.

"Oh. Excuse me. Sorry. Are you...uh...open?"

A young lady with two little kids hesitated outside the store.

Landen and I moved away from each other. I automatically wiped the counter with one of the hand towels I'd used to dry off with, which was not super sanitary.

"Just closing up," Landen said, smiling.

"Oh." All three of their faces dropped.

"No, don't go." Landen extended his hand. "The soft-serve and milk shake machines are closed down, but I can still do scoops. What can I get for you?"

I stood there, dripping, while Landen teased the little boys, asking them if they liked spiders on their ice cream. My brain kept telling me to move, to leave, but I couldn't get the message to my feet. Since the register was already closed, Landen gave them their cones for free.

With all my heart I wished he hadn't done that, or that I hadn't heard it. I knew I should have left. Probably a long time ago. There was something going on inside me that was distantly familiar and oh so scary. Something I vowed never, ever, ever to feel again.

I needed some air.

I waved my hands to get Landen's attention and mouthed, "I'm going to go." He shook his head slightly but was distracted when one of the boys asked for a napkin. I slipped into my soggy boots and left without looking back.

Okay, that's not exactly true.

I did look back.

Once I was out of sight, I turned around and watched Landen for a few minutes longer.

I don't know how I ever thought that he could have blended into the walls.

The Cromer Chronicles

ADVICE COLUMN
Sage Advice

Dear Sage,

All of my thoughts are a huge, swirling mess that will probably touch down somewhere over Kansas in a couple of days. I could really use your advice.

I've liked the same girl for a really long time, and I think it's time to tell her I like her, but I don't want to scare her off. Tell me how to make that happen, Sage, and I will give you the biggest high five you ever saw.

Sincerely, Tornado

Dear Tornado,

Sometimes when we want something super badly, we can overcompensate. You know what I mean? In my experience, it is always better to keep it simple. So, in your case, just relax! Have fun! Enjoy being in the moment with a girl you really like. The more fun you have, the more fun she will have. All the liking stuff, that will just happen naturally as an offshoot from you being yourself and having a good time.

Now, pull yourself together. Hasn't Kansas been through enough?

Love, Sage

Chapter 20

I woke up Friday morning to a belly ache and nearly continuous chimes coming from my phone. I had totally forgotten to turn my ringer off the night before. I guess I should feel grateful that all these messages came in at six in the morning and not, like, two.

With a ginormous yawn, I reached across my nightstand for my phone. There were about a billion messages from Leah. I needed to show her how to send messages without making each sentence its own text.

Don't forget!

Prom Prep after school!

Can you double check with the b-ball team about hanging lights?

I would do it myself, but I just really don't want to! :P

Come over at four to get ready! I banished Landen to Will's house, so it's just us girls. Yay!

Oh! Were you in charge of the photo backdrop?

All her exclamations and emojis made my head feel a little swimmy. The best thing to do in a situation like this was to dive right in and answer back.

I won't forget. Totally planning on meeting after school and coming over at four. B-ball team is all set. I'm not in charge of the backdrop, but I can help figure it out if you need. Hey, is it okay if Sage takes a break this weekend? All caught up.

Leah responded right away.

You are brilliant, an angel and a rockstar, and I love you forever! Thank you, and no problem!

Right back to you! See you soon.

Now I could just concentrate on getting through prom.
My stomach did a loop-de-loop.
None of that.
I could do this.
It was a whole year later. It wasn't the same. My date was different-oh boy, was he different-and the circumstances were different. I was different. I mean, there was just as much a possibility of this day being rocking awesome as there was of it being awful.
Right?
I glanced at my closet where the dress of my dreams waited. I bought it to wear with Jason, until I overheard him saying how much he loved the color red. I bought myself a whole new dress and left this gorgeous thing in my closet to gather dust. I walked over to it and held the big, poofy skirt out to see more clearly. In a way, it was better that I didn't wear it for Jason. It would have ended up in the trash can like the red one, and this dress deserved better.

I pulled on the skirt to make it swish back into place and sighed. If there was a small part of me that wished I was going to wear this dress to prom with someone special, well, I was just going to ignore that part. Going with 'someone special' totally didn't do me any favors last year.

Determination welled up inside me like rising waters. I would make this the best prom ever. I would banish all those horrible memories from last year, and I would do it all in heels with a fantastic up-do.

My phone chimed from my nightstand. When I picked it up, I saw a text from Brooklynn.

> Call me when you wake up.

I dialed her number and brought the phone to my ear.

"Hey." Brooklynn's voice was gritty.

"Hey, Brookie!" I tucked the phone between my chin and my shoulder to free up my hands. I had last week's clean laundry still stacked on my desk chair.

"Are you kidding?" she scoffed. "I've been up for an hour studying."

"I should have known," I laughed. "What's up with your voice?"

"I stayed up late watching the game."

"Ah," I nodded and then realized she couldn't see me. "That explains it. Did you win?"

"Crushed them."

"Yay!" I said, even though I wasn't sure if that was how you respond to a sports victory. It was the best I could do on short notice. "Hey, so, I got your text. I have Leah's address, but instead of sending it to you, how about you come home with me after school, and we drive over there together."

Strength in numbers, I think.

"Okay, yeah. That works. Do I need to bring anything? Like...?" Brooklynn's voice trailed off while she waited for the right words to pop into her mouth. Unfortunately, she didn't have enough experience to supply any.

I took pity on her and intervened. "Nope. I have tons of makeup and stuff. Have you thought about what you want to do with your hair?"

I swear I heard her gulp through the phone. "No."

"No worries," I said. "I'll bring a hairstyle magazine. We'll find something you love."

"Thanks, Pyper. I don't think I could do this without you. I almost called and canceled, like, fifty times already this morning."

"Don't do that! I need you there. Have I told you I'm so very glad you're going this year?"

"I wish I was there last year."

"Yeah?" My heart sped up a fraction.

"Yeah," she sighed. "I wish I was there for you. If I had been there, things would have been different. For one, I would have punched Jason in his perfect teeth."

I cleared my throat but didn't get a chance to say anything.

"I keep wondering how he did it. Don't you? It's kind of mind boggling."

"What?" I thought we were wrapping this conversation up with a big glittery bow, and now it sounded like we were just tearing off the ribbon.

"How did he fool everyone? How come no one knew what a jerk he was? He seemed so nice. It must have been exhausting to keep that act up all the time. Don't you think so?"

My hand twitched against my leg. I stood up and began pacing to use up the adrenaline I could feel rising inside me, like Mentos in Coke. "Hey, I just noticed the clock. We are totally going to be late for school if we don't get going."

"You don't want to talk about it," Brooklynn said.

"I just don't want us to be late for school."

"Pyper, you are always late for school."

"I am not!" I slid a stack of jeans into one of my drawers, getting a whiff of Tide. "Okay, sometimes I am. So, no, I don't want to talk about it. It just feels like bad juju to talk about a lousy prom before this prom. You know? Let's just focus on making tonight the best night of everyone's life."

Brooklynn hesitated. "That sounds like a lot of pressure."

"No pressure! Just high hopes. Hope is good."

"Fine, but before I let you change the subject, can I say one last thing?"

"Sure. What's up?"

"Jason was never good enough for you."

I swallowed hard. "Thanks, Brooklynn."

"It's true. He screwed up big time, and I'm positive that somewhere in his black and grody soul, he's going to regret what he did for the rest of his life."

I couldn't get words past the lump in my throat.

"There. I'll stop talking about it, and I'll never bring it up again, I promise. Are you still there? Pyper?"

"Yeah, I'm here."

"Why did I agree to go to prom? This is a terrible idea. I didn't really think it through all the way, and now I feel sick. I don't want to watch Will and Leah make goo-goo eyes all night. And I don't even know Landen very well. Help me, Pyper. I might actually die right now."

Thank the shoemaker! Advice! I could do this!

"You're not going to die, Brooklynn. It's just a dance. But, since you asked, I'm going to tell you something that should help. Will and Leah aren't a thing. I don't know for sure how Will feels, I do know for sure how Leah feels. She's friend-zoned him permanently. There will be no goo-goo eyes. Take my advice: go, have fun, and don't worry about it."

"Okay." Brooklynn took a breath. "Okay! Yeah, I can do that. But what about Landen? Do you think it will be awkward?"

My stomach did an odd little turn. I searched my feelings to see what truth was churning around in there.

I found it pretty quickly. Apparently, the thought of Landen on a date with Brooklynn didn't agree with me. Sort of like the peanut-butter-and-pickle-sandwich phase Kai went through last year.

Interesting. I would have to think about that later.

Or never again.

One of the two.

"No worries there. You'll be in a group with other people the whole time. The only time you will have to talk to him alone is when you're dancing together."

Hmmmm, that was curious. My bubbling stomach didn't like the thought of Brooklynn and Landen dancing together, either. I kept talking to drown it out.

"Just focus on having fun, okay?"

"Okay," she said. "Okay! We can do this. Just promise me one more thing, Pyper." Her voice lowered.

"Anything."

"Please don't let Leah talk me into wearing anything pink or sparkly."

My text notification chimed.

I laughed. "I promise! See you at school, Brookie."

"See ya."

I hung up and opened my messages. There was one from Carly.

Carly.

She hadn't texted me all week, hadn't even responded to the text I sent. I wasn't sure I wanted to know what she was messaging about. It could be anything from bomb threats to split ends.

> Sorry. I've been so busy. Glad you're going to prom.

See you there.

That's all it said.

I puzzled over her text the entire time I got ready for school. That didn't sound like Carly at all. Not only was it the shortest text ever, but there wasn't a single exclamation mark anywhere. Those reasons, and the fact that she had been missing in action all week, were definite causes for concern.

At first, I thought I'd blame Travis for her change of behavior. Obviously, his creepiness was wearing off on her. But she hadn't acted this way with any of her other boyfriends, and they were plenty creepy. Deep down I think I knew what the problem was and why she was avoiding me. I just didn't want to face it.

It was because of what I said to her on Monday.

I should have resolved things with her sooner. I was just irritated, and then I got busy. There were so many things going on in my brain. I guess my mom was right again; there are always zillions of excuses *not* to do something.

I knotted the bottom of my raglan tunic at my hip and looked myself sternly in the eye. Today was the day to resolve things with Carly. It was up to me.

I pulled my hair into a messy bun and pulled on my tennis shoes.

"PYPER!"

I jumped into the air and landed just like a ninja, my hands out and ready to slice through cheese. Roxie ran to me on the verge of tears.

"I can't find my lucky socks! I'm going to miss the bus, and Gavin ate all the granola bars with chocolate chips. Can you give me a ride to school?"

I turned my ninja face into a sympathetic frown. Roxie's struggle was real.

"Just breathe, Rox. I can totally take you to school. Remind me, which socks are the luckiest? I'll look while you go check the pantry for more granola bars. Mom usually buys extra."

Roxie took a shuddering breath and walked forward until her forehead rested on my shoulder. "Thank you."

"Yep." I gave her a squishy bear hug and then smacked her rear. "Hurry. If you make me later than I already am, I will tell the whole high school that you sucked your thumb until third grade."

Roxie gasped. "Only at night!" She turned to leave the room. "Glitter purple with lime llamas."

"What the what?"

"My lucky socks. Thank you!"

Then she skipped out of the room, all sunshine and butterflies once again.

Chapter 21

When I pulled into the driveway of my house after school, I had to stop and collect myself for a minute. The whole day had been like a weird, fuzzy dream. I should have been grateful that I showed up to school fully clothed and made it to all my classes in the correct order, but I was haunted by an unsettling feeling that wouldn't go away.

I slowly climbed out of the car while moments from school popped up in my mind, like flashback scenes in a movie.

After dropping Roxie off and getting stuck behind a tractor, I was super late for first period. Landen, Brooklynn, Will, and I presented our project without any bickering or outrageous confessions.

I would call that a huge win.

I was late to second period because my locker wouldn't open, and I had to wait for the janitor to unclog something in the boy's restroom before he could come help me. It took forever, but I didn't ask for the details.

I totally didn't want to know.

I saw Carly across the commons at lunch. When I called her name, she didn't look up even though everyone else in the room did. That wasn't awkward at all. By the time I pushed my way through the crowd to where she had been standing, she was gone. She never answered any of my texts.

In English, I realized that I had been wearing my shirt backwards all day. I left to change it and cursed Brooklynn for not being more fashion observant so she could have told me.

By the time I got to chemistry, I felt like I was slogging through mud. My voice sounded loud in my own ears when I arranged last-minute prom details with Sam. It might have been okay after that except we had a pop quiz, and I still didn't know what that acid thing was from the notes.

Ugh.

I was almost to the front door of my house when I realized that I had told Roxie I would pick her up from school.

Sure enough, my cell phone started a vibration tap dance in my jacket pocket. I answered it breathlessly.

"Hey, Rox! I'm sorry! I forgot, but I can come right now."

She laughed. That was a good sign. An unexpected, good sign. Roxie wasn't usually so accommodating when things didn't go the way she had planned. "Don't worry about it; I have a ride. I just wanted to make sure you weren't on your way. See ya."

Who was she getting a ride with? Obviously, none of her classmates had their driver's licenses yet. I pulled my bag onto my shoulder and decided to just be grateful she had a plan and was not mad at me.

As I opened the front door, my phone went nuts again.

"Hey, Leah."

"Hey, Pyper! Don't worry about coming to decorate; we are totally done! It went so fast with all the cheerleaders and basketball team! You're the best! Gotta go! See you at four!"

I stared at the silent phone again. I had totally forgotten about decorating the gym!

It was a good thing no one was keeping score because I was losing today. I sighed and pushed the front door the rest of the way open.

"Pyyyyyyyyyyyyyyyyyyyyyypa!" Gavin threw himself at me. I wrapped my arms around him as tight as I could and blew into his neck.

"Ew!" he squealed.

I blew again, louder this time.

"Pypppppppppa!"

"Quit messing around, Gavin. I totally have stuff to do!" I pinned his flailing arms and leaned to blow one more time, but he turned his head with a screech. I ended up with a mouth full of his hair. Which was adorable, but not very tasty.

When I set him down, he wrapped both arms around my legs and hung on while I dragged him into the kitchen where Mom was working on something bite-sized, sugary, and beautiful.

"Oh good, you're home! I'm almost done with these. Tell me your plan for the rest of today."

My phone vibrated again.

"Where's Brooklynn?" my mom asked, looking past me.

Brooklynn!

I blew out a very unflattering noise as I opened my phone and saw her text.

> Aren't we meeting at the lockers?

"Knickerbockers!" I cried.

Gavin covered his ears with his hands, his voice was unnaturally loud when he spoke. "Is that a potty word?"

"What's going on?" Mom paused in her detail work.

"I forgot Brook at school! Mom!" I wanted to pound my forehead on the counter. "This day! For reals!" My fingers flew across my phone's keyboard.

> I totally forgot! I'm so sorry!

> I'll come right now to get you.

> No worries. I have Moe. Are you home?

> I'll just come there.

> Yes, I'm home. I'm so, so, so sorry!

> No biggie. See ya in a few.

A heart emoji let me know I was forgiven.

I set my phone on the counter and buried my head in my arms.

"Aw." Mom rubbed my back.

I stayed hidden for so long that Gavin got bored and let go of my legs. With a cackle, he dove for the Lego tower he had constructed in the middle of the kitchen floor.

"I'm fine." I finally looked up, giving my mom a pained smile. "I'm fine. It's fine. It's all fine."

"Of course you are."

Those simple words gave me hope for myself. Maybe I could make it through the rest of the day. Maybe I could rally and have the best prom ever with my friends.

I stood up and wiggled my shoulders. "Right. Okay, so, my plan. Brooklynn is on her way; we're going to go to Leah's to get ready for prom. I will have my cell phone if you need me."

"Or if you need me." Mom gave me a significant look.

"Or that," I nodded. "Right now, I need to go get my makeup and hair stuff, and my dress, of course." If I said it out loud and in order, my chances of forgetting something went way down. I'm pretty sure that's how that works.

"Sounds great." Mom fixed me in her inescapable stare. "Tell me how you are feeling."

"Truth or lies?"

"You know the answer to that."

I did know the answer to that. So, I told the truth. The truth I wanted for myself, anyway. "I'm fine about prom. Prom is going to be great. Best prom ever."

Sometimes when I'm writing a word over and over, it starts to look like it's spelled wrong. The word 'prom' was starting to feel that way. Like, the more I said it, the less it sounded like a real thing and the more it sounded like a goose when it wants more breadcrumbs.

Mom raised an eyebrow.

I cleared my throat and went on. "So, um, after we get ready and the boys pick us up, we're going to dinner. I don't know where. We need to be at the dance early so Leah and I can check on things before people start showing up. I should be home by eleven-thirty."

Mom just kept looking at me.

"Are you coming over to Leah's house to take pictures?" I asked, trying to diffuse her relentless stare. "Wasn't that the plan?"

"Yes." Mom raised her eyebrows.

Obviously, she knew I was babbling to avoid talking about other things. The question was whether she was going to let me get away with it. I really hoped she would. My soul did not want to be bared just now.

"Oh, doorbell. That's probably Brooklynn." I dashed out of the kitchen before my mom could say anything else.

"Hey!" I said as I threw the door open, my smile perfectly positioned. "Ready for this?"

No," Brooklynn groaned. "Let's get this dress part over with so I can stop stressing about it. Every time I close my eyes, I see hot pink taffeta."

"Hang up, the eighties are calling." I pulled her into the house. "I just need to go grab my stuff. Mom's in the kitchen."

Brooklynn's face lit up; she loved my mom. Most people did, but Brooklynn did especially. It was only when I saw her eyes in the middle of one of my mom's hugs that I realized how much Brooklynn missed her own mom.

I hurdled up the stairs to get all my supplies, feeling a little guilty. It wasn't that I didn't want to tell my mom everything. Normally I would have sat down, snitched a finger into whatever she was making, and laid out every piece of my messy life so she could help me put it back together in a way that made sense. But today, I just couldn't do it. It was all too much. If I let any feelings out even a little bit, I was afraid they would devour me, leaving nothing but a pink rhinestone or a smidgen of glitter.

I gathered my favorite makeup into an accessory bag with my curling iron and bobby pins. Leah would probably have most of those things at her house with five older sisters and a pageant queen for a mother, but I would rather have them and not need them than the other way around. I raided Roxie's room for rhinestone clips and every headband I could find. There were plenty of choices. As much as she had a thing for pineapples, Roxie was also obsessed with headbands.

I ran back to my room for magazines with formal hairstyles. I'd marked pages of ideas for Brooklynn's short hair. Any of them would be fantastic, but I needed to see her dress to know the perfect one. Back downstairs, I gave my mom a hug goodbye. She held on a little longer than she normally would have and kissed the top of my head. I felt approximately five years old and then sort of wished I was. Things were a whole lot simpler then.

"Love you," I called on my way out the door.

It was a good thing Leah didn't live far. We were counting down the seconds to four o'clock when I knocked on the door to her house.

"Yay! Come in, come in! Landen isn't here. I kicked him out to do guy things." Leah chattered as we followed her out of the entryway and into the house. "You wouldn't believe how much Will is complaining about Sam going with us. He's such a whiner!"

I started to ask if she meant Sam was the whiner or Will-because it could have been either one of them-but Leah kept talking, and my words disappeared into the hall carpet under our feet.

"I don't know what his deal is. Sam is more mature than the rest of us put together! He almost looks like a senior; he's so tall, and he has those dreamy eyelashes." Leah sighed and turned a corner, stopping in front of a closed door. "Prepare yourselves, girls! This is my mom's mothership. She's been more excited about us getting ready then I am, which is a lot!"

With flourish, Leah opened the door into a large room. It must have been an office or guest room at one time, but today it was so much more. There were two vanity tables set up against one wall, each with those Hollywood light bulbs that framed the mirror. The rest of the room was filled with legit clothing racks, like what you find in department stores, each stuffed with ball gowns in every color. Not a joke. I spotted one that was pumpkin orange.

"Do you love it?" Leah whirled around with her arms outstretched, almost knocking a curling iron off the table. She swooped to catch it before it fell. "There, all better. Normally this isn't my scene at all, but I'm thinking I could totally get into it! Where should we start?"

"Dresses," I said, remembering Brooklynn's biggest stresser.

Brooklynn let out an audible breath, and her shoulders unhunched for the first time since we left my house.

"Yes!" Leah clapped, then attacked the nearest rack of clothing and started pawing through the dresses.

I carefully draped my dress over a chair and then went to a rack that neither Brooklynn nor Leah was looking through. A sense of awe settled through me as I took in all the floof and sparkles at my fingertips.

Brooklynn looked a little green. "No pink," she whispered to herself. "No pink, no pink, no pink."

"Done!" Leah announced, throwing her arms in the air like a champion. I looked over my shoulder to see Leah bouncing on the balls of her feet, holding a cream-colored dress with a huge chiffon skirt.

I breathed in. "That is gorgeous!"

"I know, right? My sister wore it to prom two years ago, and even though I told her at the time that she looked horrible, I secretly couldn't wait to wear it!" Leah held the dress up to her shoulders and swayed to make the skirt swish.

I shoved a bunch of dresses I'd already looked through further down the rack; the hangers made a high screech that gave me goosebumps. "Ugh! Sorry!" I rubbed my arms. "What are the sizes, Leah? Are they separated?"

"Oh!" Leah walked over and pulled a dress out so we could see the back. "They all have corsets, see? They lace up, so you can adjust them a few sizes up or down."

"Great," Brooklynn said. "Corsets."

She didn't look like she thought it was great.

"Super convenient, right? Here, I'll help you look. Do you know what you want?" Leah asked.

Brooklynn shook her head. "Something simple?" Her eyes were wide and unfocused.

"I already have a dress," I said, "and I still want to try on every single dress in this room." I flipped through a line-up of pink dresses that activated Brooklynn's gag reflex.

Leah pretended not to notice. "What are you wearing, Pyper?"

"Oh!" I turned to Leah, my eyes shining. "Let me show you!" I skipped to the chair where I had dropped my things. I unzipped the garment bag and pulled out my dress so I could hold it up for Leah and Brooklynn to see.

It was the dress of my dreams.

The mint color brought out the green in my eyes. The bodice was form-fitting to the hips with a darker green belt that accented the waistline even more. From there, the skirt flounced in layered ruffles that floated to the floor. It had cap sleeves and a boat neckline that I was completely in love with. In a dress like this one, a girl could be on a date with Frankenstein and totally not care.

"Pyper," Leah said in a hushed voice. "That dress was made for you."

"It really is perfect," Brooklynn agreed, which I thought was saying something.

I smiled and laid it back over the chair. "Thank you. Now let's find a dress made for Brooklynn."

There was relative silence as we searched through the dresses. Every so often, one of us would mumble a commentary.

"This one is just weird."

"I wish the mermaid style looked good on me."

"What color is this exactly? Puce?"

"Look, girls! The seventies and the eighties got married and made a dress! Yikes!"

"Pyper, you would look great in this red one."

I bit my lip to keep from yelling something about how much I hated the color red.

"Do you want to try it on just for fun?" Leah wiggled her eyebrows, waving the dress around in the air.

I shrugged one shoulder, keeping my voice neutral. "My prom dress last year was red. I made a personal goal never to wear the same color to a dance." And then I gave a careless, tinkly laugh.

"Oh," Leah placed it back on the rack.

"Besides, I already have the dress of my dreams. Let's concentrate on finding Brooklynn the perfect prom dress." I finished.

"Girls!" Leah stopped moving, her eyes wide. "I just realized this is our last prom! Never again, for the rest of our lives, will we get to wear a floofy dress!"

"Thank goodness," Brooklynn whispered so only I could hear.

I decided not to mention the possibility of a floofy wedding dress. It just didn't seem like the right time. "How about this one, Brookie?" I wiggled my eyebrows up and down, pulling out the orange monstrosity I'd seen earlier.

"Ah!" Brooklynn stepped back as though I were brandishing a snake.

I turned to Leah. "Yeah, where did this come from, exactly?"

"I don't know, and I don't even want to know. Put it away. It's totally burning my retinas!"

I laughed and moved to another rack, skipping my hand along the hangers. Somewhere in this bunch was the perfect dress for Brooklynn. I closed my eyes and willed it to come into my hand. I wanted her to have fun and feel gorgeous. I needed everything to be perfect.

"Pyper?"

I turned to Brooklynn, who had turned into a statue in front of the dress racks.

"Look." She slowly swung around with a navy blue dress that made me want to cry, not just because the dress was beautiful but because of the look of surprise on Brooklynn's face.

The dress was form-fitting to the knees, where it flared just enough for a person to take comfortable steps. The sleeves went to the elbows, the neck was high, and there was some ruching along the middle, but it was otherwise unadorned. It was absolutely the perfect dress for Brooklynn.

Her eyes were bright as she stood in front of the mirror.

"Try it on!" Leah said.

As Brooklynn changed, Leah and I flipped through my pages of hair styles. I already knew what I wanted, but Leah hadn't decided yet.

"All right, what do you think?" Brooklynn stepped slowly in front of the mirrors.

I couldn't even talk; I seriously got an enormous lump in my throat.

"I guess it was too much to hope that it would fit." She bit her lip. I didn't even know what she was talking about. I had never seen my best friend in a dress, and the effect was mesmerizing. She could have been a storybook princess.

"It's just a little long; we can fix that," Leah said. She walked to the door. "Mom!"

Natasha popped her head into the room. She looked like an older version of Leah, but with way more makeup and a teased hairdo. "Hey, girls!"

"Mom, can you hem this dress for Brooklynn?"

Natasha lifted her finger into the air and disappeared. In just a few seconds, she was back with a fabric tomato full of pins. She sat crisscross applesauce at Brooklynn's feet to fold the hem of the dress.

"Is this good?"

Brooklynn poked a foot out to see if it snagged. "Perfect."

Natasha finished pinning and waited for Brooklynn to change so she could leave with the dress. "Be back in a flash," she called over her shoulder.

Brooklynn sat on one of the vanity chairs to look through the magazines while I got to work on Leah. I scrutinized the picture she'd chosen and then began braiding Leah's long, brown hair into a crown around her head. It took a little while, but the result was fantastic. I added an ivory pearl headband from Roxie's collection. When Leah put on her cream dress with all the tulle pushing out wider than the door, she was totally gorgeous.

For my own hair, I did a simple side sweep with loose curls that were held in place with a zillion bobby pins and a coral-colored rose for decoration. It looked nice with the mint green from my dress.

Natasha returned, and Brooklynn put her dress on so we could see her semi-finished look.

"You know what?" Natasha said, chewing the bottom of her lip. "I think, with her hair so short, it would look beautiful to put a flower right by her ear and sweep the bangs aside."

"Do we have a navy flower?" Leah asked.

I didn't, but once again Natasha came to the rescue. She clipped the flower in Brooklynn's hair and stood back. Brooklynn gazed at herself. Her cheeks were rosy pink, and we hadn't even done makeup yet.

"It is almost six! We have to hurry!" Leah flew to a seat and went to work on her face. Her mom stuck around to help Brooklynn so I could touch up my own makeup. Brooklynn kept saying the word 'natural' over and over in a nervous voice, like a mantra.

We were just finishing when the doorbell rang.

"That's the guys?" Leah shrieked, knocking over a container of eyeshadow. "On time? What are they thinking?"

"It's just us." My mom peeked into the room. "Your husband let us in. Oh! Girls!" She clasped her hands, gazing at Brooklynn, then at Leah, then at me. We moved together in a row, gripping each other's hands.

It was an auspicious moment.

"Oh, Pyper!" My mom covered her mouth with her hands. "I wish your dad was here!"

"No, you don't!" Roxie came in behind her. "He wouldn't let her leave the house. Seriously Pyp, you look beautiful. Better than beautiful!"

I walked over and gave her a hug until she squealed, slapped my arm, and called me a weirdo.

"And Brooklynn!" Tears welled in my mom's eyes. "You are a picture!"

Brooklynn ducked her head and smiled.

"See," I whispered to her. "This is why it's fun to get dressed up!"

She stuck her tongue out at me.

"Let me get the camera," Natasha sniffed.

We posed separately for pictures and then all together. Since Natasha was the expert, we just did whatever she told us to do. She insisted that it was easier to take most of the pictures before the guys got there. Apparently, guys have a ten-minute limit before they get antsy and want to leave.

The doorbell rang while we were taking a picture with all three of us. Roxie, who was standing behind the camera, hooted. "You should totally see this!" She took the camera and held up the viewing screen.

We stood in a perfect pose, but all three of us had varying looks of alarm, and our eyes had shifted to the door. I tried to laugh with her, but the corner of my mouth insisted on wavering. In all the fun of getting ready, I kind of forgot that all of this meant I was going to prom. I suddenly wasn't positive this was a good idea.

Was I really about to do this again?

"It's not the same," I told myself over and over as I walked to the door. Sam is not Jason. Sam is *so* not Jason.

And that was a very good thing.

Will walked in first, his eyes darting from person to person until they settled.

On Brooklynn.

His face went slack. He blinked so many times that I began to wonder if he was developing a twitch. It took obvious effort for him to pull his eyes away from Brooklynn and onto his own date. If Leah noticed, it didn't bother her. She was all easy smiles.

Will stepped to the side so Sam could come in. Leah gasped. Gone were the horrible glasses and the plaid button-downs. Clark Kent had fully merged into Superman. And Leah was right; he totally didn't look like a freshman. I started to raise my hand to show him where I was. I didn't want him to feel overwhelmed with a bunch of people he didn't know. But I couldn't move. Raising my hand was way too hard; I could barely find it in me to take a breath.

Landen had just walked in.

Our eyes met across the room, like something out of a movie. A really cheesy movie. A really cheesy, romantic movie that you have to watch with a can of whipped cream. His eyes were velvety brown and warmed my insides like a mug of hot cocoa.

"Over here for pictures!" Natasha called, waving her hand at the fireplace.

We stood in formation: Will, Leah, Landen, Brooklynn, Sam, and me. After exactly ten minutes of pictures, Will's smile dropped, and he started edging towards the door.

Natasha caught my eye and grinned. So that was where Landen got his smile from.

"Not yet." She shook her head at Will. "I just need a few more couples pictures, and then you're done."

Will and Leah went first, then Sam and I. Landen and Brooklynn were last. Will shifted impatiently as he watched Natasha arrange them into a pose. His hand twitched when Landen put his arm around Brooklynn's waist.

"That's good. Let's go," he said way too loudly.

"Almost done," Natasha sang.

Will mumbled something under his breath.

"All right. You kids have fun." Natasha winked at Landen as she waved us towards the door.

"Hang on." Will stopped with his arm held up like he was about to make a right-hand turn on a bicycle. "I just had a wacky idea. What if we take pictures with other dates?"

Sam groaned.

"What?" Brooklynn asked, her eyes widening. "You want to take more pictures? I thought you wanted to go?"

"I do. And we will. It just might be funny to pose with other dates. You know, like me and Pyper, Landen and Leah... No, not them. But you get it. It would be funny," he ended lamely.

Sam pushed the bridge of his nose like he was wearing glasses, even though he wasn't. "A logic puzzle. I see it working like this: Will and Brooklynn, Leah and I, Pyper and Landen. Then no one stands with their sibling or actual date."

Leah grabbed Sam's arm. "I'm all for it!"

"See!" Will looked at Brooklynn, but gestured to Leah and Sam. "It's fun." He grabbed Brooklynn's hand and pulled her to the fireplace. Brooklynn flushed as Will wrapped his arms around her back, more like a hug than a picture pose. Her smile had never looked brighter.

"Come on, freshman!" Leah tugged Sam closer so they would be ready when Will and Brooklynn were done.

"I hope you don't think this signifies that I acquiesce to being called 'freshman' all night."

"Course not." Leah patted his arm.

I studied the puffed skirt of my dress like it was super fascinating because I was afraid to look up. The rough texture of Landen's suit coat brushed against my bare arm, making it difficult to breathe again.

"Hey." His voice was as deep and velvety as his eyes.

Was this all it took to undo me? A fairy-tale dress and something manly in a tux? I wrapped my arms around my middle, telling myself to hold it together. Since when was I the girl who came unraveled by a guy?

I mean, anymore.

My eyes flickered to Landen's for just a moment. I forgot everything and everyone around us and got totally lost in the ring of darker brown around the pupil of his eyes. I may have stayed in that moment for the rest of eternity if Roxie hadn't bumped into my elbow.

"Sorry," she said with a small smile.

I blinked about a billion times, trying to reclaim myself. It was like waking up from a realistic dream where you weren't sure if you were actually dreaming or not. There were a few moments of confusion while my brain tried to adjust to reality.

I pulled my signature smile into place and wiggled Landen's bow tie. "You clean up pretty good," I said, brushing invisible lint from his shoulders.

"Yeah?"

"Yeah. You know, almost anything is an improvement over crusty soft serve."

Landen smiled, took my hand, and gently tugged. "It's our turn."

My hand tingled all the way to my shoulder. I don't know how my brain connected enough with my legs to get my knees to bend and my feet to move, but somehow, we ended up standing against the wall, slightly facing each other. Landen, under his mother's instructions, held one of my hands and wrapped his other arm around my waist from behind.

"You look beautiful." He whispered so quietly into my ear that I couldn't be sure if he really said the words, or if I imagined them.

My whole body went rigid.

"Smile!" his mom commanded.

I pasted a smile on my face that felt as stiff as a tiki mask.

Landen poked me in the ribs lightly. "You gotta relax, or this picture is going to look like I'm with a cardboard cutout. Just have fun. Enjoy the moment."

Have fun. Enjoy the moment. That was great advice. I squirmed away from his poke and smiled for real. It wasn't until we were done taking pictures and I was away from Landen's arms that I could think clearly again. My thoughts went straight to what Landen had said.

Relax.

Have fun.

Enjoy the moment.

Why did that sound so familiar? I mean, obviously I'd heard those words a zillion times before, but those three phrases, one right after the other, were familiar for a different reason.

I puzzled over it while we gathered our things and began filing out the door. I ended up leaving last.

My mom patted me on the back. "Love you, sweetie. Just have fun."

"We should talk later," Roxie whispered with a smirky little grin; her eyes darted to Landen.

"Shhh!" I gave her a scrunched-up stink face just before she closed the front door after me. I hope she saw it and it haunted her thoughts for the rest of the night.

My steps faltered on the way down the stairs.

Wait a second.

I knew why Landen's words sounded so familiar to me.

I wrote that!

In my last Sage Advice column when I responded to Tornado. Was Landen quoting Sage Advice because he read it in the paper, or did he remember those words because it answered a question he wrote?

Was Landen Tornado?

Chapter 22

I studied Landen as he held out his elbow for Brooklynn as if maybe the way he moved would give me a clue that he wrote to Sage for advice. Of course it didn't. There was nothing in the turn of his chin or the slick of his hair to tell me anything like that. I also tried, and failed, to remember what else I'd told Tornado in the column.

Sam appeared at my side and put a tentative hand on my shoulder. I couldn't think about Landen anymore right now. Sam was my date; he deserved my attention. I would have to sort the rest out later.

Natasha followed us all the way down the driveway to the car, which was Will's family minivan. She kept snapping pictures on rapid shot all around the car like the paparazzi. She only stopped when Leah yelled that she could only see flashing lights. Will and Landen gave audible sighs of relief when Natasha disappeared inside the house.

Sam opened the sliding van door and waited for me to climb into the very back. It was not a feat for the faint of heart. I smacked my head on the roof once and almost tripped on my dress three times. It was with great relief that I finally found my seat and got my seatbelt buckled.

My dress took up so much room that Sam left the seat next to me empty, scooting all the way to the other window. Even then, he had to keep shoving satin and tulle away from his face.

"Assessment." Sam leaned across the sea of fluff. "This is going really well. Conclusion: dating is acceptable."

I laughed. "Experiment is a success."

"We'll see." He drew his lips together. "But I am beginning to see why you people date so often." He leaned back in the seat.

"Actually, I…" I started and then stopped when I realized Sam had that glazed-over expression, the one that meant he was too deep in thought to listen to me. I'm not sure what I was going to say, anyway. Probably something about me not dating people all that much.

Then I realized something.

This date with Sam was basically my first date, too.

I never dated before Jason, and he had never actually asked me out. Not even to prom. We were sitting in the commons during lunch period and all of Jason's friends buzzed about prom. One of the girls-I don't remember her name-asked Jason if he was going. He shrugged, turned to me and said, 'Yeah I guess Pyper and I will go.'

He just assumed I would.

And he was right.

I was a jellyfish and he was a shark.

My insides squirmed as I remembered how excited I was. I should have said something like, 'You assume too much,' or 'You wish I was going to prom with you,' or 'How about asking me, jerk face.'

But I didn't.

What I did was melt into a gooey puddle on the commons floor and nod like a bobble head with a vague and pathetic grin.

"Where to first?" Leah asked. She leaned over to change the radio station to country music.

Will groaned.

The minute I heard the first steel guitar, I poked Brooklynn. She turned around with a smirk. The two of us loved to sing country songs off-key while we watched Will play basketball with Brooklynn's brothers. It totally threw off his game. He wasn't tough enough for the twang.

"Dinner," Will said, changing the station back to where it had been.

I rested my hands on my lap, where they twitched like a fish out of water. As Will pulled into the street, I found my eyes wandering to the back of Landen's head.

We turned the corner, away from the house, and I twisted in my seat to look longingly at Beauty parked in the driveway. Oh, how I wished I was driving her home right now, back to my simple life where I did my thing and solved everyone else's problems while ignoring my own.

How did I get here?

"Hey guys! Ready for the best prom ever?" Leah rolled down her window and woo-wooed out into the night.

Best prom ever.

Best. Prom. Ever.

That's right!

If I had to be at prom, I was going to make it the best one ever. I'd done all I could to make that happen up until now. The time had come to stop focusing on myself and concentrate on making this the best prom ever for my friends so none of them had to look back in horror on this day.

I could do this!

"Hey, we should play a game while we drive." I leaned forward as much as I could, so Will and Leah would be able to hear me up front.

"Like, Parcheesi?" Will asked, catching my eye in the rear-view mirror with a grin.

"Does anyone actually play that game? Or do they just make lame jokes about it?" I asked.

Leah slapped Will's shoulder. "Yeah, Will. Don't be cheesy." She turned to show us a toothy, Cheshire cat grin.

"Cause that wasn't cheesy at all," Landen said.

"What kind of game?" Brooklynn, as usual, brought us back to the subject at hand.

"Truth or dare?" Leah suggested.

"Dare might be hard to do in a car." I tried not to imagine the kind of dares a bunch of teenage boys would come up with in a moving vehicle.

"No way! It would work, see? I dare you to spit on the next pedestrian," Will said.

My point exactly.

"Ew! Will!" Brooklynn cried.

"Instead of that," I said, "we could just do the truth part. Oh! Or two truths and a lie! That might be fun!"

"What game is this?" Sam leaned forward.

Leah answered. "You tell three things about yourself. Two are true, one is a lie. Everyone else has to guess which one is the lie."

"I see." Sam leaned back, assuming his contemplative scowl. "I'll play."

"I'm in," Landen said.

"Fine," Will grumbled. "I still think it would be more fun to dare."

Brooklynn muttered under her breath. "Of course you do."

"What does that mean?" He glanced behind him, his face unreadable.

"Nothing." Brooklynn held her hands out in front of her defensively. I don't think she expected him to hear.

"Whatever. Just tell me." Will turned to look at her. He could do that because we were at a stoplight, but truthfully, he probably would have done it anyway. I wondered who thought it was a good idea to put Will in charge of driving.

Brooklynn's shoulders straightened as her chin lifted to meet Will's eyes. "Fine. I meant that you only want to do things that you think are fun."

"Is that bad?" Will looked around the back of the car, appealing to the rest of us. Brooklynn didn't give anyone a chance to answer.

"It is if something is complicated or hard or messy. How are people supposed to know if they can count on you when you never take anything seriously?"

"Wow," I murmured.

"Green," Leah said, pointing.

Will turned slowly, giving his full, undivided attention to driving.

"So!" I said brightly, "two truths and a lie. Who wants to go first?"

"I will," Landen said, leaning forward with his hand resting on the shoulder of Leah's seat. "I love economics with Mr. Rypkema. I hate working at Greedy Cow. And I wish I could invent a machine to change the past."

"The machine is a truth," Leah said confidently. "Everyone wishes that."

Landen just shrugged.

"The lie has to be economics. No one likes economics," Will said.

"I like economics," Brooklynn said.

"Oh," Will drummed his thumbs on the steering wheel. "Right."

"Changing the past could change the present," I mused. "Do you hate the present?"

"Not at the moment."

"I know for sure he hates Greedy Cow." Leah peered at Landen for confirmation.

His face was expressionless.

She threw her hands in the air, exasperated. "You are so annoying, Landen! I am never playing poker with you, ever! You have the worst blank face in the world!"

"Do you think it's the worst because it's the best?"

Leah didn't answer.

"Jealous." Landen nodded.

"What is this cow place?" Sam asked.

"The ice cream shop in the mall." Leah craned her neck to see Sam better. "Have you never been?"

He shook his head. "I don't frequent the mall."

"It's really good. We were just there last Friday," Brooklyn said.

Will signaled to turn left. I couldn't figure out where we were going. It looked like he was driving us in a big circle.

"Landen's family owns Greedy Cow," Will said over his shoulder when he stopped at a stop sign.

"Then, you are heir to all the ice cream?" Sam asked Landen.

"No!" Leah protested. "I was born one minute and twenty-three seconds first. I'm the heir; he's the spare."

Landen flicked Leah's ear.

Leah swatted his hand. "It doesn't matter, anyway. None of us want the ice cream empire, so, eventually, it will fall."

"Then you are the one who detests the Cow?" Sam said thoughtfully.

"No!"

Landen coughed.

"I mean, I don't hate it. I just hate working there. I want to run the business end, but Dad thinks I'm not old enough. Gimme a break! Like, I'm student council president, run the dang school paper, and-"

"I didn't know you were in charge of the paper." Brooklyn leaned forward. "Do you know who does the advice column?"

"Wow!" I said, my voice making my own ears ring. "You guys are, like, heirs to the Ice Cream Empire. That sounds so epic. I should make a crown out of cones or paste rhinestones to the soft serve machine or something significant."

"Don't touch the soft serve machine." A smile played on the corner of Landen's lips.

I snapped my eyes away from Landen before my cheeks could flush.

"Oh, my goodness! Right?" Leah groaned. "Our soft serve machine is the worst! Landen made the biggest mess the other day when he pushed the clean button instead of turning it off. I love it when he does stuff like that. Then I'm the good child."

"Oh no!" Brooklynn said. "Did you have to clean it up?"

"I had help," Landen said, this time without looking at me.

A flush crept up my neck as I remembered how Landen had stepped closer, his thumb brushing the back of my hand. The way he looked at me. I drew in a breath as I wondered what would have happened if that woman and her kids hadn't shown up? What would Landen have done?

"Pyper? You okay?" Brooklynn peered at me.

I tried to shake my thoughts to the back corners of my brain where they were supposed to stay.

Stubborn things.

"Dude," Will said in his boomer voice, "what's with the new flavor? I saw it on the Facebook page. Maple bacon waffle berry? That sounds weird."

Landen pointed at Leah, who just shook her head and said, "It's creative, okay?"

Will flipped a U-turn, convincing me once and for all that he had no clue where he was going. "The lie is econ, I'm telling you. No one likes that class."

Landen smiled. "You sure?"

"No." Will let out a breath.

"This really shouldn't be that hard!" Leah huffed. "I'm your twin! Don't we have a psychic connection?"

"Apparently not." Landen leaned back, stretching his hands to the roof of the car.

I started thinking of all the things I knew and had observed about Landen Thom. I wanted to figure this out.

He always said what was on his mind. Not in a mean way, but in a straightforward way. He didn't beat around the bush; he wasn't mysterious or manipulative. What you saw was what you got.

I remembered he told me that he didn't want to work at Greedy Cow for the rest of his life, but did that mean he hated it? I thought about the way he smiled at the lady with her two little kids. Someone who was a good actor could have pulled that off, but Landen was transparent. He would not have been so happy at work if he hated it.

"I got it!" I sprang up so fast my seatbelt locked. "I know what the lie is. You don't hate working at Greedy Cow. Am I right?"

Landen turned slowly, his eyes making their way to mine. "You win."

I looked away.

"That's weird, bro," Will said, pulling the car into an empty parking lot surrounded by office buildings. "Economics is the worst."

"Where are we?" Brooklynn asked.

We parked right in front of a large dumpster.

"Is this dinner?" Leah wrinkled her nose as she looked around.

Landen looked out the window, saw the dumpster, and started cracking up. "Nice spot, Will."

Will shrugged. "Coincidence! No, this isn't dinner. This is where we put on blindfolds because dinner is a surprise." He and Landen whipped out handkerchiefs like synchronized choreography. Sam dangled one in front of my nose, barely holding the corner with his thumb and index finger before dropping it into my lap. Will tied Leah's into place and Landen handed his to Brooklynn so she could tie it on herself. I held mine over my eyes but didn't tie it.

"No peeking," Sam whispered.

Will started the car back up and drove a few circles around the parking lot—to throw us off, I'm sure; then went back the way we had come. My blindfold slipped when Will took a speed bump too fast, so it wasn't totally my fault that I peeked. After a few minutes, we pulled back into the driveway of Landen and Leah's house. I sat quietly until I heard a door open, then I let the handkerchief drop.

"Pyper!" Will said, his eyebrows down.

"I won't tell them where we are! I have to be able to see; I won't be able to get out of this car blindfolded. Did you see how long it took me to get settled back here?"

"Truth," Sam said.

Natasha stood at the door, waiting for us. She led us through the house, around some corners and into a back room, where Landen and Will stopped their dates to remove the blindfolds. Sam swung his arms as he looked around.

The room we were standing in must have been a sunroom because all of the walls, except for one, were floor-to-ceiling windows that overlooked the San Francisco peaks. The tippy tops of the mountains were still covered in snow that glowed a little in the darkening sky. It was beyond beautiful.

"Is this my house?" Leah looked around. "We're eating dinner at my house?"

She did not sound happy.

Will looked a tad embarrassed. "Your mom wanted to make dinner for us, but she didn't think you would go for it."

"No, I wouldn't. She already asked my opinion, and I said no way." Leah narrowed her eyes at Will and Landen. "You guys totally ganged up on me!" She turned her back on us and flounced to the table, which was laid with linen and porcelain plates. She sat down, not waiting for Will to pull out her chair.

Landen pulled out the seat next to Leah and waited for Brooklynn to sit before pushing it slowly to the table. Then he did the same for me when Sam sat down, oblivious.

"Thanks," I whispered.

"Sure." Landen smiled, then turned to Leah. "Mom's excited, Leah. She really wanted to do this for us."

Leah huffed but softened just a little. "Well, dinner had better be good."

If the smells wafting through the sunroom were any indication, it would be.

Chapter 23

"I think I'm going to explode." Sam groaned.

I thought Sam was going to explode, too. I couldn't believe how much he'd eaten. It was almost amazing. I had two little brothers with ridiculous metabolisms, and I had never seen someone pack it away like Sam just did.

Will's younger brother and Kai began clearing our plates. They looked adorable in white shirts and black slacks with white towels draped over their arms.

I winked at Kai when he took my things, but he pretended not to notice.

Sam rubbed his belly. "I didn't know food could taste this good. That dessert…" He kissed his fingers.

That was a very true statement. My mom brought over the petit fours she had been working on when I saw her after school. They were beautiful and melt-in-your-mouth yummy. I wished I had another stomach or wasn't wearing a waist-hugging dress so I could eat more of them.

Leah had been jiggling her leg for the last fifteen minutes, waiting for the boys to finish eating. As soon as the last plate disappeared from the table, she was on her feet.

"Let's go! I keep having visions of sagging lights and limp crepe paper! Let's go, let's go!"

By the time we parked the car at the school twenty minutes before prom was scheduled to start, I was as antsy as Leah. My mind was already transitioning to business mode, full of logistics and back-up plans.

Please let this prom be perfect.

I outpaced everyone else and entered the gym a few strides ahead. If I hadn't known it was the school gym, I wouldn't recognize it at all. Leah told me she made a deal with the guys that showed up to decorate. If they would finish up alone after the girls all went home to get ready, we would make them cookies. Mostly because boys take about thirty seconds to get ready, and because she admitted she didn't want to do it anymore.

Classic Leah.

As I looked up, I had to hand it to the guys. They did not disappoint. The whole room was transformed, magnificent. The twinkle lights on the ceiling made all the difference. I could almost fool myself into thinking we were outside under a sky full of stars.

Except for the lingering smell of fish sticks. I'm sure that would go away once the room filled up with an overabundance of cologne and perfume.

There was no one else in sight. The dance floor was completely empty. I couldn't resist. I walked to the center of the room and twirled until the skirt of my dress flared into a perfect circle.

It felt amazing.

Then, I heard applause.

Mrs. Larsen stood on the sidelines of the gym with a hipster dude I didn't know. I did a sweeping bow and swished across the gym to where they stood.

"That was beautiful, Pyper!" Mrs. Larsen smiled. "But you know you didn't have to come early. My husband and I took care of everything so all of you could enjoy your prom."

"Thank you," I clasped my hands.

"Are you here with a date?" Mrs. Larsen looked over my shoulder as my friends filed into the room with no small amount of noise thanks to Will.

"Yeah. Yes, I'm here with Sam."

"Sam Pederson?"

I nodded.

"That is really sweet, Pyper. I knew you would put aside your personal feelings for the greater good, but you surpassed my highest expectations. I'm proud of you."

I felt uncomfortable under the praise and mumbled, "Thanks" before escaping to check the refreshment table. Everything was perfect, but I straightened napkins and smoothed out wrinkles on the tablecloth to have something to do with my hands.

The Jensons had already been there to set out cream puffs, dainty cookies, and mini raspberry tarts on pretty porcelain cake stands. It was gorgeous; they really came through.

I needed to tell Carly how grateful I was.

Brooklynn caught my eye and waved me over to the large round table the group had claimed as their own. I nodded but took a few extra moments to finish with the tablecloth.

Leah snapped her fingers under my nose, startling me so much I almost knocked over the punch bowl. I didn't even hear her walk over.

"You are absolutely not staying behind that table all night. The tablecloth totally clashes with your dress. Let's go." She grabbed my arm and pulled me over to the table. I sat immediately, but Leah squinted at the DJ table with her hands on her hips. Weird speaker noises filled the air every couple minutes.

"I'm going to go check on that guy." She said through pressed lips.

"Look! SweeTARTS!" Sam held up the roll of candy. "I love these things."

I turned my attention to Sam so he could show me the other treasures he found in the prom treat bag. I was surprised to see how quickly the gym was filling up. Wasn't it cool to be fashionably late anymore?

Or maybe that was never cool.

Music poured into the gym without any squeaks just a moment before Leah returned to the table. She placed her palms on the top as though she was calling a student council meeting to order. "I took care of that business. You're welcome. Now let's have a prom-date meeting. Do you guys want to dance first or mingle?"

"My grandma says the word 'mingle,'" Will said in a falsetto voice. Leah whacked him in one arm the same time Brooklynn whacked him in the other arm. Will grabbed each of his arms with a look of fake pain and suffering on his face. He totally looked like he was hugging himself.

"Let's dance, doofus." Leah said, poking Will in the back with her clutch. "Come on!"

He groaned as he lifted himself grudgingly from the chair and followed Leah like a wounded gazelle. Brooklynn watched him go with an unreadable expression.

"Do you want to dance?" I asked Sam.

He looked up from his treats with real fear in his eyes.

"Because I totally don't!" I said quickly.

Sam went back to his rummaging with a breath of relief.

"Want to hit the refreshment table?" Landen asked.

I stared at him. "Are you serious?"

He couldn't be serious. I was there at dinner. I saw how much he ate.

"I was just making conversation."

"Making conversation?" Brooklynn smiled. "Are refreshments really the first things that came to your mind? Most people opt for the weather or the Diamondbacks."

"Not a big fan of baseball." He popped a piece of candy in his mouth. "Or weather."

Now I knew he was being silly. Weather was way important.

"You guys don't want to dance?" I asked Landen and Brooklynn.

Brooklynn's eyes went wide, which, on her pixie face, looked really, really big. She shook her head.

"Of course you don't. This is a horrible song." I swallowed my words. I wished I'd brought a board game or something. There is not much else to do at prom if half of us didn't want to dance. Maybe we should all follow Sam's example and meticulously fold SweeTARTS wrappers into tiny airplanes.

"Pyper? Pyper!"

Carly came flying across the gym in a cloud of pink tulle. One minute she was airborne, the next she was pulling me out of my seat and squeezing the air out of my lungs with a tight hug.

"You're here! I'm so glad!" She stepped back and narrowed her eyes. "Wait." She peered around me to one side and then the other, as if I was hiding a guy in the folds of my dress. "You didn't really come without a date, did you?"

"I'm here with Sam."

He waved without looking up.

"I texted you, like, a hundred times this week about that. Did you get them?"

Carly bounced on the balls of her feet. "My phone fell in the pond at Travis's house when he was showing me the koi fish. They are this big!" She held her hands out a few feet apart. "I didn't get anyone's texts all week! I feel like I've been in social isolation!"

"Oh, that stinks!" I pursed my lips.

Carly nodded solemnly then leaned forward and whispered behind her hand like we were co-conspirators. "Do the refreshments look okay?"

"Car!" I squeezed her arm. "They are perfect! Thank you so much, and thank your parents. Without them, we would have had fakey cookies from the grocery store. This was above and beyond."

Carly blushed a rosy pink that matched her dress. "I'm so glad. Travis and I really wanted to do something to help. You've been so stressed. I know that's why you said what you said. You're just stressed."

I wavered for a minute. I'd really said what I said because it was true, but now wasn't the time to go into that. We could talk about it more later. "I love your dress!" I picked up a side of the chiffon and let it flow back to the floor.

Carly swung her dress back and forth. "We should have gone shopping together. I love *your* dress! Where did you get it?"

"I bought it ages ago," I said. "Did you see Brooklynn?" I moved out of the way so Carly could see her sitting at the table. Carly skipped over to her for a hug.

"Hey guys, want some punch?" Will appeared out of nowhere with a bunch of paper cups balanced in his hands. I had no idea how he carried all of them across the gym without spilling on his shoes.

I took a cup and sniffed. I didn't smell anything, but I wasn't taking any chances. "Did you drink that?"

"Not yet," Will said.

"Don't," I said to Will and then turned to everyone else at the table. "It's always spiked. Someone pours cheap alcohol in the bowl every year, and then someone always barfs all over the dance floor."

"Are you serious?" Carly asked, her eyes wide.

I nodded.

"What should we do?" Brooklynn asked. "Should we empty it? Or, I don't know, hide it somewhere so no one drinks any?"

I suddenly got this mental image of Landen, Sam, and Will trying to hide the punch by pouring it in their pockets and down the neck of their tuxes. Sam looked at me quizzically, so I wiped the smile off my face.

"I'll go tell Leah. She'll want to handle it," I said. "Where did she go, Will?"

"Tell me what?" Leah appeared at my elbow as if saying her name was the equivalent of rubbing a genie lamp.

"Someone spiked the punch," Landen said.

"Again?" Leah took the punch from my hand and sniffed it. Since that didn't work, she put a droplet on the tip of her tongue and grimaced. "Juvenile! I'll be right back! I am not dancing on barf this year!"

We watched Leah march to Mrs. Larsen and don her official Student Council President Cap—metaphorically, of course. There were many things I could say about Leah; my favorite was that she got things done.

Fast.

"So," Carly said, her eyes sliding over to Landen. "Have we met?"

Landen held out his hand. "I'm Landen."

"Carly." She giggled, taking his fingers. "Pleased to meet you."

"We've met before," Landen sighed. "We had tech together last semester."

"We did?"

"Yeah." Landen looked up at the ceiling. "We were lab partners."

Poor Landen! Why was it so easy for people to overlook him? I felt his pain like it was raining down from the ceiling. I hated that I'd caused part of that pain for him, too.

"And you gave me your phone number."

Wait, what?

Carly squinted. "Did we go out?"

Landen pulled on the sleeves of his jacket. "No."

"Why not? Is it because you're an anti-dater? Or do you have a mystery girl, like Pyper and her boyfriend?" Carly grinned at me.

"Pyper has a boyfriend?" Will asked.

Brooklynn rolled her eyes. "Seriously, Will? Where have you been for the last forever?"

"Wait, are you guys serious?" He looked from me to Brooklynn to Landen.

How did we even get on this topic? One second, I'm trying to figure out how to save Landen, and the next I'm totally trying to figure out how to save myself.

Carly's face lit up. "Travis told me all about it. They are so in love! They went to prom together last year, and then he graduated, but they're still together. That's why high school boys aren't good enough for her. His name is-"

"Carly!" Brooklyn shouted.

Everyone at the table startled and stared at Brooklynn. Her face reddened and her mouth was set in a determined line. "I think you have a smudge on your dress."

"No!" Carly twisted and pawed through the layers of tulle like a fiend. "Where? Oh my goodness, where? Is it big?"

"It's, uh, right there," Brooklynn pointed.

I knew that as soon as Carly figured out there was nothing wrong with her dress, we would be right back where we started. I racked my brain to think of something to change the subject. I opened my mouth, waiting for a flash of brilliance, for the perfect thing to say to distract everyone.

It never came.

Carly was slowing down. She'd already inspected every inch of her dress without finding anything, and she was going through it again just in case. Any minute now, she'd turn around and share whatever other nonsense Travis told her. My heart sped up and my eyes started searching for the exit doors.

"I'm not an anti-dater," Landen said.

Carly's fingers stilled. "What?"

"You asked if I'm an anti-dater. The answer is no. I'm here with Brook-lynn. Even if I was anti-dating, there's nothing wrong with that. It's not a big deal. Lots of people don't date in high school."

"Like who?" Carly's eyes widened.

"I haven't been on a date before tonight," Sam said without looking up from his intricate folding.

Carly waved her hand with a laugh, "Yeah, but you're a freshman."

The skin on my arms bristled as though the little, fine hairs had morphed into needles.

"There you are." Travis sidled up behind Carly, wrapping his arms around her waist. "I thought I lost you."

"I put that app on your phone so you can track me," Carly said, twisting to look at him.

I couldn't tell if she was serious. I really hoped she was joking. But I was pretty sure she was not.

Travis just laughed. "Did you guys check out the DJ? He takes requests." He fist bumped Will, nodded to Landen, looked right through Sam, and waved to Brooklynn. Then his eyes settled on me.

"Pyper," he said evenly. "I'm really glad you came."

"Thanks?" I said, not sure why his smile was giving me the willies.

"Oh!" Carly gripped Travis's arm. "I *love* this song. Let's go dance, babe. Later, guys."

"Bye, Pyper." Travis smirked as they danced away.

I glared at his back. He was such a plague; he always had been, but especially last year. I couldn't figure out if it was because he thought I wasn't good enough for Jason, or if he just hadn't liked having a girl hanging around them all the time.

Whatever. It didn't matter. It was all in the past, and that's where it was going to stay.

Brooklynn stood up. "I need some water. Is there bottled water with the refreshments?"

I nodded.

"Cool. You guys want anything?"

The guys shook their heads. I watched Travis and Carly dance, trying to keep my lip from curling. The DJ bellowed something that made the sound system crackle, and everyone close enough to hear what he said started laughing.

"I'm going to go check on Leah," Will said. "She's taking forever."

I sank into the chair across from Landen, my cheeks in my hands. I suddenly felt very, very tired.

"Can I ask you a question?" Landen leaned forward with his elbows resting on the table.

I shrugged.

"What was that all about?"

"What was what all about?"

Landen raised his eyebrows.

I straightened up. "It's nothing. It's fine. Everything is fine." I pulled out my purse and rummaged for lip gloss. I felt horrifically unglossy.

"Pyper, we're friends, right? You don't have to pretend that everything is fine."

You don't have to pretend everything is fine.

You don't have to pretend.

We're friends.

My eyes began to sting. I blinked rapidly until the feeling went away, then I looked up with a smile. "I'm not pretending. It really is fine."

Landen studied me in a way that made me feel like my brain was being dissected. After a few moments, he leaned back. "Want to know another truth about me?" he asked. "Besides the fact that I really like econ?"

I nodded. I wanted to hear anything that would change the subject.

"I never play pretend. You can ask Leah. Even when we were kids, I wouldn't do it. It used to seriously tick her off. I like things to be real. I try to live that way, and I like it when my friends are that way, too."

I lifted my eyes, not sure what to say.

His face softened. "I know you're not being real. I also know you have your reasons, so I'm not going to force you to talk to me about it," Landen said in a low voice. "Okay?"

"Okay," I said, glancing at Sam. I felt like I should be doing something to help him have an awesome first date. He wasn't paying any attention to me. His tongue stuck out slightly as he tried to fold the heavy cardstock prom invitation into what looked like a swan.

"Hey?"

I reluctantly met Landen's eyes.

"If you need to talk, I have ears."

I burst out laughing and couldn't stop. All the pent-up feelings, all the everything, came out in loud, unladylike guffaws. I laughed until my abs ached and my throat got sore. I was still laughing when Brooklynn walked up with two bottles of water.

"What's so funny?" she asked.
Landen just smiled.

252

Chapter 24

Landen, Brooklynn, Sam, and I watched the night unfold from our table on the outskirts of the dance floor. I thought with all my pent-up energy I would want to dance my booty off, but I was strangely content to sit in silence with my friends and watch.

It was comfortable.

Cozy.

To entertain ourselves, Landen started making wacky observations. His most recent was that it is practically impossible to look cool while doing the YMCA dance, which is true. Brooklyn amused herself by copying Sam and folding all the purple paper napkins into swans, hearts, and ninja stars.

"Hey guys!" Leah landed in a chair next to me, bringing with her a puff of fruity perfume. Will sat next to her, out of breath and laughing.

"That was so fun!" Carly squealed, pulling Travis into one of the few empty chairs at our table. "I have never done a line dance at prom before! Don't you think this DJ rocks?"

I don't know why she looked at me, she knew I'd been sitting at this very table since the music started. I gave a shrug-nod and took a sip of water.

"Yeah, nice work, Travis." Leah dug through her purse. "He does rock. Who is he?"

"Brooklynn, what are you doing? Seriously?" Will tried to snatch her pile of origami napkins.

She shooed his hands away and held up her newest creation for everyone to see. "What does it look like?"

"ABC gum," Will said.

Carly tipped her head to one side. "An elephant?"

"My math teacher," Travis laughed.

"Forget it," Brooklynn said, crumbling the napkin up and arching it into a nearby trash can.

Will whistled when it swished neatly inside. "Why don't you play basketball with us, Brooklynn? You've got a great hook shot."

"You never asked," Brooklynn said, staring at Will until he turned away. His ears were an interesting shade of fuchsia.

"What was the napkin supposed to be?" I asked.

"The Millennium Falcon," Brooklynn said, but I couldn't tell if she was serious.

"Hey! The photo room is almost empty. We should take pictures, Will!" Leah said, pointing to the area we had designated for the photographer. It used to house the folding chairs, tables, and various sports equipment, but now it was sparkly and star-lined with a deep purple backdrop.

"We already took, like, an infinity of pictures at the house. How about we don't?" Will whined.

"Will!" Leah and Brooklynn said at the same time with the same impatient tone.

"Hey," Landen patted the pockets of his tux jacket and his pants. "Have you guys seen my wallet?"

"Really, Landen?" Leah rolled her eyes. "You need to duct tape that thing to your heinie."

"Weird," Landen said, but it was unclear whether he was responding to Leah or reacting to his empty suit pockets. "I had it when I left the house. I'm going to go check the car." He stood up.

"Where are you going?" My voice sounded high and squeaky. I took a deep breath to keep my heart from knocking out of my chest.

"I'm going to look for my wallet. I'll be right back." One of Landen's hands still rested on the table.

I stared at it as though I could make it stay there with the sheer force of my eyes, maybe even make him sit back down.

"I'm just going to the car. I'll be back in two seconds. Okay?" He turned to Will. "Can I use your keys, man?"

Will tossed them over, and Landen jogged from the room.

"He will be fast; he did track," Leah said as if to reassure me.

I tried to nod or shake my head or shrug or laugh or do something other than stare at the spot where Landen had been standing just a minute ago, but I couldn't. My eyes went slowly out of focus.

I sat at a table next to the gym entrance, running my fingers lightly along the sleeve of Jason's tux while he talked to his friends. I will never forget that moment. Hank, who graduated with Jason, was playing a game on his phone while his girlfriend tapped her feet to the music. He kept tipping the screen to show Jason and Travis whatever random thing he was doing. I leaned my head against Jason's arm and breathed in that tangy, Jason smell that I could never find the right words to describe in my journal.

Jason moved his arm suddenly. I tipped over; he steadied me and laughed. He said he would be right back, that he had to get something from his car.

I watched him walk out of the gym; that cool-guy strut was irresistible.

Jason's phone was on the table. I pulled it closer so that the other guys wouldn't prank it. Travis asked if I knew Jason's password. The way he looked at me was so challenging, like he didn't think I was enough of Jason's girlfriend to know his password. I took the bait and entered the password. His pictures were open. I couldn't help but see the first one. After that, I kept scrolling.

There were so many pictures.

Travis said something, but I didn't hear him over the buzzing in my ears.

"Pyper?"

I jolted as if I had been sound asleep and someone slammed a door right by my head. "Yeah?" I blinked, trying to orient myself.

Leah watched me with scrunched eyebrows. "Are you okay? You look kind of pale."

"I'm fine. Perfect. I'm fine." It was like my brain had stepped on a big wad of gum and was stuck while trying to take another step. I breathed deeply until the edges of my memories faded back into the past, where they belonged.

I leaned back in my chair like I didn't have a care in the world, even though my pulse had sped up quicker than a racehorse out of the gate.

Brooklynn touched my arm.

I smiled at her, or at least tried, to reassure both her and myself that I was totally fine. This wasn't a big deal. Everything was different now, and this for sure was not last year.

"You just need to dance. You've been sitting here forever. Travis, ask Pyper to dance," Carly said, nudging his arm.

"No, really, it's okay. I have a date I can dance with." I gestured to Sam, who ducked his head and avoided eye contact.

Travis held out his hand. "Will you dance with me?"

No way. No, no, no, no—

"Okay," I said, rising to my feet.

I did not take his hand. I brushed by him and headed towards the dance floor. My legs felt wobbly, like I'd just done leg day twice in a row. I wished I was moving for a different reason, but anything, even dancing with Travis, was better than sitting there with everyone questioning my sanity.

Including me.

Travis followed me to the dance floor, then took my hand and steered us closer to the DJ table. A slow song was just beginning. Travis looked at a spot somewhere over my head while I tried to unfreeze my brain.

"I'm actually really glad Carly suggested we dance, Pyper."

"Why?" I could not say the same thing. For me, this dance lived in the same neighborhood as medieval torture.

"I've wanted to talk to you about something for awhile."

"Okay." My voice was not encouraging.

On purpose.

Travis wiggled his shoulders to loosen them before he tried again. "Carly told me you, uh, she told me that you told her not to date me."

My eyelashes fluttered as my eyes found their way to Travis' face.

Carly did what?

What was she thinking, telling him that? Didn't she know the girl code?

"No, I get it. I think I get why you told her that." Travis said while I scanned the dance floor, looking for an escape.

There was a strand of twinkle lights sagging above our heads. Yeah, that would work. I needed to go find Leah so we could fix it before the whole thing came tumbling down.

I opened my mouth to tell Travis that our dance would have to come to a close early, but he kept talking, glancing at something over my shoulder.

I tried not to turn around.

"So, you remember last year, at prom?"

I shook my head. Not because I didn't remember, but because I wanted him to stop talking more than anything else in the world.

"Remember when you were sitting at the table, and I told you to look at the pictures on Jason's phone?"

I shook my head with more energy. I'm surprised the couples around us didn't comment on the breeze I was creating.

"I didn't get a chance to explain why I did that. I-"

"No," I finally found enough voice to croak the word out. "No, it's okay. You don't need to explain."

The corners of Travis' mouth sagged. "I want to though. I think you got the wrong idea. I was-"

"It's fine!" My voice carried enough that a few people looked over with wide eyes. I cleared my throat and tried again with lower tones. "It's really fine. Totally over it. No big deal. Do you think that light strand looks saggy?"

Travis didn't answer; he studied me thoughtfully. "Pyper, I saw the look on your face when you were scrolling his phone. I know I messed something up. I've been trying to figure out a way to make it up to you for a year."

We turned a circle, and I noticed that we were closer to the DJ table. I could feel the subdued bass of the song pulsating.

"Also, I wanted to tell you I think it's cool you stayed with Jason after that."

"Travis..." I said, my voice tight.

"I mean, I'm glad the two of you worked it out."

"Stop."

"You must really love him—"

"Don't..."

"—to forgive him like that. Anyway, I think it's cool. That's why—"

"Travis!" I said loud enough to get him to finally stop babbling. "I really don't want to talk about prom last year or about Jason." My voice cracked. "I can't."

My heart pounded up my throat and into my ears. I couldn't hear the music anymore.

My mom told me a zillion times that when we bottle up feelings, they are going to come pouring out at the most random times, and now I knew she was right. I hadn't meant to say any of that. I was almost afraid to look at Travis. When I finally found the strength to lift my head, Travis's eyes were wide with surprise.

"Pyper, I think—"

"Hey guys! Let's switch partners. Fun, huh?" Brooklynn didn't wait for an answer before she cut between Travis and I, swinging him across the dance floor. Landen took my hand and pulled me close to him.

"Are you okay?" Landen asked.

"No," I said. "No, I'm not."

Landen grinned. "Way to go, you."

Okay, maybe he was right about that upfront and honest thing. It felt really good to say those words. Tears of relief welled up behind my eyes. I leaned my forehead against Landen's shoulder and stayed there until the song ended and another slow song started.

"Grab your dates and hit the floor. This song is what prom is all about." The DJ's voice boomed through the speakers right by me.

I stopped moving. It was like someone hit the pause button. That voice. It filled all the empty space I'd cleared in my head.

"What?" Landen squeezed my hand. "What's up?"

"I know that voice." I whispered.

"The DJ?"

I didn't bother to answer as I slowly turned to face the DJ table. The lights had shifted for the new song, and I was close enough to see the scar on his chin from when he biffed it wakeboarding about ten years ago.

His hair was longer. He wore hipster sunglasses, and he'd filled out since I last saw him, but it was undeniably him.

"Jason," I whispered.

"Jason?" Landen's head snapped up. "That's Jason? The DJ? Are you sure? It doesn't look like him."

I nodded. My throat was too tight to speak.

"Did you know he was going to be here?" Landen's hand wrapped around my arm, and he tugged me until I looked at him. "Pyper?"

I didn't get a chance to answer. Carly's shriek blocked everything else out. She broke between Landen and I, squishing my waist in a tight hug.

"Are you *so* surprised? Did you guess? Oh my gosh, it was so hard to keep this a secret! I had to avoid you all week 'cause I knew I'd blab! I told you Travis is amazing! He planned this whole thing for you because you miss Jason so much! Most. Thoughtful. Ever!" She pulled back and put her hands on my shoulders. "Go to him. Go."

Before I could react, she twirled me around and gave me a push toward Jason's platform. I stumbled forward, falling into the table hard with both palms spread.

Jason looked up from his equipment and raised a hand into the air. "Hey, Pyper," he called.

I'd imagined this moment. This moment when I saw Jason again. I'd played it all out. What I would say, what Jason would say, what we would both be wearing. In all my imaginings, I never experienced the wave of red-hot rage that washed over me when I saw him there, draped over sound equipment like he didn't have a care in the world.

Anger propelled me up the two stairs like a jet engine.

I stopped in front of Jason's chair. "What are you doing here?"

He spread out his arms like it was obvious. "Playing music."

That was not what I was asking, and he knew it.

"No. I mean, why are you doing this?"

He tipped his chin forward until his glasses slid to the end of his nose. Those bright, piercing blue eyes raked over me. "You look hot, by the way."

I hugged my arms across my chest. "Why are you here?" The words were not cooperating with me. Instead of sounding powerful and indignant, they were small and pleading.

He shrugged. "Travis asked me to do the music. Sick, right?"

I took a deep breath, trying to recover myself. "You need to leave."

Jason stood up and sidled closer so he could slip an arm across my shoulders. "You're so cute, Pyper. Still the little clown."

The anger was back, and I almost welcomed it. Nothing felt worse than that small, shriveled feeling. I would rather be all mad than vulnerable.

I picked up his sleeve with two fingers and tossed his arm away from me. "Let me give you some advice, Jason. Don't you ever, ever touch me again."

Discomfort rippled across his face. He shifted to the other foot uncertainly.

So he did have feelings.

I spent a lot of time in the past year wondering if he was a cyborg.

Or a sociopath.

He laughed and swung his hair out of his eyes. "What's up with you? You didn't use to be so melodramatic. Then again," his eyebrows went up, "you didn't use to be such a babe, either. Maybe we should have dated when I was still here."

I stared at him. "We did date, Jason."

"Nuh-uh. When?"

I couldn't believe it. Was he messing with me? He had to be messing with me. We started dating exclusively at the beginning of my junior year, his senior year.

Wait.

No, that wasn't true.

I just *thought* we were dating exclusively. Judging from the contents of his phone, he did not feel the same way.

"We dated all last year."

"No way, really?" Jason slumped back into his chair and linked his hands behind his head, his elbows sticking out to the side. "Huh."

"You...you don't remember?"

How could he not remember?

"Nope. But then, that was a whole year ago. Can't really expect a guy to remember everything he did in high school." He gave a short laugh and adjusted some knobs.

A tingle started in my fingertips and jetted up my arm, then through my torso and down to my pinkie toe, where it vibrated. I shook out my hands to get rid of the after-effects.

My eyes roamed over Jason's high cheekbones and square jawline. Those crazy blue eyes and thick, black eyelashes that looked like he wore mascara.

It was like I saw him for the first time.

How had I ever thought he was handsome?

I was suddenly overcome with all the time and energy I had wasted thinking about him. The hours I spent wondering if he would ever apologize. All those tear-soaked tissues from wishing things had been different.

My knees wobbled underneath the weight. Already it was almost too much for me to hold. It was the biggest feeling I had ever, ever felt. It swelled inside my chest like a hot air balloon.

Just when I thought I would combust from all the pressure, I felt a prick, like someone stuck me with a needle.

Jason didn't know.

He didn't know he broke my heart.

All the horrible heat seeped away, taking with it the sadness and regret. All that was left was this one, dominant realization.

I was wrong.

I did this all wrong.

This whole entire year, I carried what Jason did like a backpack full of rocks. The horrible weight motivated me to change the way I looked, how I dressed, how I acted. It was almost like I was justified in changing everything about myself because I'd been hurt. I moved forward with a harder shell that affected how I interacted with my friends, the choices I made, how I spent my free time, and what I thought about people—especially guys.

My whole life revolved around Jason before he broke my heart, and it continued to revolve around him after, even though I thought I was over him.

I had let this control me for way too long.

Goosebumps rippled up my arms as my defenses crackled. I stepped back, giving myself room to breathe, and I felt the shell of that old Pyper fall at my feet.

The burden, the weight, was gone.

Now, there was nothing to keep me from floating to the ceiling.

"Jason?" I said in wonder.

"Yeah?" He glanced at me while he fiddled with some cords. Even now, in this most life-changing moment, he didn't give me his full attention.

And it was totally okay.

I didn't need his full attention. I didn't need his apology. I didn't need things to be different.

"I don't understand why you did what you did or why you are the way you are, but it's okay." I took a deep breath. "I forgive you."

"Okay…" Jason looked at me with complete confusion.

A bubbly laugh tickled my throat until I swallowed it back down. He had no idea what I was talking about! And I totally didn't care!

It felt amazing.

I was over it.

I was over him.

"Thanks for being the DJ," I smiled. "We were in a bind. That was really nice of you."

He stood up, adjusted his headphones, and grinned. "I totally rock this. I do all the dorm dances."

I nodded, staring at him just a moment longer, then turned away.

"Good-bye, Jason."

Chapter 25

I could have flown across the dance floor, I felt as light and airy as cotton candy. I floated to the edge of the tables but had to stop when Travis and Carly stepped in front of me.

The change of focus set me off balance. I grabbed the back of a chair to steady myself.

Suddenly, everything looked different.

Carly looked different, more concerned. Travis, well, all his trollish and villainous features were gone. He was just a person with a crease above his eyebrows and worry in his eyes.

"Is everything alright?"

Carly peered over my shoulder. "What happened? It didn't look happy."

"It wasn't." The corners of my mouth rose shakily.

"Oh, no! What happened?" Carly clasped her hands under her chin.

"Crap, Pyper." Travis shoved his hands in his pockets. "I messed this up again, didn't I?"

I held up a hand to stop him. "It's not your fault, Travis. I haven't been honest about Jason."

"What do you mean?" Carly's mouth puckered into a rosebud. "I don't understand."

"I...I did this all wrong." I took Carly's hand. Something heavy dropped into my belly and settled there.

"What?" Travis filled his cheeks with air and blew out the word.

My fabulous high heels were killing my feet. And my brain felt so jumbled that I had a hard time gathering my thoughts while I stood there with pinched toes. I pulled Carly to an empty table, knowing Travis would follow close behind. Carly sat in the nearest chair with Travis next to her. I swung around to the other side so I could see both of their faces and kicked off my shoes with a sigh. "Jason and I aren't a thing. I thought we were at one time, but we weren't. He never loved me the way I loved him. I let people believe we were together, but we weren't."

Carly breathed in a sharp breath.

"So, pretty much, I've been lying all year. I'm so sorry." This I directed to Carly. She was my friend; I should have told her what happened.

"Pyper," Travis said, "before you say anything else, I need to tell you something about Jason." He carefully wove his fingers together.

"Okay." I nodded, pressing my lips together to keep all the words from bubbling out. After what a beast I had been, the least I could do was hear him out.

"Okay, then." He stumbled over the words. His eyes followed the movement of his fingers instead of looking at me. "Did you know about Jason's goal?"

"Not at first, but then, yes, he told me."

Travis's face clouded over. "That-" He stopped himself by glancing at Carly. "That was not cool. The whole team thought Jason was an idiot. He had a girlfriend that adored him and...anyway, despite what you think, most guys don't think it's cool to treat girls that way."

I felt a wave of shame.

I was so unfair to Travis.

I'd been so unfair to all of them.

"I tried to tell you what he was doing all last year, but you were so into him, it never got through."

I didn't remember that. Mostly I remembered Travis giving me a hard time. I tried to think specifically what Travis had said to make me dislike him so much. As phrases went through my mind, I suddenly heard them differently.

'You shouldn't date Jason' no longer meant that I wasn't good enough for Jason.

'Jason's not the right guy for you' no longer meant I was a nerd.

'You should break up with Jason' no longer meant Travis was trying to get rid of me.

I groaned inside my soul.

"Anyway, we were all playing basketball at the park the day before prom, and Jason started mouthing off about you. I got so mad. I wanted you to know what he was doing, so I decided to show you his phone. I knew you'd never dump him without proof."

"So," I swallowed, "you showed me his phone so that I would dump him first?"

Not to rub it in.

Not to brag about how awesome Jason was.

Not to make fun of me.

"Yeah. I thought you deserved to end it on your terms, and I knew Jason had a boatload of pictures. But Pyper, seriously, I wouldn't have done it if I'd know how much that was going to hurt you."

"Why didn't you tell me this before?" I asked, even though I knew that wasn't a fair question.

Travis gave me a sad look. "You wouldn't talk to me. You never let me explain."

"It's true, Pyper," Carly said, even though she had no proof except for Travis's word. I looked at her in a new way. Maybe I didn't give Carly enough credit. Maybe there was something to be said for loyalty.

And trust.

"Travis, I'm so sorry. I've treated you terribly, and I really hope you can forgive me."

Travis reeled back in surprise, but I wasn't done yet. I leaned forward so both of his eyes were locked on to both of mine. "I'm sorry I told Carly not to date you, and I'm sorry I called you a jerk. I never should have judged you the way I did. I have been seriously unfair."

"I am a jerk sometimes." Travis ducked his head when Carly protested and smacked his arm. "No, I mean it. I've been kicking myself since last year, Pyper. I knew what Jason was doing, and I waited way too long to tell you about it. I didn't think you'd believe me."

"I wouldn't have," I said with a short laugh.

Travis sighed. "Yeah, I get it, though. I probably wouldn't have believed me, either. But I should have explained what was going on before I told you to open his phone."

The corners of my eyes prickled. "I thought you were in on it."

"No! Are you kidding me, no." He shook his head, tousling his Ken-doll hair. "I would never do that to someone. Seriously uncool. I'm just glad you believe me."

"I do." I smiled, and this time it stayed in place. "I do believe you. Carly, I never should have told you who to date. From now on, I'll stay so far out of your business that you'll need high-powered binoculars to see me."

"Pyper, I don't want that!" Carly's eyes widened. "I want you to tell me what you think. That's what friends do!"

I sucked in my bottom lip and chewed on it. I wasn't totally confident that I could tell her my thoughts without trying to control everything, but I got what she meant. "In that case, I'll tell you what I think without acting like I know everything about everything. Fair?"

Carly stood up, her arms lengthening out to the sides. "Give me a squeeze," she laughed.

I moved over to her and wrapped my arms tight around her neck. "I'm sorry, Car."

"I love you, Pyp."

I squeezed extra hard and then let her go. "I love you, too. Thank you." I included Travis in my smile. "It really was nice of you to surprise me with Jason, even though it's Jason."

Travis grinned. "It's nothing."

"You guys go have fun; I've sucked up way too much of your night."

Carly smiled up at Travis, and he nodded. They waved, then boogied their way to the dance floor.

When they were swallowed up by the crowd of sequins and bow ties, I sat heavily in a chair and laid my chin on my forearms to give myself a chance to process everything that had just happened. But my brain didn't stop with the night's events; it continued to wander through all the decisions I'd made since prom last year.

There was a lot to sort through.

I thought about my broken heart and Jason's indifference. I wish it hadn't taken me so long to realize he'd never been worth my time. But, I guess, that was all part of it. I had to go through what I went through to get where I am.

I thought about the advice column. Giving advice was fun, but now I knew what Roxie had meant that day at the mall when she said giving advice was a big responsibility.

I thought about Travis, and then people in general. A person wasn't what they looked like; a person was what they did. That's what really showed who they were because it showed who they *chose* to be.

Suddenly, I sprang out of my seat and spun in a circle, my eyes scanning the crowd of people. Looking for Landen in this mess of tuxedos was like the world's worst search and find.

I dodged tables and chairs until I got to the one my friends had claimed. For a second, no one noticed me. Leah and Sam were deep in conversation about college applications, and Will and Brooklynn played that game where you try to slap the other person's hands before they move out of the way.

I didn't see Landen, though.

Where was he?

"Hello, Pyper." Sam lifted his hand to wave.

"Hey, guys. Do you know where Landen went?"

Leah's eyes widened. "Landen?" She looked around, then under the table.

Did he often hide out under tables?

"He was here a few minutes ago." Brooklynn squinted at Will. "Wasn't he just here?"

"He went for a walk. Gotcha!" Will gave Brooklynn's hand a slap that made her yelp.

"No fair; we were paused."

"You never said 'pause.'"

"It was implied when I started talking to Pyper, you heathen."

"Sorry. Are you okay?" He took her hand and cradled it next to his chest, stroking the back like it had morphed into a puppy.

"Let me go, weirdo." She pulled her hand away from Will. "I'll walk with you," she said to me as she stood up.

"She knows where the doors are, Brooklynn," said Will. "You can't really miss them."

Broolynn shot Will a nasty look and looped her arm through mine. "Come on."

When we were a few steps away, Brooklynn squinted at me. "So, Travis brought Jason to surprise you. Are you surprised?"

I laughed until I snorted, and then we both cracked up.

"It was a nice thought."

Brooklynn stopped and looked up at me. "Pyper, you are my best friend forever and always, so I am going to say something I have wanted to say to you for a long time. Stop being so flipping nice."

Okay, that was not what I was expecting her to say.

"You always look perfect, act perfect, are perfect. You put on this pretty show, so everyone thinks you are fine all the time. But you don't have to be fine, Pyp. I give you my permission. It's okay to be a mess."

"Is it?"

"Yes." Brooklynn nodded once. "Stop pretending."

I sucked in a big breath. "I don't know if I can do that, honestly."

"Hey, no worries. I read in an advice column that it only takes three weeks to build a new habit, so if you start today, you will be totally golden by the time school is over."

I laughed a deep belly laugh and hugged Brooklynn with all my might. "You are the best friend ever, anywhere."

Brooklynn wheezed into my shoulder. "You don't have to tell me what I already know."

I stepped away and stopped myself from straightening Brooklynn's sleeve. It had flipped over during our hug. "I'm going to go find Landen."

"Good," Brooklynn put her hands on her hips. "And?"

"And I'm going to tell him about Jason."

"Fantastic! And?"

"And...and, I don't know. What else should I do?" I twisted a ring around my finger.

Brooklynn's grin stretched from cheek to cheek.

"Why are you smiling like that?" I dropped my hands to my sides. "It's creeping me out."

"Do you realize this is the first time you have ever asked me for advice? I want to savor the moment."

"Wow," I rolled my eyes.

"AND," Brooklynn spoke over me. "You need to tell him that you like him."

Chapter 26

It wasn't until I stood on the pokey asphalt parking lot that I realized I never put my shoes back on. It was too late to go back for them now, but I felt a little idiotic as I picked my way through the cars with only dim city lights to keep me from stepping on glass.

Or worse.

And what in the world did Brooklynn mean I needed to tell Landen I liked him? I mean, I did, but not the way her little smirky smirk implied. I just wanted to tell Landen about Jason. I wanted to be completely honest with him like he always was with me.

I stopped walking and listened. I don't know why that seemed like a good idea. Landen would have to be a major, chronic mouth breather for me to hear him.

"Pyper?"

I leaned forward, squinting into the dark. "Landen? Is that you?"

"Yeah."

I heard a rock scuttle across the ground. "Where are you?"

"By Will's car."

There, finally I could see him. I moved slowly in the direction of the car. Without those super high heels, my dress dragged along the ground, so I gathered it by the handfuls in front of me. I didn't want tripping and falling flat on my face to distract me from finding Landen.

He leaned against the trunk, kicking pebbles across the parking lot. Now that I stood in front of him, my mind went completely blank.

"Are you barefoot?" Landen stared at my feet.

I let my skirt drop to the ground. "Maybe."

"Where are your shoes?" He stood up and took a step towards me. "Do you know what kinds of garbage people drop on the ground out here? You're going to step on something." His words sounded right, but his tone was the same as Roxie when she yells at Gavin to stop flossing.

"I forgot them when I came looking for you." I clasped my hands in front of me.

Landen stepped around me and started brushing the ground with the sides of his shoes. "Only step once I've cleared the ground." The words were clipped and tight.

I meekly followed Landen, taking small steps, until we reached the sidewalk. There were solar lights lining the way, so it was easier to see now. I lifted my eyes to Landen's face, and my heart flip-flopped.

"Landen..." I tried to catch my breath.

"What?" He snapped as he turned to face me.

"I need to talk to you about something."

"Okay. Talk."

I couldn't say the words, not with him looking at me like he wanted to shot-put me into the next county. I choked those words down and replaced them with others. "Do you know Jason Myler?"

Landen shrugged one shoulder. "Sure, everyone knows Jason Myler."

I pushed my curls into the sleeve of my dress to keep the wind from whipping them around. If only I'd foreseen myself standing outside the school when I'd planned my hair; an updo would have been much more practical. "Did you know Jason's parents went to college with my parents?"

He shook his head.

"They were all best friends that ended up getting married."

"What are the odds?" Landen looked up at the sky, the moon was full and bright.

"It was supposed to be perfect. Like, happily ever after and stuff. They would raise their kids together, their kids would get married, and their kids would get married...forever and onward. They had it all planned out. After they graduated, my dad interviewed for a job here and decided to take it. Mr. Myler was considering opening a sporting goods store in Colorado, but they couldn't stand the thought of being so far away from each other, so Mr. Myler started his business here instead. We've lived down the street from the Mylers my whole life. They were like family." I let out a breath and started walking; there was so much nervous energy built up I couldn't stand still any longer.

"I didn't know that." Landen shifted to his other foot and followed me. "So, then, you and Jason grew up together?"

His tone was still tight, but something else in it gave me hope. I opened my mouth, and the words gushed out. "Here's the thing, Landen. I have known Jason my whole entire life, literally, but I never really knew him. I didn't see him for what he was. I've wondered so many times if that was a defect in me or in him. I honestly don't know. I thought I was in love with Jason. When I was five, he gave me a dandelion and told me we were going to get married when he turned eight." I looked sideways at Landen. "We didn't."

"This would be really awkward if you were married." Landen tossed the rock he'd been holding and reached for my hand. I fell into stride beside him as he steered us away from the school. After we'd been walking for a moment, I waited for him to let me go, but he didn't. His thumb brushed the back of my hand every few seconds.

"Go on," Landen prompted.

"So, when Jason started middle school, things changed. He was really, really good-looking, and I think that's about the time he started to realize it."

Landen snorted.

"He spent less time with me and more time with kids his age, especially girls. I was jealous all the time. My mom kept trying to distract me with things like horse lessons, dance classes, gymnastics, mall trips... All of it was way fun, but they didn't accomplish what she wanted. Jason was pretty much all I could think about. It's so stupid."

"It's not." Landen squeezed my hand. "I can think of a lot of things that are more stupid than that."

"Thanks, but really. I was so blind. There were so many things that could have shown me what Jason was like if I'd paid just a tiny bit of attention."

"Like what?"

"He never asked me questions, and he never took interest in anything I did. It was always, always all about him."

"Don't be hard on yourself, Pyper. 'Love is blind' is a saying for a reason."

"I don't know if that makes me feel better or worse, actually." I gave a short laugh. "Once Jason got into high school, he quit talking to me completely. Except for when we had dinner as families or did our yearly trip at the lake during Memorial Day weekend. I was a tag-a-long; he just barely tolerated me. Then, at the beginning of junior year, Jason started calling and texting me every day. I had almost given up on him, and suddenly he wanted to hang out with me all the time. It was like all my dreams were resurrected and coming true at once. I was so in love with him that I overlooked more red flags."

"What were those?" Landen's voice was tight.

"He checked out other girls when we were together. He didn't answer right away when I asked him something, or he answered with a question because he didn't listen to what I said and was trying to cover it up. He could never remember the names of my friends... I think I knew something was wrong, deep down. I let Jason hold my hand and hug me, but I never let him kiss me."

"That's interesting." Landen slapped at a wispy tree branch that overhung our path. "Why?"

"I don't know." I paused to think but couldn't come up with a good reason. "Maybe because I was a hopeless, ridiculous romantic. I thought I loved Jason more than life itself, but I was always waiting for that spark. You know, the kind you read about in books. I never felt it, and I tried, believe me."

"Yeah?"

"Yeah. I mean, I was giddy. I was thrilled. I was a lot of other things, but every time it came down to it, I never felt like I wanted him to kiss me. So, we never did. But then, prom..." I stopped.

"Prom?" Landen said, after the silence had stretched for a long time.

I groaned softly; this part was harder than I thought. The words wanted to stay where they were. Trying to get them out was like pulling stubborn weeds.

I took a deep breath. "We went to prom together last year. I was so excited. While I was getting ready, I vividly remember thinking that if Jason tried to kiss me that night, I would let him."

"Did you?" Landen turned his head away.

This was getting harder. "Jason picked me up. We went to dinner with another couple—some friends of his that were seniors. I hung on his arm and laughed at his jokes, and I thought I was the luckiest girl in the whole world. Then, Jason realized he left his wallet in the car."

"Really?" Landen's next step faltered. "That's an interesting coincidence."

"While Jason was gone, Travis sat next to me—"

"Travis?"

"He asked for Jason's phone, which I was holding for Jason. Travis said there was something I needed to see. I unlocked it and found myself staring at picture after picture of Jason kissing girls. There were so many. I scrolled until my thumb hurt. I didn't know there were that many girls in this town."

"Pyper." Landen wound his pinkie finger around mine.

"I must have looked awful because everyone left our table. When Jason came back, I was alone."

I took a deep breath. I was almost done. It was almost the end.

"I still remember every detail about that moment. The way he walked, the horrible taste in my mouth, a sequin I accidentally twisted off my dress. Unimportant details. Funny how that happens, huh?"

"But not hilarious."

I laughed, the knot in my stomach unwinding. "I asked Jason what those pictures were, and he explained that he made a bet with one of his friends that he could kiss every girl in the school by the time he graduated."

"Are you serious?"

"He scrolled through and pointed out things about the girls, telling me who used cinnamon toothpaste or who has excessive spit. He didn't even care. It was like the perfect Jason I knew had morphed into a disgusting monster."

"Did you punch him? You should have punched him."

"I wish I had." I smiled at the thought. "No. Instead, I started cry-ing–like, ugly crying."

"Pyper." Landen stopped walking. His hands hovered at my shoulders like he wanted to wrap me up, protect me from the past. Instead, he raked both hands through his hair, totally destroying Leah's gel work.

"It's fine, Landen." And for the first time in a year, it was. Instead of saying those words to cover up the truth, I felt them swell inside me. I stepped away from Landen and stood taller. Jason couldn't hurt me anymore.

"Jason told me he knew I would never kiss him unless we were dating, so he gave it a try. He said it all nonchalantly, like he was going for the ninth hole at mini golf instead of ripping my heart to pieces. I told Jason that I wanted to go home, but he wasn't ready to leave, so I had to call my mom. She was so mad that she tried to go to the Mylers' right then. I talked her out of it; I wanted Jason to tell his parents. I wanted him to own it, take responsibility for it, or something. Both our parents had been as excited as I was that we were together for those few months, and I wanted them to know it was Jason's fault things did not work out the way everyone hoped."

I saw all this play behind my eyes like I was watching it happen to someone else, except a flutter in my belly felt now more like hope than horror. It didn't hurt anymore. I'd been waiting for a year to find this sense of peace.

"So, did he? Own it?"

I shook my head. "Of course not. I was so angry I gave myself a make-over with the intention that when I saw him again, he would see what he missed out on. I let everyone at school think we were still together because I didn't want to date anyone else ever again. I was so hurt and jaded. I thought it was the way to handle it, but I was wrong."

Silence took over the conversation, but it wasn't uncomfortable. I ig-nored the echoes of the words I'd said and focused instead on the sounds of rustling leaves and the cool mountain breeze that brought the delectable scent of pine.

Landen cleared his throat. "Thank you for telling me. I wanted to—"

"You know what, Landen?" I interrupted. I just had to say it; this thought had been eating me alive for an entire year. "I'm no better than he is. I didn't talk about it, either, for different reasons, but doesn't it all come down to the same thing? We were both saving face; we were both protecting our pride and only thinking about ourselves. I stuffed it all down inside and quit dating. I quit everything that reminded me of Jason and what he did."

"Pyper, you are not the same as Jason."

I couldn't look at him. "I'm not so sure."

"Really?" Landen's voice held a challenge. "What else have you done this year?"

"What?" I cleared my throat. "What do you mean?"

"Were you mean to people because you were hurting? Did you push all your friends away? Did you hide in your room all the time and ignore your family?"

My eyes widened as I looked at Landen.

"Pyper, you go out of your way to be nice to everyone, no matter who they are or what they look like or smell like or where they buy their clothes."

I shook my head ruefully. "Not everyone. I have not been very nice to guys. I kind of think they are genetically flawed."

Landen waved a hand in the air. "That makes complete sense, considering what Jason put you through. And I wasn't done yet. You have thrown yourself into volunteering for every committee, club, and service project all year. Even prom, which you hate."

I laughed at the way he said 'prom', like it was evil and must be destroyed. I plucked a leaf off one of the Aspen branches that waved near my head. It was translucent in the moonlight. "I guess, then, I'm a hopeless optimist pretending to be a cynic. Or maybe I'm just a complete control freak." I shivered.

Landen shrugged off his jacket, then held it out to me.

"You'll get cold."

He nudged it forward. "Take it."

I slipped my arms in the sleeves and pulled the sides around, then tucked them in place by crossing my arms. This must be the reason mothers swaddle their infants. I felt safe and warm and, holy cow, his jacket smelled good.

"You know," Landen said, "everyone is having a blast in there."

"Are they?" I looked up, feeling a bubble of hope.

"You should have seen Sam. When you were talking to Jason, Leah was teaching him how to swing dance."

"No way! I'm so sad I missed that!"

"And that's another thing, Pyper. You came to prom with Sam. That makes you a very different sort of person than Jason."

I looked up at the sky to escape Landen's gaze. I followed along, tracing a pine tree all the way to the top. Layers of lacy branches reached for the sky. I breathed in the tangy sweetness and felt my whole body relax.

"You really think so?"

"I do." Landen brushed a stray hair off my cheek. His fingers paused at the edge of my face before his hand dropped back to his side. "And I'm not the only one. Leah loves your guts for taking over the advice column. She was stressing that fierce."

Wait, what?

I looked up slowly. "You know I write the advice column?"

Landen's face fell into an expressionless mask. "Yes."

"That was supposed to be a secret. Leah promised she wouldn't tell anyone it was me."

Landen held up both hands. "She didn't tell me on purpose. I overheard."

I crossed my arms and took a step away from Landen. "Have you ever written in with a question?"

"Yes, I did."

"How many?"

"Hold on now," he said, holding up both hands. "That was two questions in a row. Isn't that against your rules?"

I couldn't have smiled if I wanted to. My face felt like someone had dipped it in papier mâché and left it to dry.

After a moment, Landen sighed. "I wrote in twice."

"Tornado?"

"Yes."

"And?"

Landen took a deep breath, his eyes steadily on mine. "Bad Timing."

I sucked in a breath and looked away. Bad timing? Bad timing was the guy who liked a girl since seventh grade. In fact, now that I thought about it, Tornado said the same thing. Did Landen say the same thing in both questions on purpose?

"Why did you do that?" The words clipped like stiletto heels.

"I—"

"Were you..." My voice wavered. I swallowed and tried again. "Were you messing with me?"

"What do you mean by 'messing with you?'" Landen's eyebrows lowered.

"You wrote in for advice. You followed it, and the whole time you knew it was me giving you the advice. Was it like a game?"

It didn't matter what explanation he gave. I should have known better than to let my guard down. My heart hammered in my chest and tears burned behind my eyes. I thought Landen was different. I thought I could trust him. I was the worst judge of character. I couldn't believe I did this to myself.

Again.

Landen's face softened. He reached for my hand and wouldn't let me pull away. "Look at my face, Pyper. This is important. I told you I don't play games. I wasn't messing with you."

"Then why did you do it?" I hated that my voice cracked.

"Pyper." He waited again until my eyes met his. "I really, really like you. I have since the seventh grade. That's all true."

He gripped my hand tighter, tugging me closer.

"I thought you were dating Jason. I couldn't compete with him, so I gave up. When we ended up in econ together and Jason had been gone for almost a year, I thought I might finally have a chance. I tried all semester to get your attention. It wasn't until that day at Greedy Cow when you didn't know my name that I realized I was doomed."

"I said I was sorry," I said defensively.

"That's not why I brought it up!" His chest heaved; it took a few breaths before he spoke again. "I just want you to know exactly where I'm coming from. I thought if I wrote for advice, you might—"

"You wrote to me, knowing it was me, for advice about me. Landen!" My anger was like lava that couldn't decide whether to erupt or go dormant. "That is totally a mind game. You weren't being honest; you were manipulating me."

Landen grew very serious. "I wrote to you to get your attention. I have literally tried everything else I could think of. I thought that if I wrote to you and followed your advice, it would be like a clue and you would finally notice me. I have tried so hard to be your friend. The more I try, the more I realize I want us to be more than friends."

I slipped my hand out of his loosened grip and backed away, shaking my head. "Why would you say that? Why can't we just be friends? We could, you know? We could just be friends."

"We could." Landen pressed his lips together. "But that might be awkward now that you know how I feel." He took a step forward, closing the gap I had created between us.

"Landen, I can't date you now. I don't know you that well. We need more time."

"Okay, how long?"

"How long, what?"

"How long do you have to know me before you decide I'm safe to date?"

I shook my head. "I— I don't know. I—"

"You knew Jason your whole life, and he wasn't who you thought he was. So, I need you to tell me how long it's going to take for you to feel like you know me well enough to date me."

My thoughts were like shredded paper in the wind; I couldn't grasp a single one. I stuttered and fidgeted, but no words came into my mind that I could say out loud.

"Pyper?" Landen's face and tone were void of emotion.

Flustered, I said, "I don't know, Landen. I don't know what to do! I just know I don't want to get hurt like that again, ever."

His face hardened. "I am not Jason."

"I didn't say you were."

"Not in words." He crossed his arms. "I know that he hurt you. That was bad, and you have every right to feel the way you feel about him. But, can't you just let all that go? That was the past; it has nothing to do with right now. We are talking about you and me, and what is happening right here, between us, today."

I opened my mouth, but Landen held up a hand to stop me.

"Dating is a risk. I get it. I am a risk. No matter how long you know me or how well, it's always a risk. I might do more dumb things; in fact, I guarantee I will. I'm going to change because that's what people do. I'm never going to be perfect. I have a ton of bad habits—Leah could give you an itemized list." He shoved his hands into his pockets. "I am willing to take that risk for you, Pyper. Will you take it for me?"

I looked away.

"Pyper." His voice was husky. "Please, just give me a chance."

The seconds stretched out between us. I wished so badly that I could trust what he was saying. I even wanted to, deep down. The song from Frozen and the phrase, 'A risk worth taking' twirled a frantic waltz through my mind. That phrase was probably advice I'd given someone else. How much of a hypocrite was I for giving advice I couldn't follow?

I tried to look at Landen, but images of Jason's smirk kept waving in front of my eyes, blurring over Landen's face.

I stepped away.

"I can't."

Then, I turned and ran.

Chapter 27

My eyelashes were stuck together.

I didn't take my makeup off the night before because I came home and went straight to bed. Which also meant I didn't brush my teeth.

Clearly, that was a series of mistakes.

I moved my tongue around the inside my mouth a few times before letting it out to get some air. Yeah, not good. My breath was the opposite of delicious. I rolled out of bed, flung a blanket over my shoulders in case I ran into any of my family in the hall, and slogged to the bathroom to brush my teeth. There was no way I was eating breakfast with this mouth; everything would taste nasty.

Minty fresh and feeling more human, I started back to my room but didn't make it in time. The hall erupted with chaos that is also known as my family. They herded me away from my room and into the kitchen

"Hey, honey." Mom waved with Gavin on her hip.

"Pypa! You look scary! Like a monster raccoon."

"Hey, Pyper. You need to buy more of your cereal." Kai walked by with a bowl balanced in his hand. "All we have left is Cheerios. No marshmallows. No nothing."

"There's a box of Pypa cereal behind the vacuum," Gavin said.

"Nah, all that's left is the gross powder at the bottom."

"What's in your bowl then?" I leaned in to look.

"The gross powder from the bottom."

"Oh, ew!" Mom and I said at the same time.

"Pyper, finally. I've been waiting forever!" Roxie crossed her arms. "It is your job as the oldest to save me from these maniacs. What are we going to do today?"

What were we going to do? I hadn't thought about it. It seemed strange that there would be life as usual after a night like last night. I shook my head, the way I do when I had a water-clogged ear.

"I have to work today." My stomach clenched. "I'm supposed to be at Greedy Cow at nine."

Was it too late to put in my two weeks' notice? Was that required if you hadn't worked even one day yet? I couldn't go work with Landen after what happened last night.

I couldn't.

"Awwwwwwwww." Gavin gave a super sad face. "I want to play Armor Egg tag!" He hopped up and down with each word.

"What is he saying?" Mom asked.

"Arm and Leg tag." Kai rolled his eyes. "It's the only game he ever wants to play."

Mom nodded and then turned to me with her signature shrink look, the I-know-there-is-something-you-aren't-telling-me look.

I just smiled sweetly.

"Roxie and Kai could play with you."

Roxie shrugged. "Fine. But I don't want to be it first."

"Kai?" I asked.

"Whatever." He lifted his free arm to show me a thumbs up and then let it drop back to his side.

"YES!" Gavin shrieked.

"I'll be ready in ten," Roxie said. "Can you drop us off at the park? I don't want to play in the backyard. Someone," she fixed Kai with a pointed look, "hasn't picked up Donny Doo in, like, a week. And it rained."

"Kai!" Mom scolded. "You have to scoop every day! Dogs will go in the same place all the time if you keep it clean. If not, they go all over, and the backyard becomes—."

Mom was wasting her breath. Kai had magically disappeared before Mom could give him an ultimatum he couldn't refuse.

Mom sighed at his retreating back. "Poor Donny Osmond."

"Don't look at me!" Roxie held both hands up in the air and backed away. "I wanted a bunny." She turned and sprinted into her room, leaving me and Mom alone.

Mom turned her shrink eyes on me full blast. "I am feeling a little bit worried about you. Do you want to tell me why I'm feeling that way?"

"Um," I wiggled my toes through the carpet. "Indigestion?"

Mom nodded. "Or it could be that I picked you up from prom last night two hours before it was over, and we didn't talk about it."

"I was tired."

Mom tipped her head to the side to look at me. "That hasn't stopped you in the past."

Good point.

I shuffled my feet, digging my toes into the fluffy carpet. "Jason was at prom."

"What?" Mom's mouth worked around, then settled into a thin line. "What do you mean?"

"He was the DJ." I wished I could have talked to my mom about this right after I finished with Jason. My floaty feeling from getting over him was totally eclipsed by what happened with Landen afterward. My stomach felt heavy, like I'd swallowed a brontosaurus.

Gavin squirmed, so Mom set him down and patted his bottom to get him moving. "Go get dressed, sweetie. I'll come help you in a minute."

Gavin padded out of the kitchen and disappeared.

"What happened?" Mom folded her arms, her voice tight.

I knew I would feel better after I told her; I always did It was just hard to get the words out. I took a deep breath and went for it. At first, my sentences came out choppy and halted, and just like I thought, it didn't take long for the words to flow on their own, almost without me having to think about them.

I told my mom everything: my realization about Jason, how wrong I was about Travis, and how I ran away from Landen.

"When I went back to the dance, Sam and Leah were leading the whole student body in a conga line. Sam was laughing his head off, which I have never seen before, so I didn't feel bad telling him I was leaving early. I got all my stuff and went outside to call you. I don't know where Landen went. I didn't see him again." I stared at the minty green polish on my toes and wondered what my mom was thinking.

I didn't have to wonder for long.

"Honey, look at me."

I did.

"How do you feel about Landen?"

That wasn't the question I was expecting. It made my insides curdle like buttermilk. I thought she would ask me about Jason or announce we were going over to the Mylers' to straighten all this out or tell me to clean my room before I left for work.

All of that would have been better than talking about Landen.

"Why do you hesitate? Is that a hard question?"

I finally looked up as a tear slid down my cheek. "I really like him, Mom."

Mom's face softened. She wiped my tear with her thumb and pulled my head into her shoulder. "But you're scared?"

I nodded, dropping my forehead against her collar bone.

"Are you scared because you think he's going to hurt you like Jason did?"

I took a shuddery breath. "Yes. It's stupid though. I know he's not Jason."

"It's okay, honey. You're just making comparisons to keep yourself safe; that's what we do."

"Don't try and make me look normal!" I laughed and then hiccupped. "I'm a disaster, Mom! I spent all year trying to control everything and nothing worked the way it was supposed to."

"That sounds like a valuable lesson learned."

"I..." I pulled back so I could see my mom's face. "Can I ask you a question?"

"Of course, Pyper. Always."

I twisted my fingers through each other. "Do you think I'm broken?"

"Honey."

"No, really, Mom. What if my heart is ruined forever? Like, what if I can never trust anyone ever again? What if I can't love people?"

Mom's lips turned up. "Pyper, do you trust me? Do you trust your dad?"

"Of course." I didn't even have to think about that.

"Mooooooooooooooooooooooom!" We could hear Gavin before we saw him turn the corner, his little legs pumping until he ran into Mom's knees. "Kai said Batman is better than Superman!"

Mom bent down. "That's just an opinion, sweetie."

"But Superman can blast things with his eyes balls. Batman can't do that."

"Guess what?" Mom tipped his chin toward her. "Both you and Kai get to be right! Isn't that fun? He can think Batman is better, and you can think Superman is better, and you are both right! Yay!"

Gavin pursed his lips in his famous thinking monkey face, then nodded. "Okay."

"Okay," Mom stood. "Now run back to your room; I'm talking to Pyper right now."

He wrapped his arms around my legs, squeezing like a python, and looked up with his big baby blues framed by lashes that were totally wasted on a boy. He blinked as I ran my fingers through his hair.

"Pypa?"

"Gavi?"

"I love you the mostest of anybody, except Mommy and Daddy and Grandma and Gramps and Grammie and Superman."

"I love you too, buddy."

He kissed my knee with a big, sloppy, squishy smack. "Know what else, Pypa? You are more prettier than my dump truck."

I smiled down at him, my heart growing three sizes in that one second.

That was the sweetest thing anyone had ever said to me.

"Run along," Mom said as she patted his head. Gavin gave us both a lopsided grin and took off.

Mom looked at me now. "Do you love Gavin?"

"Yes!" That was the silliest question in the world.

Mom leaned against the wall. "So, you trust me and Dad, you love Gavin…"

Oh, wait! I see what she did there.

"I mean boys, Mom. I mean, what if I can't trust boys or really love them?"

"Dad is a boy; Gavin is a boy."

I wrinkled my eyebrows. "It's different, though."

"Is it?"

Okay, was it? I thought it was, but if my mom didn't think so, maybe I was wrong about that.

"Honey, tell me, plain as day, what you're really worried about."

I didn't give myself time to think or filter my words. "I'm worried that I wrecked things with Landen last night. I— I'm scared I lost him."

"Why does this worry you? He's just a boy, right? He's untrustworthy, unloveable..." Mom's eyes crinkled at the corners.

"No!" I said, before I could stop myself. "Landen's not like that. He's super sweet and totally honest and..." I gave my mom a look. "Nice job, Mom."

"Reverse psychology. Works every time."

I chewed on that for a few seconds. "What do I do now? He told me he likes me, and I freaked out and ran away. How do I fix that?"

Mom raised her eyebrows but didn't say anything.

Okay, so I guess I needed to figure it out on my own.

I screwed up pretty big last night, so I needed to fix it pretty big. I could make a huge candy gram poster that had a sorry message.

Or I could...

Oh!

I could get the glee club to help me rewrite a song to apologize and sing it to him in front of everyone! That would be big! He couldn't turn away from all that effort and time. Especially if we threw in costumes and a dance number.

I bet Holly and the cheer squad would help me.

"Tell me what you're thinking," Mom said.

I outlined the plan, ideas firing at rapid speed. The more I talked, the better I felt. This was a grand gesture. Landen would have to know I liked him after this.

"What do you think?"

Mom hesitated. "That is a fun idea; I love it."

"But?" There had to be a but; I could see it lurking behind her eyes.

"But I wonder if that's the best way to speak to Landen."

I blinked.

My mom continued. "Dressing up in costumes, singing an apology song with back-up dancers, that's something! It would knock the socks off some guys, but do you think Landen wants a big show?"

I bit my lip. "I have to do something epic. I seriously screwed up. I don't know how else to make him see how sorry I am."

"Consider this." Mom held up her hands. "What if you just go to work today, look him in the eyes, and say 'I'm sorry?'"

I wrinkled my nose. "That sounds lame sauce."

Mom laughed. "Maybe so, but I think that will mean more to Landen than a big production. What do you think?"

I agreed, but I hated to admit it.

"Honey, you don't have to jazz things up to make them meaningful."

"You sound like Grandpa when you say 'jazz.'"

"I will take that as a compliment. Now, go get ready. You can do this." Mom flipped my hair over my shoulder. "Remember, from small and simple things comes great things."

"You really think it will work?"

"Absolutely. Have fun. I can't wait to hear all about it."

Chapter 28

I stood outside Greedy Cow, my heart trying to pound its way out of my chest. I was only a couple of steps away from Landen, and I could sense him on the other side of the wall as though I had Superman vision.

My brain ran wild, telling me I should have done the epic song and dance thing. Or, at the very least, I should have dressed super cute. At home, when I was safe and comfortable, I decided to wear a simple t-shirt and my favorite jeans that were faded in all the right places. I threw my hair into a messy bun, and I didn't even put on a thin layer of mascara. At home, I felt like I was enough without all the embellishments. Standing here now, I felt like an idiot.

I needed something pink and sparkly, stat.

I leaned against the wall to do some deep breathing and tried to sort through all the things I wanted to say. I wasn't convinced Mom was right anymore. A big, grand gesture seemed like a way better way to win Landen back. Plus, with Landen's attention on background dancers and the lyrics to the song, there would be less focus on me.

My hands were ice cold, but I had to keep wiping them on my jeans to keep the sweat down. How was that even possible? I should have paid better attention in sophomore biology.

I caught a glimpse of myself in a store window and noticed my shirt was crooked. As I tried to straighten it with my frozen, sweaty hands, I heard Brooklynn's voice in my head.

"It's okay to be a mess."

I stopped tugging at my clothes.

If I went in there and apologized to Landen and he still hated my guts, it wouldn't be because my shirt was crooked.

As much as it devastated me to realize it, there was nothing I could do to make him want to try again with me.

Except walk in there, just me, exactly the way I was, and apologize with all my heart.

But was that enough?

I argued with myself for a couple more seconds, then I silenced all of it. None of that mattered. Whether it was enough or not, I had to try.

Suddenly I understood what Landen meant last night.

He was totally worth the risk.

With a sassy toss of my head, I tucked in one side of my shirt. It gave me a disheveled look, but I gloried in it. I was half mess and half marvelous; my shirt was proof.

Courage welled up in my belly and filled my head. If I was Scottish and lived a few hundred years ago, I would have wiped paint across my face and blown a horn.

I was ready.

I walked into Greedy Cow.

There were a few people at the tables, but I didn't let that stop me. My eyes were fixed on Landen's face as I moved across the floor to the counter where he stood.

"Can I help—." He looked up and then stared over my head. "Pyper, you're late."

Only by, like, three minutes. I had to ignore that and stick to the plan, or I was going to lose my nerve. "Hey, Landen." My voice sounded shaky, so I paused to breathe in. "How are you?"

He grabbed a rag and started wiping the counter. I knew he did that so he wouldn't have to see my face, which meant he felt something. All was not lost.

That gave me the boost I needed.

"Hey." I followed him until we reached the end of the counter. "Can I talk to you for a second? Before we start training?"

"Excuse me." A girl waved from the register. "The napkins are all gone." She placed the dispenser on the counter with a bang.

Landen left me standing alone to get her a handful of napkins. Then he had to fill the empty dispenser and go from table to table to check all the others.

That was a little excessive.

When he came back to the counter, the phone rang.

I didn't hear a word he said until he hung up and his attention was mine again. "This isn't really a good time."

"I know, but—"

"Great. Then let's get to work." He turned his back and started moving around, messing with things but not really doing anything.

I stepped around the counter and trailed along after him. "Landen?"

He didn't respond; he just kept clanging things as loudly as he could.

I reached for his hand.

He breathed in sharply; his fingertips were colder than mine, which was saying something. I raised my eyes to his and was surprised to see him looking back at me.

"Landen, I'm so, so sorry."

He stared without blinking for several breaths, then slipped his hand out of mine. "I'm not sure what you mean by that."

I was suddenly aware of the hum of the soft-serve machine, the chatter of customers, the clicking of the clock, and Landen stepping away from me. I reached out a hand. He didn't come closer, but at least he stopped moving away.

"Really? You can't think of anything I should be sorry about?"

A small smile gave me hope. "Oh, I can think of plenty of things. I'm just not sure what *you* think you should be sorry about."

Tears welled up in my eyes. They were so unexpected that my breath caught in my throat. "I'm sorry for all of it, Landen. I'm sorry I never noticed you. I'm sorry I let you and everyone think I was still with Jason. I'm sorry I've been so stuck on him for so long. I'm sorry I ran away from you last night. I know I hurt you; I know I was an idiot. I wish I could do an epic redo of all of it, but I can't. All I can do is tell you how sincerely, desperately sorry I am and hope you will forgive me."

A long silence spread between us. It crept through me, leaving goose-bumps on my arms. This was the moment I'd been dreading. This was why

I wanted to do a grand gesture. All I had to offer Landen was myself, and at the moment, I found myself horribly lacking.

What if I wasn't enough?

"Forgive you?" Landen leaned against the counter, a slow smile lengthening his lips. "That sounds risky."

My heart lifted. That familiar, Landen-y smile gave me the boost of courage I needed to say, "I'm willing to take that risk for you, Landen. Will you take it for me?"

Landen held out his hand. "Come here."

The air between us suddenly went electric.

I took his hand and slowly moved forward.

Then, my sneakers hit a slick spot on the tile. My feet flew out from under me. Landen yanked me by the hand to keep me from falling, careening me upwards and into his arms. The momentum knocked the two of us into the soft-serve machine.

There was a mechanical sputter, then ice cream gushed out all over our feet.

"Oh my gosh! I'm so sorry!" I pulled away from Landen, fumbling around for the button to make it stop. My fingers were so stiff that it was like I was working with popsicle sticks. What button was it? Why weren't they labeled better?

I gave up on the button and cupped my hands under the spout. So much ice cream was spewing out that my hands were overflowing in less than a second. I looked around, trying to figure out where to empty my handful.

Landen bent in half, hands on knees, his face an interesting shade of puce.

"What are you doing?" I shrieked to be heard over the machine and the splattering noises on the tile. "Stop laughing and help me! I think we hit the self-clean button, but I don't remember how to turn it off. Why are you just standing there? Landen!"

Landen moved closer, then took my slippery arms and wound them around his neck. His eyes warmed my insides all the way to my toes. He wrapped his arms around my waist and leaned his forehead gently against mine.

"Let me give you some advice," he murmured, his eyes half closed as he leaned closer. His head tipped to the side. "Just let it go."

295

Acknowledgments

Let me tell you about this book! When I first submitted to my wondermous editor, Staci, it was a very different story. Someone gave me feedback after writing Bake Believe that my style was too silly, it was hard to take seriously, so I thought I'd take a stab at something less so.

Oh my goodness, guys, it was a disaster! Luckily for me, and I hope for you too, Staci and her team at Immortal Works saw the potential in the story and gave me a chance to rewrite it. This is what came from that.

And you know what? I adore this story to the moon and back! Pyper gets to experience a version of what I did in high school* and it was just a super joy to write it.

Why am I telling you this? Because I learned a very important lesson from Sage Advice that I think is valuable to everyone: Be true to who you are! Don't be less to become what you think others want. Figure out what makes you, you, and then let it shine!

I know some people might hate my work, but I also know some people might love it. I write for those people. For you!

Thank you for reading!

No, really, THANK YOU!

*Asterisk after high school? Yeah, because, disclaimer, all the people and events in this book are the work of my own brain. If you went to high school with me and think you see yourself in one of the characters or think you experienced something described, it's purely coincidental. This is a work of fiction people, come on! Don't make it weird.

About the Author

Cori Cooper has never been great with advice. In high school, she gave some advice to a friend that backfired so hard core it caused the biggest drama of all time. There's probably still a crater somewhere where people can go to view the aftermath. It most likely costs admission though, so be aware of that.

Since that ridiculous experience, Cori has learned to use her ears instead of her mouth. It's not all bad news though. She has literally become the bestest listener in the whole entire world. For reals. In fact, she's considered trying out for America's Got Talent to demonstrate her extraordinary talent for listening, but she can't seem to find the time to do it between writing stories and hanging out with her totally fantasticalistic family.

Maybe next year.

Besides listening, writing and hanging out, Cori loves fluffy blankets, snow days, sunshine, reading next to a large body of water (lake or beach, she's not picky) and trying out recipes that involve her sourdough start, Clarence.

Connect with Cori

If you liked this book, be sure to check out the others!

The Bake Believe Trilogy
Bake Believe – Bake Off – Bake Happy

The Senior Year at Cromer High Series
Sage Advice – The Importance of Being Roxie – The Perfect Girl for Kai –
Gavin to the Rescue

Ways to Improve Baily
A Tale of Two Crushes
One Quarter Villain
Tears into Gold
Drama, Drama, Drama
Merry's Christmas

www.ingramcontent.com/pod-product-compliance
Lightning Source LLC
Chambersburg PA
CBHW061521210726
48287CB00006B/1777